Janet Evanovich is the No. 1 *New York Times* bestselling author of the Stephanie Plum series, the Lizzy and Diesel series, twelve romance novels, the Alexandra Barnaby novels and Trouble Maker graphic novels, and *How I Write: Secrets of a Bestselling Author*.

Lee Goldberg is a screenwriter, TV producer, and the author of several books, including *King City, The Walk,* and the bestselling *Monk* series of mysteries. He has earned two Edgar Award nominations and was the 2012 recipient of the Poirot Award from Malice Domestic.

Raves for Evanovich:

'Pithy, witty and fast-paced' *Sunday Times*

'Among the great joys of contemporary crime fiction' *GQ*

'Slapstick, steam and suspense' *People*

'Evanovich's characters are eccentric and exaggerated, the violence often surreal and the plot dizzily speedy: but she produces as many laughs as anyone writing crime today' *The Times*

'A laugh-out-loud page-turner' *Heat*

'Undeniably funny' *Scotsman*

'Romantic and gripping . . . an absolute tonic' *Good Housekeeping*

'Fast, funny and furious . . . keeps the reader breathless' *Publishers Weekly*

'The pace never [illegible] s off the page' *Irish Time*[illegible]

By Janet Evanovich

The Fox and O'Hare novels
with Lee Goldberg

The Heist
The Chase

The Stephanie Plum novels

One For The Money
Two For The Dough
Three To Get Deadly
Four To Score
High Five
Hot Six
Seven Up
Hard Eight
To The Nines
Ten Big Ones
Eleven On Top
Twelve Sharp
Lean Mean Thirteen
Fearless Fourteen
Finger Lickin' Fifteen
Sizzling Sixteen
Smokin' Seventeen
Explosive Eighteen
Notorious Nineteen
Takedown Twenty
Top Secret Twenty-One

The Diesel & Tucker series

Wicked Appetite
Wicked Business

The Between the Numbers novels

Visions of Sugar Plums
Plum Lovin'
Plum Lucky
Plum Spooky

And writing with Charlotte Hughes

Full House
Full Tilt
Full Speed
Full Blast

JANET

EVANOVICH

AND

LEE

GOLDBERG

THE CHASE

headline
review

Published by arrangement with Bantam Books, an imprint of The Random House Publishing Group, a division of Random House LLC, a Penguin Random House Company, New York.

First published in Great Britain in 2014
by HEADLINE REVIEW
An imprint of HEADLINE PUBLISHING GROUP

First published in paperback in Great Britain in 2014
by HEADLINE REVIEW

4

Cataloguing in Publication Data is available from the British Library

ISBN 978 1 4722 1614 4 (A-format)
ISBN 978 1 4722 0179 9 (B-format)

Typeset in New Caledonia by Palimpsest Book Production Ltd, Falkirk, Stirlingshire

Printed and bound in Great Britain by Clays Ltd, Elcograf S.p.A.

Headline's policy is to use papers that are natural, renewable and recyclable products and made from wood grown in well-managed forests and other controlled sources. The logging and manufacturing processes are expected to conform to the environmental regulations of the country of origin.

HEADLINE PUBLISHING GROUP
An Hachette UK Company
338 Euston Road
London NW1 3BH

www.headline.co.uk
www.hachette.co.uk

Acknowledgments

We'd like to thank James T. Clemente, Mark Safarik, Jay Stringer, Laurence Light, D. P. Lyle, Graham Smith, Jamie Freveletti, Christopher Reich, Alan Guthrie, Sam Barer, Gregory Nunn, Tim Hallinan, Cassandra Troy, Howard Shrier, Zoe Sharp, Lisa Brackmann, and Kate Kinchen for sharing their expertise with us. Any creative liberties we've taken with the facts, or any mistakes we've made, are our fault and shouldn't be blamed on these innocent bystanders.

One

It was 10 AM on a warm Sunday morning when the bomb exploded at the First Sunland Bank in downtown Los Angeles, setting off alarms in every parked car and building within a square mile.

The bank occupied the ground floor of an office tower on the north side of Wilshire Boulevard, midblock between Flower Street to the east and Figueroa to the west, in the heart of the financial district.

LAPD headquarters was just a few blocks away, so the dust, shards of glass, and chunks of mortar had barely settled on the ground when the bomb squad, a SWAT team, and scores of uniformed officers swarmed onto the scene.

FBI Special Agent Kate O'Hare got the call ten minutes later from agent Seth Ryerson. Kate was pulling away from the drive-through window of a McDonald's in West Los Angeles.

'A bomb just exploded at a bank downtown,' Ryerson said. 'We're up at bat.'

'Was anyone hurt?' Kate asked, setting her Coke between her legs and the bag with her two hot Bacon, Egg & Cheese Biscuits on the seat beside her.

'Nope. The bank was closed, and the financial district is a ghost town on Sundays.'

'I'll meet you out front in two minutes.'

Kate sped east on Wilshire Boulevard. The Federal Building was in Westwood, only a few blocks away, just past the San Diego Freeway overpass.

Ryerson was waiting for her on the sidewalk when she got there. He wore a blue dress shirt and red-striped tie under a blue FBI windbreaker. He was in his early thirties, tall and pale with a rapidly receding hairline. She'd noticed that the faster he lost his hair, the more he lifted weights. Soon he'd be a bald man with grossly inflated biceps.

Kate was about the same age as Ryerson but a lot less concerned with her hair, partly because she had a lot of it, and partly because she could care less. At the moment, her shoulder-length chestnut brown hair was pulled into a ponytail, and her slim, athletic body was appropriately clothed in a dress-for-success dove gray pantsuit, the jacket left unbuttoned to allow her easy access to her Glock 9mm. Kate was ex–Special Forces, she believed in law and order, God, and her country, and she suspected that through no fault of her own she'd lost control of her career and her life.

Ryerson opened the passenger door, picked up the McDonald's bag, and wiped the seat to check for grease before he sat down.

Kate made an illegal U-turn across Wilshire Boulevard and minutes later made a sharp turn onto the southbound San Diego Freeway. She steered onto the transition to the eastbound Santa Monica Freeway and could see that traffic was backed up behind an overloaded, rusted-out truck that had spilled wooden crates across three lanes.

'There's no rush,' Ryerson said, nervously tightening his shoulder harness, sensing that there was a maniac behind the wheel. 'We're just along for the ride. The police will already have everything locked down.'

'Blowing up a bank is a federal offense.'

'True, but we're a formality. We're only answering this because we're on call this weekend. Someone else will pick this up tomorrow morning, and you'll be back chasing Nick Fox.'

Kate mentally rolled her big blue eyes. If only Ryerson knew! She'd be chasing Nick a lot sooner than tomorrow morning. This whole bank event was a fake. A sham. A gigantic waste of taxpayer money, and God knows how many police officers' time. And she was involved! The very thought made her cringe. All her life she'd tried to do the right thing and uphold the law. And now it was a confusing mess. And it was all Nick Fox's fault.

'I hate him,' Kate said.

'Who?'

'Nick Fox. I wish I'd never laid eyes on him. I wish I'd never heard of him.'

Now it was Ryerson's chance to roll his eyes. 'He's your obsession. You've chased him for five years. You even *caught* him once. You're practically *married* to him.'

She veered onto the shoulder, speeding along the narrow strip between the concrete divider to her left and the stalled traffic on her right. A large wooden crate was on the shoulder directly in front of them. She tightened her grip on the wheel and sped up. Ryerson put one hand on the dash and turned his head away, as if that would make any difference if the windshield shattered.

Kate yanked the wheel just before impact, clipping the box and sending it skidding into the divider. She cleared the pickup truck and the crates and swerved into the fast lane, cutting off a bus on Ryerson's side by mere inches. He let out an involuntary yelp of fear, which she found sort of satisfying.

Ordinarily, a trip from Westwood to downtown Los Angeles took an hour. But Kate drove with the pedal to the floor, weaving wildly through traffic. She got there in twenty minutes and even managed to eat one of her Bacon, Egg & Cheese Biscuits on the way.

The windows of the bank were blown out and there was rubble on the street. There wasn't any fire or smoke, only swirls of dust kicked up by the wind. SWAT officers were positioned around the building, waiting for something to happen.

Kate parked beside the cluster of police vehicles that formed the LAPD command center. She got out of her car and approached a barrel-chested, square-jawed officer who looked to be in his fifties. He was leaning over a map he'd spread out on the hood of the black-and-white. He wore a Kevlar vest over a starched white shirt and a red-white-and-blue-striped tie. The patch on his vest read: CAPTAIN MAIBAUM.

'I'm FBI Special Agent Kate O'Hare and this is Special Agent Seth Ryerson,' Kate said to Maibaum. 'What have we got here?'

'I don't know yet. The bomb squad sent a robot inside with a camera. There's debris everywhere, but the front counter is reasonably intact and the vault is secure. If it was money they were after, they screwed up.'

'How smart could they be if they hit a bank that's three blocks from police headquarters?' Ryerson asked.

Maibaum shrugged. 'Could be a disgruntled employee, or maybe a frustrated customer lobbed a grenade in there to make a statement. Maybe some sicko is waiting for me to send men into a booby-trapped building so he can blow them up.'

Kate nodded. She knew it was none of the above, but she wasn't sharing that information just yet.

'I'm not letting anybody near the building until the bomb squad gives me the all-clear,' Maibaum said.

'Okay, we'll get out of your way until then,' Kate said, turning and walking into the middle of the street.

She looked to her left and then to her right. There were cop cars blocking both ends of the street. In between were several office buildings with banks, restaurants, and other storefront businesses, all closed for the day.

'Captain Maibaum,' Kate called over her shoulder. 'Did the blast set off alarms in any of the other buildings in the area?'

'Yeah,' he yelled back. 'There were alarms going off all up and down the street.'

'Did anyone respond to those alarms?'

'I saw a couple private security guards checking things out, but we weren't asked for aid.'

Kate turned back to Ryerson. 'How many banks do you figure there are on this block and the next one over?'

Ryerson's eyes widened as the meaning of what she was saying dawned on him. 'Too many.'

There was a narrow alley in front of her that ran down to Seventh Street alongside a branch of Westgate Bank. There was a black-and-white parked in front of the bank. The black-and-white looked empty. A uniformed police officer ambled out of the bank carrying a bulging gym bag.

Kate started toward him. 'Excuse me, Officer,' Kate yelled, holding her badge up in front of her. 'FBI. Could we have a word with you?'

The officer ignored her, opened the driver's side door of his black-and-white, and casually tossed his bag inside.

Kate drew her Glock. 'Don't move!'

Ryerson grabbed her wrist and tipped his head up at the choppers in the sky. 'Have you lost your mind? We're on live TV. You can't pull a gun on a cop.'

The officer got into the car and, with one foot still on the street, looked back at Kate. He lowered his Ray-Bans and smiled at her like she was Little Red Riding Hood standing at the foot of her grandma's bed and he was the Big Bad Wolf.

Kate grimaced. 'That's not a cop. That's Nick Fox.'

Nick blew Kate a kiss and sped off in the black-and-white.

Good lord, Kate thought, he's such a grandstander . . . and a flirt. She was caught between wanting to wring his neck and wanting to nibble on it. She spun around and ran flat out for her car with Ryerson close on her heels. He was barely in his seat when she floored the gas pedal and took off, making a hard right turn into the alley. She cut the corner so close, she sheared off her passenger side mirror on the edge of a building.

'Are you sure it's him?' Ryerson asked as he buckled up.

'Yeah,' she said. 'I'm sure it's him.'

Especially since she'd spoken to him two days ago when he'd come up with this scheme. And now she could add aiding and abetting a bank robber to her laundry list of hideous crimes! She'd go to church and ask God's forgiveness, but that ship had sailed long ago.

'You only caught a glimpse of him,' Ryerson said.

'I'd recognize him in the dark, a mile away, underwater.'

How could she not recognize him? Six feet tall with soft brown hair and a boyish grin that brought out the laugh lines around his eyes. He had the agile body of a tennis pro. Lean and firm. The kind of body she'd like to curl up next to if only he wasn't such a jerk. The man was a felon, for crying out loud. He was a con man. And he loved it!

She sped down the alley, made a tire-screeching left onto Seventh, and, when she didn't see Nick's black-and-white anywhere on the long stretch of road ahead, made a fast right onto Flower, a one-way street heading south. And there he was, a block ahead of them, siren and lights on, the few cars that were on Flower quickly moving out of his way.

Ryerson leaned forward and looked up at the sky. 'The LAPD chopper is on top of him and so is every TV station in town. There's no place for him to hide. You can ease up.'

She narrowed her eyes. 'I don't think so.'

Nick made a right onto Eighth Street and then a left onto Figueroa, a one-way northbound street. He sped south, weaving through four lanes of oncoming traffic. Kate stayed on his tail. Ryerson swore and placed his hands on the dashboard to brace himself as Kate narrowly avoided one head-on collision after another.

The Los Angeles Convention Center loomed ahead of them. A banner across the intersection depicted the starship *Enterprise* and welcomed attendees to WorldStarCon 43, the Ultimate Trekker Experience.

Nick turned right, crashed through the wooden gate arm at the entrance to the parking lot, and skidded to a stop in front of the Convention Center. He bolted out of his police car and into the building.

Kate stopped behind Nick's black-and-white. She and Ryerson jumped out of their car and ran inside after him but came to an abrupt stop as soon as they stepped through the doors. They faced 720,000 square feet of exhibition space packed with thousands of Starfleet officers, Klingon warriors, Romulan centurions, Andorian ambassadors, and Ferengi traders.

'How can we possibly secure this building before he slips out?' Ryerson asked.

'We can't,' Kate said.

It was a hard truth Ryerson didn't want to swallow. Kate marched into the crowd to look for Nick while Ryerson stayed where he was. A Vulcan Starfleet science officer in a blue velour shirt walked toward Ryerson. The pointy-eared alien raised his right hand in the traditional Vulcan greeting as he passed.

'Live long and prosper,' the Vulcan said.

Ryerson rolled his eyes as Nick Fox, the tenth man on the FBI's Ten Most Wanted list, walked casually out the door.

Two

Kate left Ryerson at the Convention Center to coordinate the search for Nick with the LAPD. She confiscated Nick's gym bag from the black-and-white as evidence and took it back to the Federal Building for processing, completing the necessary paperwork in ten minutes. Twenty minutes later she was on her way up the Pacific Coast Highway to Malibu when her father called.

'That was a hell of a chase,' Jake O'Hare said. 'I wish you could have put it off until the US Open was over, though. The stations cut in with their live coverage just as Tiger was trying to swing his way out of a sand trap.'

'How did you know it was me?'

'I recognized your car. But you could have been driving a tank and I would've known it was you. You drive like a maniac. You corner too hard.'

When Kate was sixteen, she and her younger sister, Megan, lived with their dad on an army base in Germany. Every weekend, Jake would take Kate to a defensive driving course to teach her how to drive in all kinds of conditions. After she'd learned how to maneuver on an oil-slicked road, he'd shot out her tires so she could master that, too. By comparison, her driver's license test was a snooze.

'Who were you chasing?' Jake asked.

'Nick Fox.'

That had Jake smiling. 'I thought it was him. Did you catch him?'

'I'm closing in,' Kate said. 'I'll call you later.'

She drove into the cobblestone motor court of a sprawling estate off Kanan Dume Road and parked her nondescript, slightly dented car that was missing a mirror beside a pristine black Aston Martin Vanquish. A FOR SALE sign was staked into the manicured lawn.

She knew there'd been a time when a real estate investor could dump fifteen million dollars into building a spec home in the hills above Malibu, dress it up with an infinity pool, a screening room, a bowling alley, and a kitchen Gordon Ramsay would love, and count on selling it at a five-million-dollar profit. Those days were over years ago and they weren't coming back. That's why this place sat vacant while three banks fought over ownership.

Kate walked into the house without knocking, strode across the vast entry hall and into the gourmet kitchen. Nick Fox stood at the cooktop in the center island, sautéing some fish in a pan. He wore a polo shirt and faded jeans, and had a chef's apron tied around his waist.

'That was fun,' Nick said. 'There's nothing like ending the week with a restful Sunday drive.'

'Did you have to go the wrong direction on a one-way street?'

'I was worried you weren't feeling challenged.'

'That was very considerate of you.' She took a seat on a stool at the counter. To her left, a farmhouse table nestled beside a large picture window with a commanding view of Santa Monica Bay. The table was set for three. A bottle of wine in a cooler and a pitcher of iced tea had been placed on the table.

'What's for lunch?' Kate asked.

'I was pressed for time, so all I was able to whip up was deviled eggs with a dollop of Tsar Nicoulai caviar on top, a selection of fruit and artisanal cheeses, and sautéed Dover sole with lemon and capers.'

Kate's idea of preparing a quick meal was eating Cap'n Crunch out of the box, so this was Christmas dinner by comparison.

The house alarm pinged when the front door was opened and closed. A moment later, Kate's boss, Carl Jessup, special agent in charge of the FBI's Los Angeles office, ambled into the kitchen. He was carrying a folder under his arm.

Jessup was in his fifties, a native Kentuckian with the tanned, deeply lined face and sinewy body of a man who worked outdoors with his hands. It was a country look that had served him well during the many years he'd spent undercover before he got kicked up to a desk.

'Nice place,' Jessup said, taking in the décor. 'How did you get furniture in here and the utilities turned on?'

'I'm the broker,' Nick replied with a smooth, absolutely perfect British accent. 'John Steed, Sotheby's International Realty, London office, at your service. I have some very motivated clients overseas who are eager to purchase vacation homes in Malibu. So I obviously needed to turn the lights on and dress the house.'

Jessup eyed Nick suspiciously. 'You haven't sold it, have you?'

'Not yet.'

'Not ever,' Jessup said.

'You're no fun,' Nick said, dropping the accent.

'I just let you rob a bank and go on a high-speed chase through downtown Los Angeles in a police car, which reminds me—' Jessup held his hand out to Nick, palm up. 'Have you got something for me?'

Nick reached into his pocket and dropped a thumb drive into Jessup's hand. 'Here are all the dirty photos and videos that Fred Bose was using to blackmail regulators to get his company's flawed but wildly profitable medications approved. I don't think Fred will be declaring this thumb drive among the items missing from his safety deposit box.'

Jessup put the drive into his coat pocket. 'What happened to everything else you stole from the bank vault?'

Nick placed the servings of sole onto plates and spooned on lemon caper sauce. 'I left them in the squad car. Even the uncut conflict diamonds.'

'What was Bose doing with those?' Jessup asked.

'Not him,' Nick said. 'You might want to check out whoever kept safety deposit box number 7210. They have been very naughty.'

'Those diamonds are untraceable,' Kate said. 'I'm surprised you didn't keep them.'

Nick smiled at her. 'I'm on the side of the angels now.'

'And thanks to your effort in downtown LA today, nobody will ever suspect it,' Jessup said. 'Or question that Kate is absolutely committed to catching you. It was a win-win all around. I just wish you hadn't caused so much property and vehicle damage.'

'We had to make it exciting for the viewers at home,' Nick said. 'Or they might have switched to *Judge Judy* instead.'

'TV ratings weren't one of my concerns,' Jessup said.

His biggest concern was that Nick would get caught,

and it would be revealed that the FBI had sprung him from jail and was using him to help nail major crooks, even as he'd become one of the Bureau's Ten Most Wanted criminals. Kate's job was to be Nick's handler and protector while, at the same time, leading the FBI's manhunt for him. Only Jessup and Deputy Director Fletcher Bolton, who picked their targets and ran the secret slush fund that financed Nick's swindles, knew the truth. And if any of it ever became public, they'd all end up in prison.

They took their plates of Dover sole and went to the table. Nick brought the fruit, cheese, and deviled eggs, and Kate took the white wine from the stoneware cooler.

Jessup helped himself to iced tea, selected an egg with caviar, and slid a file across the table to Kate. 'This is for you. It's the details on your next assignment.'

Kate poured a glass of wine for herself and one for Nick. 'Who are we going after this time?'

'No one,' Jessup said. He glanced at Nick. 'We want you to break into the Smithsonian.'

'Always a pleasure,' Nick said.

Kate raised an eyebrow at Nick. 'You've done it before?'

Nick shrugged. 'Nobody goes to DC without visiting the Smithsonian.'

'Most people go when it's open.'

'I don't like crowds.'

Jessup took a sip of his iced tea. 'In 1860, British and French forces sacked the Old Summer Palace outside of Beijing and pillaged the twelve bronze animal heads from a century-old Zodiac fountain in the Imperial Gardens. Each of those Ping Dynasty heads is worth about twenty million dollars. The Chinese are determined to retrieve all of them.'

'We have the rooster in this country,' Nick said. 'It's been on display in the Smithsonian for over a hundred years.'

'I'm surprised you know about it,' Jessup said.

'Of course he does,' Kate said. 'It's a one-of-a-kind piece worth twenty million dollars. I'm more surprised it's still in the Smithsonian and not a doorstop in Nick's house.'

'During the financial meltdown, China became our government's biggest lender,' Jessup said. 'So now they are demanding the immediate return of the bronze rooster as a sign of good faith.'

'Give it to them,' Kate said.

'There's a complication,' Jessup said. 'Actually, that's not accurate. It's more like a ticking bomb.'

'The Smithsonian won't give it up,' Nick said. 'And now you want us to steal it from them and give it to the Chinese.'

Jessup shook his head. 'The Smithsonian has already agreed to return it, at the president's personal request.

The problem is that neither the president nor the current director of the Smithsonian knows that the bronze rooster on display is actually a fake. The real one was stolen from the Smithsonian ten years ago, something the museum and the FBI never disclosed and have diligently covered up ever since.'

'Why would the Bureau and the museum do that?' Kate asked.

'Pride,' Nick said. 'They can't admit that the nation's most prestigious and secure museum, standing in the shadow of the White House and the US Capitol, was broken into and that the FBI, the nation's top law enforcement agency, doesn't have a single lead in the case. Can you imagine how humiliating that would be?' Nick smiled and shook his head. 'It's one of the most successful art thefts in criminal history. The bragging rights alone make it the score of a lifetime.'

Jessup and Kate stared at Nick.

'Is the rooster a doorstop in your house?' Kate asked.

'I don't have any doorstops. I'm not a doorstop kind of guy,' he said.

Kate and Jessup stared at him.

'C'mon, really? You think I stole the rooster?'

'You said that you've broken into the Smithsonian before,' Jessup said. 'In fact, you implied that you'd done it many times.'

'I was thinking about stealing the T. rex,' Nick said.

'How could you possibly steal a T. rex?' Kate asked.

'I have no idea,' he said. 'That's what makes the idea of actually *doing* it so intriguing to me. I still haven't figured it out. But I didn't steal the rooster. Somebody beat me to it.'

Jessup sighed and dabbed at his lips with his napkin. 'That's a shame, because that's going to make things a lot harder. We need you to find the real rooster and switch it with the fake one before we have to give it to the Chinese.'

'How much time do we have?' Kate asked.

'Two weeks. That's when billionaire businessman Stanley Fu is coming to DC in his own Airbus 380 to personally transport the artifact to Shanghai. Once his plane lands, the Chinese government's antiquities expert will inspect the rooster and discover it's a fraud, which will spark a major diplomatic crisis, infuriate the Chinese, and humiliate the United States.'

'You need to buy us more time,' Kate told Jessup.

Nick stabbed a small wedge of New Zealand cheddar and dropped it onto his plate next to a slice of melon. 'Two weeks is plenty.'

'The FBI has been trying to find the rooster for a decade,' Kate said. 'What makes you think we can do it in two weeks?'

'Because I know who stole it.'

Three

Nicolas Fox and Kate O'Hare couldn't risk being seen traveling together on commercial flights or walking through airports, train stations, and other key choke points where they might be recognized by law enforcement officers or captured on surveillance cameras.

So at nine the next morning, Nick flew first class to London under a pseudonym, using one of his many impeccable fake passports. He was served a fairly edible meal and a glass of decent champagne, and arrived rested and relaxed at Heathrow at seven AM the following day. He then took a short flight to Inverness, Scotland, where he rented a Range Rover and drove south in the pouring rain, his journey interrupted on two occasions by sheep crossing the road.

Kate, meanwhile, flew economy class to Newark, New Jersey, and then on to Glasgow. For a woman who'd spent years in the military riding in the cargo bays of transport planes, economy class commercial air travel still felt comfortable to her. She even liked the food. On arrival at Glasgow Airport, she rented a compact Vauxhall Corsa and headed northwest, to a village so tiny that it consisted of just one building, a lopsided centuries-old tavern.

Kate and Nick arrived at the tavern within a few minutes of each other and got together at a table by the stone fireplace in the dining room. They stripped off their jackets, settled down in front of the roaring fire, and ordered a late but heavy lunch of minced mutton Scotch pies, mashed potatoes, and Belhaven ale.

'I schlepped all the way over here on faith, Nick. It's time to tell me who we're seeing and where we're going. I'm not going any farther in the dark.'

'We need to have an understanding first. You can't use anything you might learn today against the person we're going to meet. You're granting him blanket immunity.'

'I can't do that, but I can promise that anything I learn will be confidential and that I won't share it with anybody. You have my word on that. But if you ever break the deal you have with us, and try to run, I'll use everything I know to hunt you down and arrest you and all your known associates.'

'You're so sexy when you get tough,' Nick said. 'Your little nose wrinkles up and your eyes get smoky.'

Kate thought it was a good thing she didn't have her

Glock, because she might be tempted to shoot him. Nothing serious. Slice into his little toe, maybe. Of course she could always stab him with her fork.

'Who are we seeing?' she asked.

'Duff MacTaggert.'

'Never heard of him.'

'Of course you haven't, he's that good. Duff is the Obi-Wan Kenobi of thieves and was one of my mentors. He's retired now and runs a pub in Kilmarny, a very small, remote village about three hours from here. But don't be fooled by his charm or his age. If Duff suspects you're a cop, he will kill us.'

'He can try.'

'Duff is going to smell your self-confidence. And if anything goes down and you go into fight mode, he'll know you're a pro. So rather than try to hide it, I've built it into your cover.'

'Which is what?'

'You're my bodyguard and lover.'

She shook her head. 'Just your bodyguard.'

'He'll never believe I'm not sleeping with you.'

'You aren't.'

'Even I find that unbelievable,' Nick said.

'What makes you think Duff will give us the bronze rooster?'

'He won't, but I'm hoping he'll give us the name of the person who eventually received it.'

'And then we'll steal it from *him.*'

'That's the plan,' Nick said.

Kate left her car parked on the street and tossed her bag into Nick's Range Rover. She slid into the passenger seat, and they headed for Kilmarny.

There was a somber beauty to the misty peaks and the lush green rolling hills. They passed crumbling rock walls, ancient farmhouses, flocks of sheep, and dark, icy lochs.

'Where we're headed is smack between Heaven and Hell,' Nick said.

'Aren't you being a bit overdramatic?'

'I'm being literal. Kilmarny is on a cape between Loch Nevis and Loch Hourn. That's Gaelic for Lake Heaven and Lake Hell. You can only reach Kilmarny by boat across Loch Nevis or on foot over sixteen miles of harsh, mountainous terrain.'

'Seems like a lousy place to retire.'

'Not if you're a world-class thief who is still wanted for crimes in several countries.'

'And if you have a flair for drama.'

'That, too.'

'Is that something else that Duff MacTaggert taught you?'

'On the contrary. Drama is no fun. Theatricality and spectacle are more my thing.'

'I suppose we're taking a boat to Kilmarny. I can't picture you hiking through the wilderness.'

'We're catching a ferry from Mallaig harbor. It's about a forty-five-minute trip across Loch Nevis. I've called ahead to arrange a crossing.'

It was pouring rain when they arrived at Mallaig, a busy little fishing port overlooking Loch Nevis. The waters of the loch were choppy, and the Kilmarny ferry, a modified fishing boat, bobbed on the whitecaps that slapped against the pier. Nick and Kate were the only passengers.

By the time the ferry reached Kilmarny the rain had eased into a cold drizzle, and Kate squinted through the rain at whitewashed cottages tucked between steep green hills and the white-sand shoreline of the loch. Several weatherbeaten fishing boats were tied up at the ferry dock. A single road ran through the small village and up into the hills. Kate could see a farmhouse and, beyond that, the ruins of a castle in the mist.

Nick followed her gaze. 'That's Kilmarny Castle. This town was built for the workers who tended to the land and cattle in the days of yore.'

'Yore? Are we having a conversation, or are you narrating *The Hobbit*?'

'We're in Scotland now. I'm fitting in.'

'I'm pretty sure the Scots don't say "yore" either,'

Kate said, though all she knew about the Scots was what she'd learned from watching the Travel Channel.

'There are maybe forty people living in Kilmarny full-time. The rest are hikers and nature-loving tourists,' Nick said. 'There's only one store, one hotel, one restaurant, and the Hideaway, the most remote pub in the UK. Duff owns it and lives upstairs. He's the unofficial mayor of this place.'

Kate picked out the only building that could possibly be a pub. It was a low-slung, lopsided two-story cottage that hunkered down on a barren patch of land at the edge of the village. Several rustic picnic tables and benches had been placed out front. Smoke curled from the chimney.

'Not exactly Beverly Hills,' Kate said.

'And Duff isn't Cary Grant.'

The path to the pub was uphill and slick with rain, but it wasn't a far walk. Nick pushed the heavy wooden pub door open and they stepped inside. A massive fireplace with a stone hearth dominated one wall. A fire was roaring in the fireplace, and the surrounding wall was black with soot. Clearly the flue didn't always work perfectly. The ceiling was low, with exposed beams supported by posts that were squared-off tree trunks. The tables and chairs were hand-carved from thick blocks of wood that had been smoothed by centuries of use. The bar seemed to have been constructed out of found objects, a mix of stone, brick, bottle glass, and mortar topped with a shiny, varnished wood counter. The temperature in the room was tropical, and the air was heavy with the smell of charred applewood.

There were three men in the room, two sitting at the bar and one standing behind it. The men looked like found objects themselves, as rough as the countryside, their skin weathered and tough from years of being lashed by the wind and sea. The man behind the counter, whom Kate judged to be in his late sixties, looked like the result of an insane scientific experiment to cross a Scottish terrier with a man. His brown eyes and bulbous nose peeked out from bushy eyebrows and a grizzly, overgrown mustache and beard, all of which combined to practically cover his entire face with hair. She figured this had to be Duff MacTaggert.

'Nicolas Fox. You're the last man I ever expected to see walk through my door,' Duff said in a heavy Scottish accent. 'I can still feel your knife in my back.'

'My God, you've become a fat, hairy old bastard,' Nick said, dropping his bag by the door and closing the distance to the bar.

The two men at the bar tensed. They were big and brawny, with hands like baseball mitts. Kate could see the faint bulge of guns tucked into their pants under their cable-knit sweaters. Apparently they thought that if trouble came, it would wait for them to lift up their sweaters to get at their weapons before it struck. She set her bag down beside Nick's and stood ready by the door.

Duff marched out from behind the bar and got in Nick's face. 'You've become a soft, pretty boy with nice teeth.'

Nick smiled. 'Life has been good to us both.'

Duff looked over Nick's shoulder at Kate. 'Who is she?'

'My bodyguard.'

Duff cocked a bushy eyebrow. 'That wee lass? You must be joking. Since when do you need protection anyway?'

'Since I became number ten on the FBI's Ten Most Wanted list.'

'I heard about your escape.'

'Way out here?'

'We're remote, Nicky boy, but nobody can hide from Google. Speak your piece and make it quick. The ferry leaves in five minutes.'

'That isn't very hospitable.'

'Neither is bringing to my doorstep all the law that's hunting you.'

'They aren't even close.'

'Says a man who got caught to a man who's never been. Give me one good reason why I shouldn't kill you now and bury you in the hills just to play it safe.'

'Me,' Kate said.

Duff laughed and looked at Nick. 'I've got a mind to let the lads test her out to see what happens.'

One of the lads wore a turtleneck sweater, the other a crewneck, and they both looked at Kate like two dogs eager to fight over a bone.

Nick shrugged. 'Go ahead. I've got a proposal to discuss with you, and some privacy would be nice.'

Duff waved his men away. 'Don't muss her hair too much, lads.'

Turtleneck and Crewneck slid off their stools, walked past Kate, and headed outside. Nick turned to her and nodded toward the door. Kate sighed and walked out, too, closing the door behind her.

'Make your pitch, Nicky boy,' Duff said, leading Nick to a table. 'It better be a good one.'

Nick took a chair that had its back to the door. 'I have a friend who'd like to add the bronze rooster to his art collection.'

'What's that got to do with me?' Duff asked.

'You know who has it,' Nick replied.

'I can guarantee you that the rooster isn't for sale.'

'I didn't say my friend wanted to buy it.'

Suddenly, Turtleneck crashed through the window behind Nick and landed dazed in a heap on the floor beside the table. A moment later, Crewneck crashed through the other window and faceplanted on the floor not far from Turtleneck.

Kate walked through the door, brushing gravel off her clothes, and went to the bar. Duff looked down at the two men and shook his head with disgust.

'Do you have any idea how hard it is to get windows replaced out here?' Duff asked Kate.

Kate smiled and pulled herself a mug of draft ale. She was starting to enjoy herself.

Duff turned back to Nick. 'Why couldn't she throw them through the door?'

'She likes windows. It's showier.'

'That's your bad influence on her. You always loved to put on a show.'

'That's what makes it fun.'

'That's what gets you sent to prison.'

'What do you call living way out here?' Nick asked.

Duff shrugged. 'I have my comforts. Good ale. Good single malt. Satellite television on an eighty-four-inch flat screen.'

Turtleneck and Crewneck limped over to a couple barstools. Kate drew them each an ale and placed the mugs in front of them as a peace offering. They nodded their thanks, sipped their ale, and Crewneck dabbed at his bloody nose with a bar napkin.

'So you've got someone who wants the rooster,' Duff said to Nick. 'What's in it for me?'

'A million dollars.'

Kate nearly choked. *A million dollars?*

Duff shook his head. 'I'd be breaching a sacred trust.'

'Did I say a million? I meant to say two. I'll even throw in a couple of stained glass windows.'

'This isn't a church, laddie.'

'You're the one who brought sacred trust into the conversation.'

'I was referring to my code of honor.'

'You don't have one.'

'I've never revealed the identity of a client before.'

'Because no one ever asked you. Besides, you're retired. What do you care?'

Duff stroked his beard. 'I have to look at myself in the mirror.'

'Hard to believe. If you'd ever looked in a mirror, you'd have shaved off that mangy beard ages ago.'

Duff scraped his chair back and stood. 'I'll sleep on it.'

Nick leaned forward. 'C'mon, Duff, stop being so ornery. It's early, and it's been years since we saw each other. Let's have a few pints and talk about old times.'

'If we do that, I might remember that I want to kill you.'

'Good point.' Nick pushed away from the table and walked to the door, motioning for Kate to get the bags. 'See you in the morning.'

Four

Kate waited until they were down the road, out of sight and out of earshot of the pub, before she dropped Nick's bag into a puddle.

'I'm your bodyguard, not your Sherpa,' she said. 'And two million dollars? Are you insane?'

'The rooster is worth twenty million. I think a ten percent commission for telling us where to find it is fair and reasonable.'

'You never said anything before we left LA about making a multimillion-dollar payoff to a crook.'

'It's the cost of doing business.'

'We're the FBI. We don't do business with international criminals.'

'What do you think *I* am? You should know better than anyone that sometimes you have to get in bed with the Devil. Speaking of which, we need to get a room. The hotel is the last building on the street.'

Kate stared ahead at the whitewashed building. It looked less like a hotel than an overgrown bed-and-breakfast –

two stories high, plus small windows on the third floor that might belong to attic rooms.

The sturdy woman at the desk informed them that there was just one room left. 'Very nice, though,' she said. 'Got a four-poster bed.'

Nick thanked the woman, gave her his credit card, and took the key. The room was on the second floor. No elevator. Just a narrow, creaky staircase. He unlocked the door and pushed it open.

'Maybe I should carry you across the threshold,' he said to Kate.

'Maybe you should be careful you don't run into my fist with your face,' Kate said.

The room was cozy and snug, barely big enough to hold the single four-poster bed, which was covered with a handmade quilt, a heavy comforter, and several pillows.

Nick stepped into the room and dropped his bag. 'It's perfect.'

Except that there was no furniture to sleep on besides the bed, Kate thought. That left the floor. In the military, Kate had slept in the wet mud of a South American jungle and on the hot sands of the Afghan desert, so she supposed she could spend the night on a hardwood floor if she had to.

'We'll flip for it,' Kate said.

'For what?'

'The bed.'

'Don't be ridiculous. We're sharing it.'

'In your dreams.'

'I think we can share a bed together without giving in to our raging desires.'

'I don't have any desires, raging or otherwise, that involve you.'

'So what are you worried about? Are you afraid I'm going to attack you? You're a trained commando and crack FBI agent who just threw a couple of muscle-bound, besweatered apes through a window.'

When he put it like that, it did seem pretty ridiculous.

'*Two* windows,' she said with a smile. 'And there's no such word as besweatered.'

'It's like bespectacled, only with a sweater.'

'I get the meaning, but there's no such word.'

'Sure there is. It was common in the days of yore. Trust me, I'm a very educated man. I went to Harvard.'

'They threw you out for cheating.'

'But not before I learned many things about the days of yore. I'll tell you about them over dinner.'

There was only one restaurant in town, and only one item on the restaurant's dinner menu. It was haggis, a dish made of boiled and minced sheep's lung, heart, liver, and esophagus mixed with onion, toasted oatmeal, and beef fat. The mix was then stuffed into the sheep's stomach, sewn shut, and boiled again.

Kate pushed the haggis around on her plate with her fork. 'This looks like dog food,' she said. 'And I think I saw an eyeball.'

'Haggis is an old Scottish dish,' Nick told her, 'and it doesn't contain eyeballs . . . usually.'

Kate took some for a test drive. 'It's not going to replace a Big Mac, but I can manage it if I wash it down with a lot of beer. And good thing it comes with mashed potatoes.'

'It's an acquired taste.'

Like you, Kate thought.

'Tell me about you and Duff,' she said to Nick. 'How did you betray him?'

'I didn't.'

'And yet he can still feel your knife in his back and wants to kill you.'

Nick looked around the restaurant. Two hikers were absorbed in their guidebooks and hiking maps. A local sat nursing a mug of tea at another table. The waitress and the cook were in the kitchen.

Nick leaned forward and lowered his voice. 'After I left Harvard, I decided to go to London for a change of scenery. One day, I was sitting in the Tate Gallery, admiring the paintings, when I saw Duff casing the place.'

'I never thought of you as an admirer of fine art.'

'Why do you think I steal it?'

'For the money,' she said. 'Maybe for the thrill.'

'The value of art to me is who owns it, how hard it is to steal, and how looking at it makes me feel. What it's worth monetarily is the least of my considerations.'

'What does it matter who owns it?'

'I only steal things from people who, on some level, are just asking to be taken.'

'How did you know Duff wasn't just another admirer of fine art?'

'I was still new at the game, but I was a con man at heart, I could tell when someone was playing a role. He was trying way too hard to let everyone know he was a tourist. He made a show of taking pictures of his wife in front of the paintings, but he was actually shooting the layout of the room, the location of the security cameras and the exits. So I started shadowing him. It only took a few days for me to figure out that the woman wasn't his wife and that he was plotting a heist. But what was he going to steal and how was he going to pull it off? I was totally obsessed with the mystery.'

'You weren't worried about what might happen if he caught you?'

'He did. The night of the job. He and his crew showed up and there I was, waiting for them at the Tate Gallery.'

'How did you know it would be that night?'

'The details of the heist aren't important.'

'I want details.'

'I'd be betraying Duff.'

'You already have.'

'That's debatable, which is why I'm telling you this story, so you'll see my side of things. When he found me waiting for him, I told him I wanted in. He beat the crap out of me, bound and gagged me with duct tape, and threw me in the back of their van while they pulled off the theft. They got away with a Picasso and a Matisse.'

She knew about that heist. It was still one of the great unsolved art thefts. Until now. Now she knew Duff MacTaggert had done it. And she couldn't tell anybody what she knew. Or arrest anyone for it.

'I thought Duff was going to kill me, and I think he did, too,' Nick said. 'But somewhere along the way, he changed his mind and invited me to join his crew. Over the next couple years, we did heists all over Europe. I learned how to case a location, put together a crew, and pull off the physical, logistical, and engineering aspects of a first-class heist. It was great fun. Money, adventure, exotic locales. That's when I knew I had to go.'

'Why leave if you were having such a good time?'

'I didn't want to be just a thief or part of someone's crew. Duff stole strictly for the money. It was the game of it that I enjoyed. I wanted to be my own man, equally adept at swindling and thievery. And to prove that I was, to myself and to him, I stole a Van Gogh from a museum in Amsterdam two days before Duff planned to steal it himself.'

'What a jerk. You ripped off his scheme and stole the painting for yourself. You didn't prove your mastery of theft. You proved you're a backstabbing weasel.'

'But I didn't use his plan. I came up with a brilliant plan of my own and stole the painting by myself. I didn't even cheat him out of the plunder. I left the painting on the wall of his living room as a gift. But for some insane reason he didn't take it that way.'

'What a *jerk.*'

'You mean *him* this time.'

'I mean *you.*'

'Why? I was showing my respect.'

'You were showing off and ridiculing him at the same time.'

'I don't see how.'

'What you were saying was: "Look at me, I'm so much more clever and capable than you. See you 'round, sucker."'

'That wasn't what I meant at all.'

'Well, that's what you said. You may be a great con man, but you still have a few things to learn about human nature.'

'So that's why he wants to kill me.'

'Yes, plus you have way better eyebrows.'

Nick ran his finger across his right eyebrow. 'You think that's a factor?'

'It would be for me.'

Five

Kate's nose was cold, but the rest of her was deliciously warm. She came awake slowly, taking inventory of her situation. T-shirt, check. Silky pajama bottoms, check. Location, unknown. She hit the pause button and filled in the blank. Location, Scotland. And she wasn't alone. She was totally snuggled into a man, her arm resting across his chest, her leg draped over his thigh, and her face nuzzled against his neck. There was a moment of panic and then horrified enlightenment.

She opened one eye and grimaced. 'Crap.'

'I was hoping for something more positive,' Nick said.

'Sorry, I'm afraid I accidentally gravitated to the warm side.'

'Warm is a gross understatement. Especially after you snaked your leg between mine.'

'Sorry.'

'You could give it a happy ending.'

'A happy ending for me would be half a loaf of bread, toasted, and a gallon of coffee.'

'It's occurring to me that I must be much *healthier* than you.'

Kate eased away from him. 'I'm perfectly healthy. I'm just very selective. I don't do it with just *anyone*.'

'So you're saying I don't measure up?'

From what she could tell was going on under the covers, Nick more than measured up, so probably 'measured up' wasn't the appropriate phrase.

'I have standards,' Kate said, rolling out of bed. 'I don't consider felons to be boyfriend material.'

Nick switched on the bedside light so he could get a better look at her in her T-shirt and silky pajama bottoms. 'How about one-night stands? Would you consider dropping your standards for a one-night stand?'

'Good grief, you're hopeless!'

'True, but I'm fun.'

Nick and Kate had a hearty breakfast of hot buttered potato scones, eggs, and what looked like boiled bacon, checked out of the hotel, and went over to the pub to see Duff MacTaggert.

The Sweater Brothers had finished putting boards up over the windows and were sitting at the picnic table outside, sipping hot mugs of something. They acknowledged Kate with a nod. She nodded back. In the unspoken parlance of tough guys, it meant there were no hard feelings.

'Is Duff around?' Nick asked.

'He's inside,' Turtleneck said. 'He'd like the lady to wait outside.'

Kate had no problem with that, but she did have a role to play. 'How do I know MacTaggert isn't going to do anything stupid, like shoot him?'

'He's never shot anyone before,' Crewneck said.

'He stabbed a man once,' Turtleneck said.

'Multiple times, if it's the bloke I'm thinking of,' Crewneck said. 'But he's never sliced a man open in the morning, and never in his pub.'

'Wouldn't be sanitary,' Turtleneck said.

'I'm reassured,' Nick said to Kate. 'How about you?'

She shrugged. 'It's your life.'

Ten minutes later Kate returned from a walk on the beach as Nick emerged from the pub. They grabbed their bags and headed to the dock just as the ferry was arriving.

'What did he say?' Kate asked.

'He gave up the buyer. Duff figures the son of a bitch has had the rooster long enough and that it's fair game now. Somebody is bound to steal it eventually. At least this way, Duff will make some money.'

'I thought he'd refuse to give you the name out of spite.'

'I started off by telling him that I was sorry about

what I did, that I was young, ambitious, and cocky. He told me that I still am and that's what he's always liked about me.'

'See? Sometimes being honest pays off.'

'Yes, but it doesn't pay nearly as well as dishonesty. Look how much Duff just earned.'

'So who has the bronze rooster now?'

'We'll find out once you've wired the first million to Duff's bank account.'

'He doesn't trust you?'

'Of course not,' Nick said. 'He knows me too well.'

It was a bright, beautiful day in Mallaig, but it was after one in the morning in Los Angeles when Kate reached Jessup. She knew Jessup's phone was secure, but she was still careful.

'We'll have the name when the money is wired into his account,' Kate said.

'How much money?' Jessup asked.

'A million.'

Silence on Jessup's end.

Kate imagined him not liking this, staring down at his bare feet, shaking his head. Best not to tell him about the second million, she thought. After all, why give him the bad news now when lots of things could happen in the meantime . . . like nuclear destruction or an uprising of zombies.

'I'll need wiring instructions,' Jessup said, sounding as if his sphincter muscles were painfully contracted.

'So how'd that go?' Nick asked when Kate disconnected.

'He's transferring money from the slush fund in the Caymans to Duff's account.'

'Did he sound happy?'

Kate did a small grimace, and Nick gave a bark of laughter.

The call from Duff came through at three PM. Kate and Nick were drinking coffee in a café in Mallaig, checking the Internet for possible flights home. Nick listened to the name Duff gave him, and promised the second payment would be made upon confirmation of the information he'd just received. His voice stayed calm and matter-of-fact with Duff, but Kate could see Nick's eyes narrow ever so slightly.

'So?' Kate asked when Nick pocketed his phone.

'Carter Grove has the rooster,' Nick said.

'Whoa! I didn't see that coming. I think we should scrap the operation. I have a rule against stealing from the White House chief of staff.'

'Ex–chief of staff,' Nick said.

'Him too,' she said.

Kate kept the bad news to herself for the twenty or so hours it took her to get back to Los Angeles and meet with Carl Jessup face-to-face. She arrived at LAX at 5 PM and took a shuttle bus to pick up her car at the Parking Spot on Sepulveda Boulevard. She met Jessup at the In-N-Out Burger next door to the parking structure. They ordered fries, shakes, and 3x3s–burgers with three meat patties and three slices of cheese. The 3x3 was an unadvertised delight on In-N-Out's secret menu. They ate them in the front seat of her car.

'Canceling the operation is out of the question,' Jessup said. 'We have to get the rooster back.'

'You will,' Kate said. 'Right after you arrest Carter Grove for stealing the damn thing.'

A glob of sauce oozed out of her 3x3 and dripped onto her jeans.

Jessup handed her a napkin. 'Even if we could get a search warrant, which is highly unlikely, the last thing we want to do is reveal that not only was the Smithsonian broken into, and that we covered up the crime, but that the man responsible for the theft was the White House chief of staff. It would be an even bigger scandal and embarrassment than the one we're trying to avoid.'

'Carter Grove isn't White House chief of staff anymore,' Kate said, dabbing at the sauce on her jeans with the napkin. 'He hasn't been in years.'

'But he was, and if that wasn't bad enough, now he runs BlackRhino, the elite private security agency the

Pentagon has been using to outsource the ugliest, dirtiest aspects of fighting our wars in Iraq and Afghanistan. If we go after Carter head-on for stealing the rooster, he'll expose every black op the Pentagon has ever hired him to do, which would only whip up the scandal into a media firestorm of epic proportions. You've got to steal the rooster from him. It's the most expedient option.'

'It's not a run-of-the-mill break-in we're talking about here,' Kate said. 'Carter Grove's house is going to be protected by a state-of-the-art alarm system and a bunch of BlackRhino operatives, the best-trained and best-armed mercenaries money can buy. If we're caught, they'll torture us to find out who we work for and then feed us into a tree shredder.'

'So don't get caught. I thought you were a tough cookie.'

'I am. But I'm not suicidal.'

'I'm sure Nick can come up with something,' Jessup said. 'You can remind him that this is exactly the kind of situation we broke him out of prison to solve.'

'Uh-huh,' Kate said, slurping up the last of her shake. 'And when he talked you into doing that for him, did it ever occur to you that you were being conned?'

'Sure it did,' Jessup said. 'That's why we teamed him up with you.'

* * *

A little over an hour after her meeting with Jessup, Kate sat at the kitchen table in her sister Megan's house in Calabasas, a San Fernando Valley community of guard-gated tract house neighborhoods. The neighborhoods were built around a shopping center with a clock tower that held the biggest Rolex on earth.

Megan shared her chair at the kitchen table with Jack Russell, her Jack Russell terrier, who'd squeezed himself between her butt and the backrest. The sisters were eating the remaining half of a banana cream pie.

Megan was married, had two kids, and was three years younger and thirty pounds heavier than Kate.

'You should take advantage of all the opportunities that being single, childless, and disgustingly thin give you,' Megan said.

'I am,' Kate said. 'I'm eating this pie after having a three-by-three, fries, and a shake at In-N-Out.'

'I hate you, but that's not what I was referring to.'

'I know what you're leading up to, and I'm telling you right now that I am not going on a blind date with some guy you met in line at Costco.'

'He's not *some guy*. He's an accountant at Roger's firm, and I've thoroughly vetted him. He could be the man of your dreams.'

Roger was Megan's husband. He was watching *Iron Man 2* in the den with their two kids, four-year-old Tyler and six-year-old Sara.

'Forget it, Megan.'

'He is stable, rational, and dependable.'

'Gee, he sounds thrilling,' Kate said. 'I've heard cars described in more passionate terms.'

'He's also a fantastic lover.'

'How do you know that?'

'Because he's an accountant,' Megan said.

Kate scraped up the last of the pie. 'I don't see the connection.'

'They are very tactile. They have amazing fingers from tapping their calculators all day. And they are extremely methodical in their work. So what you get is a man who will tirelessly explore every line item until he can file a strong return and get you a whopping refund.'

The analogy was totally disturbing, and yet it made sense to Kate. 'I'm doing fine. I can get my own dates, thank you.'

'The only man in your life is Nicolas Fox, and he's a criminal that you're chasing. That's just sad.'

'Do I look sad to you?'

Megan studied her sister. 'No, you don't, and you should. So what aren't you telling me?'

Jack Russell suddenly lifted his head and perked up his ears. An instant later Kate heard the front door open, and the dog launched himself off the chair and ran skittering across the tile floor to greet Kate's dad.

'What a terrific guard dog we have,' Megan said. 'He

doesn't bark until the intruder is already in the house hacking us to pieces.'

Jake O'Hare was a stocky, square-shouldered man in his sixties who'd retired from the military years ago but still kept his gray hair buzz-cut to army regs and did a hundred push-ups every morning.

'You don't need a guard dog,' Kate said. 'You've got Dad living in the garage.'

'*Casita,*' Jake said. 'This is a classy neighborhood.' He looked down at the empty pie pan. 'Looks like I'm late to the party.'

'You're just in time,' Kate said. 'I need to talk to you.'

'If this is going to be gun talk you have to take it outside,' Megan said. 'We don't allow gun talk in the house. We're a hundred percent PC.'

'Sad and pathetic,' Jake said. 'This country was founded on guns.'

Kate dropped her fork into the empty pie pan and stood. 'We can talk in your *casita*.'

Six

Megan had two detached garages, and she'd turned one of them into an apartment for Jake. The apartment still had faux garage doors in front to conform to the gated community's rigid architectural guidelines, and while they called it a *casita*, the interior was more Embassy Suites.

Kate sat on her dad's Naugahyde sofa in his *casita* and told him about the Smithsonian, the bronze rooster, and Carter Grove. She could talk to her father about her secret life because he'd had one, too. Most of his missions for the military were still classified.

'How much do you know about Carter Grove?' Jake asked.

'Just what I read in the newspapers. Plus the scuttlebutt I heard around the FBI water cooler.'

She knew that Carter Grove had been a hatchet man. His relationship with the former president went back to their wildcatting days in the Texas oil fields. Back then, the president was the 'vision guy,' the smooth talker who made the big deals. Carter Grove was the iron fist who hired thugs to blackmail politicians, to strong-arm stubborn landowners into selling their mineral rights, and to silence any discontent among the underpaid workforce. He employed those same techniques in DC and used the FBI and the CIA as his thugs. Agents who chafed at doing his dirty work were fired, blackballed in law enforcement, and, if they were lucky, found jobs in shopping mall security.

'Then you know only half the story,' Jake said. 'Carter almost single-handedly made BlackRhino the elite international army-for-hire that it is today. While he was chief of staff he threw lucrative defense contracts their way and encouraged the president to wage wars. BlackRhino paid Carter back handsomely by making him their CEO ten minutes after he left the White House.'

'Did you ever work with BlackRhino in your military days?'

'Not directly. I saw them on the fringes, training rebels in countries where the US wasn't supposed to be involved but had an active interest in the outcome of events.'

'So the Pentagon had BlackRhino do their dirty work.'

'It gave them deniability.'

'With your covert experience, you'd seem like a perfect pick for BlackRhino. Did they try to hire you after you left the military?'

'No, and do you want to know why?'

'Because you don't play well with others.'

'Because it's not enough for BlackRhino that you know how to kill. It's important that you like to do it. If you do, you're not going to care who lives or who dies as a consequence of your actions. That's not me. You don't want to mess with these guys, Kate.'

'I don't plan to. Whatever plan Nick comes up with to get the rooster, I'm sure it's going to be a con of some kind, not a straight break-in. We're not going to confront these guys in battle.'

'You will if the con goes wrong,' Jake said. 'And you will lose. I suggest you consider a combat option.'

'Like what?'

Jake got a couple bottles of beer out of his fridge and gave one to Kate. 'Like me.'

At ten the next morning, Kate pulled into Nick's Malibu driveway just as a Bentley convertible was leaving. The Bentley's driver was a bald Hispanic man with tattoos on his arms and neck. He was accompanied by a beautiful dark-haired, dark-skinned woman.

Kate parked and met Nick at the front door.

'Looks like you had visitors,' Kate said. 'Are you serving brunch?'

'That was Enrique Montoya, the new owner of this house.'

'You sold it?'

'It sold itself. It's spacious, secluded, and the views are spectacular. It was a steal at fifteen million.'

'You're damn right it's a steal. It isn't your house to sell.'

Nick gestured to a bulging gym bag on the floor in the entry hall. 'He even left a two-million-dollar cash deposit, which will more than cover the incidental expenses of our heist. How great is that?'

'You aren't listening to me. We can't keep that money.'

'Sure we can,' Nick said.

Kate was about to argue the absurdity of his proposal when something else crossed her mind. 'Wait a minute. That guy just handed you two million in cash in a gym bag?'

'I know what you're thinking. How inconsiderate was that? Who wants to lug that much cash around over their shoulder? It weighs a ton. One of those suitcases with wheels would have made more sense and been a lot more thoughtful.' Nick led her into the kitchen, where there was a fresh pot of coffee and a platter of pastries on the counter. He held the platter out to her. 'Bear claw?'

She took one. 'He's a drug dealer, isn't he?'

'He's bigger than that,' Nick said, picking out a cinnamon roll for himself. 'He's the point man for the Vibora cartel's entire Southern California drug distribution network. He's looking to launder some of his profits in real estate. This is going to be an all-cash deal. The balance is coming on Friday.'

'When you'll already be long gone with his money.'

'That's the plan.'

'The Viboras are bloodthirsty, homicidal maniacs. They've been known to cut off a man's arm and beat him to death with it. Aren't you worried about the Viboras hunting you down?'

Nick waved off her concern. 'I'm already on the run from all sorts of mobsters and countless law enforcement agencies. What's one more? Besides, I've got you protecting me.'

'We're about to take on Carter Grove and BlackRhino. The last thing we need is a Mexican drug cartel chasing us.'

'They won't be. When Montoya comes back on Friday, one of my associates at the real estate company can be here to handle the sale.'

'Who?'

'I don't know. You tell me. It'll be whichever FBI agent wants to accept Montoya's thirteen million dollars in drug money. You could either nail Montoya on the spot for immediate gratification, or you could bug the place, let him live here for a while, and use all the juicy intel you'll get to bring down the Viboras' operation.'

Jessup would like that. A fringe benefit of their secret op. 'And what about the two-million-dollar deposit?'

'Consider it a donation to our operating capital.'

Jessup would like that, too. She had to admire Nick's initiative. There was a reason he'd been such a successful con man right up until the moment she'd caught him.

'I don't want to ruin the moment for you,' Kate said, flicking bear claw crumbs from her shirt, 'but have you given any thought to our rooster dilemma?'

'I have it all figured out. I was inspired by Montoya when he showed up for the open house.'

'So you know how we're going to break into Carter Grove's fortress?'

'We aren't going to break in. He's going to invite us in.'

'Really? And will he give us the grand tour?'

'As a matter of fact,' Nick said, 'he will.'

Kate drank half the pot of coffee and had two more bear claws in the time it took Nick to tell her the broad strokes of his plan to run a con as a television show producer. Kate didn't know what astonished her more, the audacity of his scheme or that she ended up believing it could actually work.

There were still a lot of logistical and technical details to figure out, and a million ways that everything could go horribly wrong, but the outrageous, imaginative nature of the hustle was trademark Nick Fox, which was its biggest plus.

'So what's our first move?' she asked.

'We call the Geek Squad,' he replied.

When Joe Morey was six years old, a ramshackle traveling circus came to Northridge and erected its tattered big-top tent in a vacant parking lot next to Levitz Furniture. Joe's mother took him to see the show, which opened with a parade of elephants trailed by a clown driving a yellow Volkswagen Beetle with an enormous red bow tied on top. The clown stepped out of the Beetle and immediately slipped in a pile of elephant poop. The crowd roared with laughter. It wasn't part of the act, but it was by far the funniest thing the clown did and something Joe thought about now every day, almost thirty years later. It was hard not to, since Joe had basically become the clown himself, Dumbo dung and all.

His big top was the San Fernando Valley, and his clown car was a Beetle painted black-and-white to look like an LAPD cruiser with the orange-and-black Geek Squad logo on the doors. Joe was a Geek Squad 'Double Agent,' one of the computer repair technicians dispatched to homes and businesses from the Canoga Park Best Buy store. His clown costume was a short-sleeved white dress shirt with black clip-on tie, black trousers, white socks, and black shoes. His elephant poop was the chrome police-style Geek Squad badge he was required to clip to his belt and which doubled as guaranteed repellent to any attractive woman within a hundred yards.

Joe might have been able to live with all this if he was more like his co-workers, who saw the $18-an-hour job as a stepping-stone to something bigger, like becoming the next Steve Jobs or Mark Zuckerberg. But Joe was a paunchy guy in his thirties who through no fault of his own was a victim of an economy in the toilet. Joe used to make six figures a year in a corporate position commanding a crew that installed high-end security systems in Malibu mansions much like the one he was visiting right now. Joe's Geek Squad job was a step down with no chance of stepping up. He had a monstrous mortgage on a house that was worth half of what he'd originally paid for it. His wife had left him and taken the dog. And his Lexus had been repossessed. He sometimes thought he'd like to become an alcoholic, but he couldn't afford the liquor.

Joe parked his Geek Squad car next to a sweet Aston Martin, hiked up his black trousers, and trudged up to the front door prepared to face yet another frustrated customer who couldn't keep up with the ever-changing technology. He rang the bell, and Nick Fox answered.

'Welcome,' Nick Fox said. 'It's so good to see you, Joe. Please come in.'

'How do you know my name?' Joe asked, stepping

into the entry hall, nearly tripping over a bulging gym bag.

'I asked for you personally.'

'Have we met before?'

'No, but I'm a big admirer of your work.'

Nick closed the door and led Joe into the kitchen, where Kate sat at the counter. A bottle of Cristal was chilling in a silver ice bucket. Beside it were three fluted glasses.

Joe had been on Nick's watch list for some time. Nick always kept his eye out for talented people with special skills, mostly civilians in a bind he could use as leverage to recruit them.

Joe pulled the Geek Squad work order from his pocket and checked it. 'Says here you're having problems with your network. Point me to the router and modem, and I'll see what I can do.'

'Actually, your repair skills aren't what we're interested in,' Nick said. 'It's your work with Gant Security Systems that impressed us.'

Joe felt a twinge of anxiety grip his bowels. The one benefit of working for the Geek Squad was that it had given him complete anonymity. Nobody knew who he was or what he had done. He'd been able to leave his brief moment of infamy behind him.

'Three years ago, you discovered that Gant Security, the company you worked for as an installation supervisor, was running a scam,' Kate said. 'Gant sold celebrities high-end ultraexpensive home security systems, then used those systems' surveillance devices to spy on them, selling the dirt they discovered to gossip magazines and private detectives. You figured it out and blew the whistle to the LAPD. It was the honest and honorable thing to do. I admire that. Thanks to you, your boss and the installers who were getting kickbacks from him all went to jail.

'But instead of being congratulated for what you did, you were fired, sued for violating the confidentiality clause in your contract, and blackballed in the corporate world,' Kate said. 'Even your motives were impugned. The news media implied that the only reason you went to the authorities was resentment over being the one guy in the office not getting a piece of the action. Now you're buried in debt and wearing a Geek Squad badge. How would you like to get back at the people who wronged you and earn a hundred fifty thousand dollars at the same time?'

It would take Joe five years to earn that much money in his current job, and it was close to his annual paycheck at Gant before he'd let his conscience get him into trouble.

Joe narrowed his eyes and wondered if he was being set up in some way. 'What's the catch?'

'You'll be committing a felony,' Kate said. If she and

Nick were going to use civilians in their schemes, she wanted to be sure they knew exactly what they were getting into. 'You could end up spending ten years in a federal prison.'

'Who *are* you people?' Joe asked.

'We're with a private security company called Intertect,' Nick said. 'We've been hired by a major museum to recover a stolen artifact that is in the possession of Carter Grove, CEO of BlackRhino, the parent company of Gant Security Systems.'

'By "recover,"' Joe said, 'you mean steal it back.'

'Yes,' Kate said.

'Will I be in any physical jeopardy?'

Nick shook his head. 'You won't be part of the actual recovery effort. You will be a safe distance away, handling the technical side of things.'

'What happens to Carter Grove if you pull this off?'

'Legally? Nothing.' Nick said. 'However, since the item in question was stolen to begin with, he can't report the theft to the police or collect any insurance on it. So in a cosmic sense, he's getting royally screwed.'

Joe liked that idea. What he liked even more was that he'd be paid a lot of money to see it happen. He yanked the Geek Squad badge off his belt, pulled the clip-on tie from his collar, and tossed both onto the floor.

'Pop the cork on that Cristal, and let's get to it,' Joe said.

Seven

Artificial sunshine created by movie lights bathed the cheery kitchen of a Santa Clarita tract house that was serving as the location for a TV commercial. Two freckle-faced children, nine-year-old Missy and eleven-year-old Tommy, sat at the cottage table eating cereal from colorful bowls that perfectly complemented the placemats, the walls, the cupboards, and even the flowered apron their youthful mother was wearing.

'Bran flakes for breakfast *again*?' whined Missy, listlessly poking at her cereal with her spoon.

Tommy pushed his bowl away. 'Why can't we have something fun to eat?'

'Because that usually means a bowl of sugar,' their mother said.

'But it tastes good,' Missy said.

Mom wagged a finger at her daughter. 'That doesn't mean it's good for you.'

That's when an enormous jovial-looking pancake with

arms and legs and a pat of melting butter on its head bounded into the kitchen carrying two platters stacked high with hotcakes.

'A healthy breakfast doesn't have to be bland and boring anymore. Not if you're serving Percy Pancakes,' the pancake said.

'We love pancakes!' Missy exclaimed.

The giant pancake set the platters down and shook his head. 'I'm sorry, everyone, but this just isn't working for me.'

'Oh, for God's sake,' said the mother.

'CUT!' yelled the director.

A bell rang, and the fifty members of the film crew relaxed. The soundman lowered the boom mike he'd been holding up over the giant pancake's head, and a makeup woman came out to touch up the mother's face.

Boyd Capwell was the actor in the pancake costume, and he knew that the commercial was his shot at joining the pantheon of legendary food characters such as the Pillsbury Doughboy, Mr Peanut, the Kool-Aid Man, Mayor McCheese, Charlie the Tuna, Mrs Butterworth, and the California Raisins. It could lead to a steady, lucrative gig, something Boyd had been chasing for twenty years as an itinerant, unknown actor. But he was an artist above all else and had to be true to his muse. And his muse had issues with the scene.

The director was Stan Deakins, a fifty-two-year-old

veteran of the commercial business who preferred working with inanimate objects, like cars and cheeseburgers, specifically to avoid aggravation like this. He rose from his chair behind the camera and approached Boyd. 'What's the problem?'

'A complete stranger – a giant pancake, no less – has just appeared in their home,' Boyd said. 'Why isn't anyone reacting to this? Wouldn't they be screaming in terror?'

'They love pancakes,' Stan said.

'What would they do if a fried chicken leg walked in?'

'I'm not sure a chicken leg could walk in,' said the script supervisor, a lady who wore three layers of shirts and sucked on a pencil as if it were a pacifier. 'I suppose it could hop.'

Stan looked over his shoulder at her. 'Let me handle this.' He turned back to Boyd. 'The family knows you. You're not just another pancake off the street. You're a celebrity pancake, the Jay Leno of breakfast foods. Would anyone throw Leno out of their house?'

'Okay, assuming you're right, I'm a pancake asking this family to eat me. Am I suicidal or simply filled with self-loathing?'

'Take your pick,' Stan said. 'Whatever will get you through the scene.'

Boyd thought for a moment. 'Got it. I'm ready to go.'

'Glad to hear it.' Stan settled back into his seat. 'Okay, let's do a pickup from Missy's line.'

Boyd went back to his mark at the table. The actress playing the mother got back into her position. The makeup lady returned to her spot. The soundman positioned the boom microphone over the actors. An assistant director stood in front of the camera and held the electronic clapboard in front of the lens.

'Scene one, take fifteen,' the AD said, clapping the sticks.

'Action!' Stan yelled.

'We love pancakes!' Missy said.

The mother turned to Boyd. 'But growing children need vitamins and minerals.'

'I'm loaded with fiber and eight essential vitamins,' Boyd said. 'With our six great flavors, you get incredible taste and no more problems with regularity.'

'You're a pancake for the whole family,' the mother said.

Boyd dropped to his knees and took the mother's hands, startling the actress. 'Please, you've got to serve me to the kids. Being eaten is the only thing that gives my life any meaning. Without it, I'm nothing, just flour and buttermilk without a soul.'

Stan whispered to the script supervisor, 'What the hell is he saying? Is that in the script?'

The script supervisor shook her head. Stan groaned.

'And once I'm gone, be sure to try our new gluten-free recipe,' Boyd said to the now visibly confused actress. 'It's every bit as good as our classic mix.'

Stan closed his eyes and massaged his brow. 'CUT!'

Boyd got to his feet and turned to the director. 'That felt good to me. It resonated with emotional legitimacy.'

Stan looked up at Boyd with a pained expression. 'You're a pancake.'

'Thank you,' Boyd said, giving Stan a slight bow of gratitude. 'If you believe that, then I have succeeded. Shall we do it again?'

'No way in hell,' Stan said. 'You're history. Turn in your butter patty and pancake suit. I'm shooting the scene with a computer-generated pancake in postproduction.'

Boyd was on his way to the wardrobe truck when he saw Kate O'Hare leaning against the side of a storage locker. He hadn't seen Kate in months, not since he'd helped her, Nick, and the mysterious private security agency they worked for find a fugitive and recover half a billion dollars in stolen money. Boyd didn't know who Kate and Nick *really* were, but they'd given him a juicy role to play and paid in cash, and that's what mattered to him.

'Those people have no artistic integrity,' Boyd said, pointing at the house he'd just left.

'They didn't appreciate your psychologically tortured pancake,' Kate said.

She'd never had a conversation with someone in a pancake suit before. But even in that costume, Boyd somehow managed to maintain his dignity.

'You saw my performance?'

She nodded. 'The costumers were watching it on monitors in the wardrobe truck. I peeked while I was waiting for you.'

'Then you know that my portrayal was dead-on. He breaks into homes and asks children to eat him. He's obviously not a well-adjusted pancake.'

'Look at the bright side, Boyd. Now you're available for another job. One that pays a lot more than this and doesn't require you to wear a hat of melting butter.'

'What's the role?'

'Star of a reality TV show shot on location in Palm Beach, Florida.'

'I'm in.'

'Wait a minute. You don't know what we're really going to be doing.' She looked around. There was no one close enough to eavesdrop, but she lowered her voice to a whisper anyway. 'We're stealing back a stolen object from someone and returning it to its rightful owner.'

'A noble cause and a great part. What more does an actor need to know?'

'If we're caught, we could be killed, or if we're really lucky, sent to prison for ten years.'

Boyd waved off Kate's concern. 'It's still better than playing a pancake for philistines.'

Carter Grove was living in a forty-nine-million-dollar, twenty-three-thousand-square-foot beachfront estate in Palm Beach. The mansion had taken him three years to build and an additional two years to furnish. The house had a massive, domed rotunda in its center and twin two-story limestone-clad wings branching out on either side. It even had gargoyles carved in stone perched in the eaves.

'Carter modeled his place after Château de Vaux-le-Vicomte, Louis XIV's inspiration for the Palace of Versailles,' Nick said, standing with Kate on the beach in front of the house. 'That should tell you something about Carter's delusions of grandeur.'

'The only thing missing is a moat.'

'Château de Vaux-le-Vicomte was built starting in 1658 by Nicolas Fouquet, Louis XIV's state treasurer,' Nick said. 'In 1661, Fouquet invited his boss, Louis, over for a big housewarming party. The king took one look at the opulent castle and was so jealous, he confiscated it and threw Fouquet in prison for life. Maybe that's why Carter waited until he left the White House to build this.'

Kate thought the house looked as out of place on the white sand beach as a tuna casserole at the Last Supper. But Nick fit right in with the beach scene. He wore

Ray-Bans, a Tommy Bahama silk shirt, khaki shorts, and leather flip-flops. Kate was dressed in an H&M tank top, Gap boyfriend shorts, and Nike running shoes. It was a warm and sunny morning, two days after they'd recruited Joe Morey and Boyd Capwell for the con. They had only six more days until the Chinese arrived in DC to get their rooster back.

'I've done the research,' Kate said. 'Carter has a Gant Supermax Security system, the gold standard in security. Surveillance cameras watch every square inch of the property, inside and out. Infrared beams crisscross the rooms in constantly changing patterns that, if broken by anything larger than a dust particle, immediately set off the alarms. Even if you can get past all that, they have temperature sensors that can pick up an intruder's body heat.'

'No problem.'

'A dozen armed BlackRhino operatives patrol the property at all times. Every one of them is a trained killer. They're pros, with vast resources. They aren't going to take us at face value or be fooled by smooth talk. They are going to do background checks and verify everything we say.'

'Relax,' Nick said. 'My data forger in Hong Kong has built solid fake identities for us in every bank, government, law enforcement, and search engine database that BlackRhino is likely to check. They'll hold up, at least long enough for us to get the rooster.'

They walked the length of the property to a short boardwalk that led to the cul-de-sac where Kate had parked their rented Escalade.

At the end of the cul-de-sac, and next door to Carter Grove's estate, was a weedy construction site where work on a spec home had stopped early in the framing stage. An unmarked panel van was parked beside the office trailer that remained on the lot.

If Kate and Nick had walked into the trailer, they would have found Joe Morey inside, setting up computers, flat-screen monitors, and other equipment. But they ignored the trailer and got into the Escalade.

Kate turned to Nick in the passenger seat. 'This entire operation falls apart if Carter says no.'

'He won't say no,' Nick said. 'Nobody builds a house like that unless they crave attention. And we're going to give it to him in a big way.'

Carter Grove wasn't a king, but he was a kingmaker. He was on the phone, talking to Muktar Diriye Abdullahi, the brutal dictator of a small African nation. Botan Omar Wehliye, the hotheaded, idealistic rebel leader who was trying to topple the regime, was simultaneously on a different line with Carter. Both men wanted to hire BlackRhino to bolster their forces with mercenaries, military advisers, and cutting-edge weapons.

'You may be fighting for your country's ethnic heritage

and religious values, Muktar, but that means nothing to me,' Carter said. 'But when you overthrew the government twenty years ago, you nationalized the gold mines. *That* means something to me. You want us in your fight? It will cost you fifty million now and five percent of your annual mining profits for as long as your regime remains in power. Think about that for a minute, I've got another call I need to take.'

Carter put Muktar on hold and switched over to the line with the rebel leader.

'Sorry to keep you waiting, Botan. I don't care about the atrocities your people have suffered or the righteousness of your cause. You don't have any cash to pay me. But if you overthrow the government, you're going to control the gold mines. We want an irrevocable fifty-year lease on Frobe Valley. And don't think you can say yes now and renege on the deal later, because we'll assassinate your entire family and mutilate the corpses. That's a promise. What do you say?'

Fifteen minutes later, Carter strolled out of his office onto a balcony overlooking the Atlantic. He was sixty-two years old, round-faced and round-cheeked, with a thin mustache and beard that he maintained to create the illusion of a chin. He was unmarried but had no shortage of young women willing to party with him.

Veronica Dell, Carter's thirty-seven-year-old personal assistant, knocked and entered his office. She had a graduate degree in economics from Yale, a black belt in taekwondo, and the sexiest British accent Carter had ever heard, even though he knew it was fake. She'd been born and raised in Phoenix.

'How did the negotiations go?' she asked.

Carter left the balcony and returned to his office. 'Perfectly.'

'Which side are we supporting?'

'Both,' he said.

'So we win either way.'

'That's my idea of good business. Any calls?'

She nodded. 'The CEO of AeroSystem. He's sniffing around to see if you're interested in buying some drones. Now that the war effort in Afghanistan is winding down, he's overstocked.'

He liked the way Veronica said 'overstocked.' 'I didn't catch that. What did he say he was again?'

'Overstocked.'

Carter smiled. It was like having a younger, sexier Mary Poppins working for him. He wondered if she'd sing 'Supercalifragilisticexpialidocious' if he asked her to.

'Anything else?'

'Marissa Clopp at Emerald Coast Realty called,' Veronica said. Marissa was the Realtor who'd sold Carter the house he'd demolished to build this one. 'She's got two producers in her office from the TV show *The Most*

Spectacular Homes on Earth. They'd like to feature your house in an episode.'

Carter knew the show. It was on Home & Style Television. He'd watched it several times and didn't think that any of the houses they'd featured so far came close to matching his in splendor, grandeur, or artistic vision.

'What are the names of the producers?'

'Jim Rockford and Lucy Carmichael.'

Carter thought about it. His privacy was important to him. But he also imagined the envy that his friends and enemies in Washington would feel when they saw how he lived. The fact that his house was on a show called *The Most Spectacular Homes on Earth* would say it all.

'Have the New York office check them out. In the meantime, get the president of Home & Style Television on the phone for me.'

Eight

The Palm Gardens office complex was a sprawling five-story building that wrapped around a man-made lake in a formerly industrial area of Santa Monica, California. The building was home to several cable TV channels, advertising agencies, and production companies. The most recent tenant was Rififi Studios, which occupied a cramped three-hundred-square-foot space above the entrance to the parking garage and below the headquarters of Home & Style Television.

The phone lines that served HSTV passed through one of Rififi's walls. A hole had been cut through the wall, and a MacBook was wired into the bundle of phone lines. The MacBook was programmed to intercept any call from a Florida area code and redirect it to the phone in Rififi's office. Boyd Capwell was by himself in the office playing solitaire when the phone finally rang for the first time.

'Home & Style Television, how may I direct your call?' Capwell said.

'This is Carter Grove's office calling for Warren Kane.'

It was a woman speaking with the worst British accent Boyd had ever heard. Her dialect coach must have had a terrible speech impediment.

'One moment, please,' Boyd said. 'I'll transfer you to his office.' He put her on hold, then resumed the call with a voice that had dropped an octave. 'Warren Kane's office. Is Mr Grove ready to speak to Mr Kane?'

'He is.'

There was a click, and after a good thirty seconds had passed Carter Grove came on the line.

'Hey there, Warren. Glad you were available to talk. Are you familiar with who I am?'

'Of course I am, Mr Grove. We just sent two field producers out to Palm Beach to knock on your door. We can't continue calling our show *The Most Spectacular Homes on Earth* if we don't feature your house.'

'I think you're right, and that's why I'm willing to consider letting cameras into my home for the first time. But I have some conditions.'

'Name them.'

'I want full editorial control over the episode and final cut. Not just the editing, but the narration and music as well. Nothing goes on the air that I haven't approved first. I also want all the unused footage destroyed.'

'You've got a deal.'

'Really? I was expecting an argument and an impassioned speech about journalistic integrity, objectivity, and all of that crap.'

Boyd gave a hearty laugh. 'We aren't *60 Minutes,* Mr Grove. We're an aspirational network offering viewers a vision of a better life through home ownership and improvement. Or, to put it another way, we broadcast property porn designed to sell paint, hardware, appliances, and furniture. Our goal here is to make your house look even more spectacular than it already is.'

'I'm not sure that's possible,' Carter said. 'But I'm willing to let your team give it a shot.'

'I'm thrilled to hear that.'

'My people will need to run background checks on every crew member before they set foot in my house.'

'Take their DNA if you want. Give them colonoscopies, too. Do whatever it takes to make you feel comfortable so that we can show off your fabulous taste and magnificent home to millions of people around the world.'

'I think we're going to get along just fine,' Carter said.

Nick went off to hire a local film crew and Kate returned to her room at the four-star Regal Shores Hotel, a plantation-style beach-front resort. She changed into a bikini and found a chaise by the pool that gave her a nice view of the pristine beach and the two fourth-floor rooms she and Nick had rented in the main tower.

Kate was paging through the latest issue of *People*, but her eyes were on the fourth-floor rooms. A shadow passed behind Nick's window. Too late for maid service, too early for turndown service. Kate was guessing the room was being searched.

A muscled man in his thirties, wearing striped board shorts and reading an iPad, was lying on a chaise across the pool from her. Above his navel was a telltale star-shaped scar from a bullet wound. He was paying close attention to his iPad, but Kate didn't think he was reading, because his lips weren't moving. She suspected he was watching her on the iPad's camera.

A drop-dead-gorgeous woman with a Victoria's Secret body strolled out in a barely-there bikini with a top like pasties on strings. Bullet Belly flicked a glance at her and immediately returned to his iPad. Not normal, Kate thought. Even if he was gay, he'd check her out. BlackRhino operative, she decided. She was pleased they had Carter Grove's attention. It meant he hadn't dismissed their offer yet.

She spent the next hour reading her magazine. She swam a few laps, then Nick strolled out of the lobby and came down to the pool just as Kate pulled herself out of the water.

'That was quick,' Kate said. 'You hired an entire film crew already?'

'One-stop shopping. I hired a local production

company that shoots cheap commercials for car dealerships, restaurants, that kind of thing. They jumped at the chance to work on a network TV show. They're on standby until we hear from Carter.'

Kate grabbed her towel. 'We already have.'

'I take it you're referring to GI Joe across the way and the bikini model.'

'Our rooms have probably been searched and bugged,' Kate said. 'I hope you don't talk in your sleep.'

Nick's cell phone rang. He reached into his shirt pocket, pulled out the phone, and answered it. 'Jim Rockford.' He listened for a moment, then smiled. 'Excellent. Have a pleasant flight. We'll see you tomorrow.' He ended the call.

'Boyd?' she asked.

Nick nodded. 'We're on. Carter Grove will see us at nine AM tomorrow.'

Kate awoke shortly after sunrise, changed into a tank top and running shorts, and took off on a jog down the deserted beach. The sky was clear, cloudless, and bright blue. Water birds scurried out of her way into the surf. Brown pelicans dive-bombed into the water for their breakfasts while gulls swirled around them, hoping to snag some table scraps.

About a hundred yards ahead, Bullet Belly emerged from one of the access roads and paused on the beach to do some warm-up exercises. It was a clumsy tail, she thought, but justifiably so. It wasn't easy following someone on an empty beach, and they believed they were dealing with a civilian, somebody who wouldn't notice sloppy surveillance. Before Kate reached him, the guy started running ahead of her, keeping a good distance between them. She assumed, without looking back, that there was somebody behind her by now, too.

She maintained a steady, even pace and was barely winded as she climbed the steps to the old wooden pier. There were already quite a few fishermen along the wood rails. Kate knew that her dad would be one of them.

Kate walked to the end of the pier. She stopped in front of a guy wearing a Lakers ball cap and a ratty gray sweatshirt.

'Nice hat,' Kate said.

'Gotta support the home team.'

'We're meeting Carter Grove today,' Kate said. 'So the job will be tomorrow.'

'I'll be ready,' Jake O'Hare said. 'Does Nick know I'm here?'

'I told him last night.'

'And what did he say?'

'He said he would have been disappointed if you didn't find a way to hog some of the action.'

Well he got that right, Jake thought. No way was he

going to be left out of a mission like this. There'd been too many times when Kate was a kid that he'd missed parent-teacher meetings, school plays, birthday parties, and God knows what else because he'd been on a black op in Burma or a slash-and-burn in Pakistan. He figured the least he could do now was cover her back. Not to mention: Retirement was killing him.

Nine

The wrought-iron gates at Carter Grove's estate opened onto a large cobblestone motor court where a silver Lamborghini Aventador, a gold Bentley Continental Supersports convertible, and a white Mercedes-Benz SLS AMG were carefully staged around a huge marble fountain. Kate parked her rented Taurus beside the gleaming Lamborghini.

'Careful not to ding the Lambo,' Nick said, his eye on a security guard who stood on the lawn with a leashed Doberman at his side. 'Or they might sic the dogs on us.'

'I'm surprised they even let us park in the driveway in this heap,' Kate said. 'What will the neighbors say?'

'That the gardener has arrived.'

Nick got out of the Taurus, and his entire body language changed as he slipped instantly into character. There was a swagger to his walk that reminded Kate of John Travolta in *Saturday Night Fever*.

'I can see it now,' Nick said. 'We begin with a high crane shot over the property. The camera swoops down over the motor court, past the fountain and the cars, and settles on the front doors. And there he is.'

As if on cue, the tall, elaborately carved front doors opened and Carter Grove strode out like a talk show host greeting his adoring audience. His assistant, Veronica Dell, came out two steps behind him in a low-cut, body-hugging sleeveless bandage dress.

'Welcome to Château du Roi,' Carter said.

Of course the house had a name, Kate thought, and one about as subtle as the three cars out front. Castle of the King. She decided to name her apartment something classy when she got back to LA. Her place overlooked a gas station, so maybe Château du Chevronview.

'Castle of the King,' Nick said. 'It looks like it will live up to its name.'

'You must be Jim,' Carter said, shaking Nick's hand. 'You've come a long way from producing local news in Toledo.'

Nick nodded. 'You've been checking up on me.'

Kate offered her hand to Carter. 'I'm Lucy Carmichael.'

Carter gave her hand a gentle squeeze and looked her in the eye. 'You're as beautiful today as you were when you were crowned Fresno's Junior Miss Avocado in 1998.'

'Now you're just showing off,' Kate said with a smile.

'Guilty as charged,' Carter said, raising his hands in mock surrender. 'I have to screen everybody who comes into my house. You can't be a former right-hand man to the president and run the world's leading private security firm without making enemies. Do you have a list of crew members for me?'

Kate handed him a sheet of paper. 'The crew is all local except for our unit production manager and our new host.'

Carter passed the paper on to Veronica, who went back into the house. 'That should make the background checks fast and easy. Well, now that we've got that settled, are you ready for the grand tour?'

'Absolutely,' Nick said.

Carter led them into a two-story circular foyer ringed with a pair of sweeping staircases that dramatically framed the spectacular view of the ocean through the living room windows. Kate could see a thirty-foot center console fishing boat anchored off the shoreline. If she'd had binoculars, she would have seen her father and his old army buddy José Rodarte on deck, drinking beers and watching their lines for bites.

'This entryway is inspired by the Grand Salon of Vaux-le-Vicomte,' Carter said. 'The stained glass skylight in the dome depicts Apollo, Bacchus, Venus, and Mercury looking down upon the Earth from the heavens.'

Kate looked up at the skylight and was surprised to see that Carter hadn't included himself among the gods in stained glass.

'Impressive,' Nick said. 'Do you mind if I do some preliminary filming with my iPhone?'

Carter smiled. 'Not at all, but I'll have you killed if you show it to anyone without my permission.'

'A sense of humor!' Nick said. 'I like that.'

'No,' Carter said. 'I really *will* have you killed.'

He led Kate and Nick down a corridor into what he called his 'game room.' It was in fact a full-scale casino packed with dozens of vintage slot machines.

'I needed a place to show off my collection of slots from the fifties and early sixties, so I re-created the Sands Hotel and Casino as it was when Frank, Dean, Sammy, and the rest of the Rat Pack hung out there,' Carter said. 'There's fifty thousand dollars in coins in these machines.'

'This is fun,' Nick said. 'All that's missing is cigarette smoke and the cocktail waitresses.'

'And a gaming license,' Carter said. 'I'm the only one who gets to play in here. I can do it for hours. It relaxes me.'

'How often do you win?' Kate asked.

'Even in this casino the odds favor the house. Luckily, the house is also me, or I wouldn't play.'

Kate had a feeling that was his approach to everything. If things weren't rigged in his favor, he didn't participate.

Carter took them through his library, his wine cellar, his ultramodern kitchen, and then turned onto another corridor. He stopped in front of a thick, weather-beaten old door that had clearly battled the elements somewhere for decades and survived.

'This is one of my favorite rooms in the house,' he said.

He grabbed the big iron handle and opened the heavy door, the large hinges creaking from the strain. Nick and Kate stepped past him and walked into an old pub. The walls were mottled brick framed by dark, elaborately carved paneling that was chipped and faded from age. The hardwood floors were scratched, stained, and worn smooth by years of use. The bar was made of thick, honey-colored wood and trimmed with brass. The barstools and booths were upholstered in scratched red leather.

'This was a pub I visited in London. I liked it so much that I bought it, had it dismantled brick by brick, and reconstructed it here,' Carter said. 'Everything is original. Nothing is replicated.'

'I love the original brick,' Nick said. 'I've seen houses where they'd attempted to reproduce this look, but it's never as beautiful.'

'We've taken great pains to keep it pure,' Carter said. 'We didn't clean the walls, floor, or countertops beyond a simple wipe-down with a wet rag or mop. I believe the buildup of smoke, spillage, spit, and grime over the years is an essential part of a pub's character. This looks, feels, and smells real because it is.'

Kate thought the whole idea was weird. She liked McDonald's, but she wouldn't want to take one apart, dirty floors and all, and reassemble it in her apartment.

Down the hall from the pub was Carter's home theater. The entrance was the exterior of an old movie house, with THE MAJESTIC written in neon above a lighted marquee and a stand-alone ticket booth. Beyond the glass lobby doors Kate could see a concession stand with a full-size popcorn machine, hot dog warmer, soft drink dispenser, and a display case full of candy.

'This is the Majestic Theater from my hometown of Bigleton, Indiana,' Carter said. 'This is where I went to watch movies when I was a kid. It closed down years ago and fell into disrepair. So I salvaged what I could and brought it here. Only the marquee, ticket booth, and lobby concession stand are from the original Majestic. The screening room is much smaller and outfitted with the latest advances in digital projection and sound technology.'

Nick raised his iPhone to the marquee and panned down to the ticket booth. 'What if we put the title of our series up there in lights and then panned down to you in the ticket booth, inviting the viewer to watch? That would make a kick-ass teaser for the episode.'

'I like it,' Carter said, leading them through the lobby and into the theater.

Art Deco sconces lighted the walnut-paneled room.

There were three rows of seats, each with four custom leather recliners facing an eight-by-eighteen-foot screen.

'This room is couch potato heaven,' Kate said. 'Every man in America is going to envy you.'

This got a smile from Carter, since it was exactly what he wanted to hear.

He went on to show them his six bedrooms and eight bathrooms. Then he showed them his home security center, a small, windowless room on the first floor manned by a black-suited BlackRhino operative. The operative sat in front of a bank of monitors that displayed video feeds from all the security cameras.

'A lizard can't step on my property without me knowing about it,' Carter said.

Carter ended the tour by taking them outside and showing them his pool area, a tropical paradise of waterfalls, lazy streams, and grottoes.

'Paradise,' Nick said. 'I don't know how we're ever going to top this house in future episodes.'

'Somebody had to set the bar,' Carter said. 'So what's the next step?'

'Today we'll prelight the rooms we intend to shoot and do some camera tests. That way, all you have to do tomorrow is give our host and our cameramen the same tour you just gave us.'

'Sounds good to me,' Carter said. 'Veronica will give

you a call once your crew has been cleared. It shouldn't take more than a couple hours.'

'I didn't see the rooster,' Kate said as they drove off, heading for the airport to pick up Boyd. 'Not that I expected to. How are we going to find it?'

They came to a stop at an intersection and Nick showed her a photo on his iPhone. It was one of the walls of the home theater.

'I think this is a secret door leading to a secret room,' Nick said. 'There are two security cameras aimed at it. Why else would he want to watch a blank wall?'

'Even if it *is* a door, and we are able to get inside the room, how do we avoid setting off all the alarms?'

'They'll be turned off. He can't have the alarms on with a film crew walking through the house all day.'

'But the crew won't be going into the secret room.'

'There probably aren't any alarms in there,' Nick said.

'Probably?'

'I'm ninety-eight percent sure.'

'It's where all his treasures are hidden. Why wouldn't the room be protected with all of his security measures?'

'Because to get there, a thief would have to get past his fence, his armed guards, his vicious dogs, infrared beams, heat sensors, pressure pads, motion detectors, surveillance cameras, and whatever else he's got in the house. I'm sure Carter doesn't think that's possible. But even if someone could surmount those obstacles, he's got the wall, his secret doorway to the secret room, under constant surveillance. So why go the extra step of rigging the secret room itself with security measures?'

'To protect all of his stolen treasures.'

Nick shook his head. 'That'd be overkill.'

'Have you seen his house? It's a monument to overkill.'

'There won't be any security in the secret room. Think of it as a vault. How many vaults have you seen that also have alarms inside? Everybody thinks the big door, and everything outside of it, is enough protection.'

'But you know it's not,' Kate said. 'And so does he.'

Nick shook his head. 'I don't think so. He's arrogant. He's got too much confidence in himself and his men.'

'You're still guessing,' Kate said.

'It's an educated guess.'

'What if you're wrong?'

'We'll need a distraction.'

'What do you have in mind?'

'Your dad,' Nick said. 'What's Jake got with him?'

'A handheld rocket launcher.'

'You have a very overprotective father,' Nick said. 'When you were a teenager, how did he greet your dates? With a flame-thrower?'

'With a foot-long combat machete, just like the one he gave me on my twelfth birthday.'

'Every girl should have one,' Nick said.

'Dad's on a fishing boat in front of Carter's estate. If we get into trouble, all I have to do is press the button on the tiny transmitter in my pocket and he'll destroy the dome on top of Carter's house. Is that enough of a distraction for you?'

'Maybe we can work out something a little more subtle.'

Ten

Nick, Kate, and Joe met in Boyd's suite at the Regal later that afternoon to discuss the plan.

'Carter Grove has graciously turned off his alarm system and invited us into his house, saving us the trouble of breaking in,' Nick said. 'While he gives Boyd and the film crew the grand tour, Kate and I will sneak into the home theater, open the hidden door, and steal the bronze rooster from the secret room. We'll stash the rooster in a carrying case for a piece of the lighting equipment and take it out with us when the filming is done.'

'The alarm system will be turned off, but what about the security cameras?' Boyd asked. 'You said there were cameras all over the place. How are you going to get around the cameras?'

'That's what Joe is here for,' Nick said. 'Yesterday, he set up shop in a construction trailer in an empty lot next door to Carter's house. The trailer is located beside the utility boxes for the neighborhood's electric, cable, and telephone services. He tapped into those lines and breached Carter's security system. While we were picking you up at the airport and bringing you here, Joe supervised the crew that was setting up the movie lights in Carter's house.'

'I don't know anything about lighting,' Joe said, 'but I made sure there were some tall light stands placed throughout the house at the same height and angle as Carter's security cameras. I hid tiny cameras of my own on the stands and filmed the empty rooms. When Kate and Nick slip into the theater, I'm going to replace the video feed from Carter's surveillance cameras with a continuous loop of the footage I shot of the empty room.'

'Very clever,' Boyd said.

'And that's not the only reason we have our own cameras everywhere,' Nick said. 'Joe is going to be our guardian angel. He'll be in the trailer watching everything that's happening on all the cameras and will alert us if there's any trouble.'

Boyd looked at Joe. 'You'll have to tell me where the cameras are so I can make sure they get my best angle.'

Kate groaned. 'The only cameras you have to worry about are the ones filming the show.'

'Au contraire,' Boyd said. 'An actor has to be constantly aware of his audience, whether they are in the front row or the cheap seats, if he is going to give a convincing performance.'

'Carter is the only one who has to be convinced,' Kate said.

'And the guards watching on the security cameras,' Boyd said. 'If they don't believe my performance, then the entire show fails.'

'We'll make sure you know where all the cameras are,' Nick said to Boyd. 'Just don't look into them.'

'You're talking to a professional,' Boyd said.

Joe handed Kate, Nick, and Boyd flesh-colored devices that looked like tiny hearing aids. 'We'll keep in touch with one another using these earbuds. They're both earphones and mikes. They go deep in the ear and are pretty much undetectable unless someone gets very close.'

Boyd examined his earpiece with disdain. 'I knew a Broadway actor who wore one of these so someone offstage could read him his lines. Nobody in the audience knew about it, of course. The critics thought the long pauses in his performance provided profound dramatic impact. In fact, he was just waiting to hear his next line. The fraud won a Tony Award.'

'That's not what you'll be using it for,' Nick said. 'There's no script and no lines to learn on this caper. Your job is to make the tour glamorous and entertaining for the viewer. So feel free to improvise, to find your character as you go.'

'This is why I love working with you,' Boyd said. 'You

know how to treat actors. Speaking of that, you mentioned Joe's trailer. What about mine?'

'You don't have one,' Kate said.

'But I'm the star of the show,' Boyd said. 'The star always gets a trailer.'

'It's a fake show,' she said.

'Then I need a fake trailer.'

'You'll have to settle for an imaginary one,' Kate said.

The next day, the film crew arrived at the Carter Grove estate at 9 AM in a convoy of cars, trucks, and vans led by Kate's Ford Taurus. Dozens of people spilled out of the vehicles and swarmed over the property, lugging cables, monitors, director's chairs, microphones, lights, and all kinds of other paraphernalia. It was a lot of commotion, which was what Nick wanted. He'd purposely hired far more people and brought in more equipment than was necessary so there would be plenty of activity to keep the security guards busy.

Nick and Kate brought Boyd into the kitchen, where Carter Grove sat on a barstool having his makeup applied by a slim young woman.

'Mr Grove, I'd like to introduce you to Boyd Capwell,' Kate said. 'Our new host this season.'

Carter stood and Boyd offered him his hand. 'This is a big thrill for me. I couldn't possibly be more excited about this opportunity.'

Nick led them outside, where he introduced Carter and Boyd to the two shaggy cameramen, each of whom carried a lightweight digital camera and looked as if he washed his hair with bacon grease.

'We're going to start here and go slowly through the house.' Nick turned to the cameramen. 'Your job is to stay on Boyd and Mr Grove and whatever they are reacting to.'

The cameramen nodded.

Nick turned to Carter. 'Just do exactly what you did yesterday. Pretend the cameras aren't here. We'll try to keep ourselves and the crew out of your way, so we don't end up in your line of vision. We want you to feel as if it's just the two of you.'

'I can do that,' Carter said.

'Terrific,' Nick said. 'Let's make a TV show.' The first room Carter took Boyd into was the Grand Salon with its domed skylight depicting the Roman gods. Boyd looked up at it while Carter told the story of the room pretty much word-for-word the way he had for Nick and Kate.

'You must get some monster cobwebs up there,' Boyd said. 'How do you get rid of them?'

'I send some guys up on ladders once a month.'

'I wouldn't want your window cleaning bills.' Boyd tapped his foot on the floor. 'Is this real marble?'

'Imported from Italy. From Pietrasanta, to be precise,

the same quarry where Michelangelo mined the stone he used to sculpt David.'

'Did you know that they have linoleum at Home Depot that looks just like marble now? It's much cheaper.'

'It's not the same,' Carter said, his eyes slightly narrowed.

'That's for sure,' Boyd said. 'Good luck trying to sculpt David out of it.'

Boyd laughed. Carter didn't. Nick and Kate stood by the front door, far behind the cameramen.

Kate leaned over to Nick and whispered, 'What the hell is Boyd doing?'

'He's representing the audience by being the common man.'

'The common man is pissing Carter off.'

'It's keeping Carter engaged and his attention focused on Boyd, which is what we want,' Nick said. 'You do know that Boyd can hear you on his earbud, right?'

'Of course I do,' Kate said, but that was a lie. She'd forgotten.

'Carter is going to show Boyd his slot machine collection now,' Nick said. 'This would be a good time for us to go to the theater. Joe, can you make us invisible?'

'No problem,' Joe replied, his voice transmitted to their earbuds from where he sat in the construction trailer on the empty lot next door. 'Just wait until Boyd and Carter make their move down the corridor to the game room.'

Boyd took that as his cue to head toward one of the corridors off the foyer. 'So where does this lead?'

'To the Sands Hotel and Casino, circa 1962,' Carter said.

'You're kidding,' Boyd said. 'This I've got to see.'

'Follow me.' Carter walked past him down the hall. Boyd and the cameramen went after him. At the same moment, Nick and Kate slipped away down another hall that branched off the foyer.

Nick had total faith that Joe, sitting out in the trailer, was tracking them and deftly replacing the live security camera feed with the footage he'd shot earlier of empty corridors and rooms.

'This is fun,' Nick said, stopping in front of the theater's ticket booth.

'I'd be more comfortable doing this at night,' Kate said, 'armed to the teeth, and wearing night vision goggles.'

'You'd be more comfortable doing *everything* that way.'

Nick and Kate slipped on disposable gloves, eased open the glass door to the theater, hurried past the concession stand, and stepped into the auditorium. The stage lights for filming were arranged on tall stands, but they hadn't been powered up yet. Only the sconces were on.

Nick ran his hands over the blank wall as if he were smoothing out wrinkles on a bedspread.

'What are you doing?' Kate asked.

'Trying to find a switch.'

Nick looked at the sconces. He reached up and tugged on one of them. It held fast. He tried the other one. It turned, there was a click, and he stepped back just as the wall swung out toward them, releasing a burst of cool air from the room beyond.

'Voilà,' he said and stepped inside.

Eleven

Of course Kate knew they were looking for a secret door, but when the wall actually opened, she felt a childish thrill. She'd never actually seen a secret door before. It was like something out of *Scooby-Doo.* She half expected a cartoon mummy to come running out, arms outstretched, trailing a tattered strip of bandage behind him.

Nick stopped on the first of two steps that led down into the room. Kate came up beside him and they stood there for a moment, getting the lay of the land.

The walls were painted black and adorned with paintings illuminated by carefully positioned pinpoint halogens. Pedestals and glass cases with sculptures, pottery, masks, and jewels were arrayed throughout the space and lit from below and above for full dramatic effect. Benches upholstered with red velvet cushions were placed in key positions that offered the best views of the artwork and displays.

Nick let his breath out slowly. 'Holy crap.'

'What's wrong?'

'This isn't just a secret room. It's the secret room to end all secret rooms.'

'It's pretty nice, but it's no Batcave.'

'It's better than the Batcave. You're looking at the hall of fame of art thievery.' Nick began pointing to various paintings and objects. 'That's an Edgar Degas drawing, part of the haul from the Gardner Museum in 1990, the biggest art theft in US history. Over there is a Picasso taken from the Museu da Chácara do Céu in Rio de Janeiro in 2006. And in that display case on your left is a rare Abraham-Louis Breguet clock stolen from a museum in Paris in 1981.'

Kate pointed to a pedestal at the far end of the room. 'And there's the bronze rooster.'

Nick reached into his breast pocket, took out what appeared to be a pair of sunglasses, and slipped them on. 'Damn.'

'What is it now?'

He removed the glasses and handed them to her. 'See for yourself.'

Kate put them on and looked out at the room. The glasses allowed her to see beams of red light crisscrossing the room from floor to ceiling. The pattern of the lights shifted every few seconds. They'd never be able to get past them. And if any of the beams were broken, the alarms would go off.

She took the glasses off and gave Nick a sidewise look. 'I thought you said there wouldn't be any security in here.'

'I didn't know about all of the extraordinary art treasures that Carter has or that he's a generous patron of the greatest thieves on earth. If I'd known that, I would have done a lot of things differently.'

'So what do we do now?'

'We need a distraction,' he said. 'Obviously, Carter flipped the switch for those areas where the film crew would be operating but left some of his security in place. Let's hope the roof is still wired for impact.'

Kate put her hand in her pocket, found the tiny transmitter, and pressed the button.

Both Joe and Boyd heard the conversation and knew what was coming. They'd been briefed on 'the distraction.'

Boyd was in the casino with the two cameramen and Carter. Carter was explaining that all of the 1960s light fixtures in the room were genuine.

'Only the carpets from the Sands had to be re-created,' Carter said. 'Everything else is authentic.'

'Do you pay out slot winnings in 1960s dollars or have you adjusted for inflation?'

Boyd slipped a nickel into a slot machine and pulled the lever. The wheels of fortune spun.

* * *

Joe sat at a table in the trailer. In front of him were four computer monitors. The first screen showed live video feeds from every camera on Carter Grove's property. The middle screen showed thumbnails of all the prerecorded footage that Joe had on tape. And the third screen showed him what the security guards were seeing on their monitors in the command center.

He clicked his mouse and enlarged the video feed from the surveillance cameras that covered the beach side of Carter's estate. He could see a speedboat cruising across the water, pulling a man through the air on a parasail. Suddenly the line to the boat snapped loose and the freed parasailer began a rapid descent toward Carter's estate.

In the casino, Boyd rolled cherries on all three reels of a slot machine. Bells rang, and coins spilled into the metal tray with a loud clatter. Boyd let out a whoop, and Carter Grove clenched his teeth hard enough to give himself a headache.

'Do I get to keep this?' Boyd asked.

The jackpot was pure luck, but what happened next was planned with precision. Jake O'Hare landed on the roof of Carter Grove's mansion, setting off alarms that were so loud they shook the building.

The instant the alarms blared, Nick and Kate made a mad dash across the floor of the secret room to the rooster. Nick lifted the rooster carefully from its pedestal and handed it to her.

'Take this,' he said. 'I need my hands free to grab the Degas and that Rembrandt over there.'

'This isn't a buffet. We came for the rooster, that's all we're taking.'

'Everything in here is stolen. That Rembrandt alone is worth much more than this rooster. We can't just walk away from all this.'

Kate understood his temptation. She felt it too, only it wasn't the urge to steal that she was fighting. She wanted to immediately arrest Carter Grove for aiding and abetting the theft of tens of millions of dollars' worth of art treasures. But since she'd discovered the crime while searching the house without a warrant, and in the company of an international fugitive she was supposed to be chasing, she'd be the one sent to prison, not Carter.

'We have to go *now,*' she said, 'before the alarm stops ringing and we get caught down here. And if you take anything other than the rooster I'll personally shoot you as soon as I lay my hands on my gun.'

'It's a crime leaving all of that behind,' Nick said.

'You and I have fundamentally different ideas about crime.'

'That's the story of our lives.'

* * *

Carter abandoned Boyd and the film crew and ran straight for the command center. The militaristic-looking young BlackRhino operative manning the console stood up as soon as Carter entered.

'What have we got?' Carter demanded.

The operative pointed to the monitors. 'There's an old guy on the roof.'

'What the hell?' Carter pushed the operative aside and looked for himself. Sure enough, there was an old guy in a bright yellow life vest up there. He was all tangled up in the rigging of a parasail and trying to get free.

'I don't believe this,' Carter said. 'Where did he come from?'

'He broke loose from a parasailing boat. There is a water sports outfit that runs them.'

'Damn tourists. Get someone up on the roof to bring him down,' Carter said. 'And turn off the alarm.'

'Yes, sir,' the operative said. He flicked a switch and the alarm stopped ringing.

Carter turned around to see Boyd and the cameramen standing behind him. Boyd clutched a vintage plastic Sands bucket full of coins.

'Cut!' Carter said, waving his hands at the cameramen. 'This isn't part of the tour.'

'But it adds so much excitement to the show,' Boyd said.

'Stay here,' Carter said. 'I'll let you know when we're ready to shoot again.'

Back in the theater, Kate straightened the sconce, closing the doorway to the secret room, while Nick went to a metal equipment case that was beside one of the lighting stands. He opened the case, gently placed the rooster inside, and closed it. Then the two of them walked out of the theater and peeled off their gloves.

Kate didn't like leaving the rooster, but it was too risky to try taking it with them now. They'd retrieve the case when the tour was finished and the crew packed up. At that point, carrying an equipment case out of the building wouldn't attract attention.

'We're clear,' Kate said, notifying Boyd and Joe.

It took ten minutes for Carter's guards to find a ladder, set it up in the yard, and climb to the roof. Jake stood and held out a disposable camera to the first man who showed up.

'You've got to take a picture of me,' Jake said. 'Or my wife will never believe this.'

Nick and Kate joined Carter, Veronica, and a handful of BlackRhino operatives in the yard to meet the uninvited guest. Jake came slowly down the ladder, holding on to it for dear life as he went along. His bright yellow life vest was open now and showed the white IT'S ALWAYS SUNNY IN FLORIDA T-shirt he wore underneath. He had on a pair of Bermuda shorts, white tube socks, and running shoes that closed with Velcro straps. Sunblock was smeared heavily on his nose. Once his feet touched solid ground, Jake turned to the gathered crowd with a big smile.

'Woo-wee, what a wild ride that was. Sure got my fifty bucks' worth.'

Carter stepped up to him. 'Who are you?'

'J. W. Saltz from Baxter Springs, Kansas. I own the Chevy dealership in town. Come by and I'll make you the deal of a century on the Impala of your dreams.'

It was hard for Kate not to laugh.

Jake shaded his eyes with his hand and scanned the ocean. 'Looks like Pedro headed back to Cuba after my line broke. Can't really blame him. He probably thinks I'm tangled in a tree with a broken neck. Hell, I'm surprised I'm not. I've never steered a parachute before. I just pulled this and pulled that and made a bunch of promises to God that I hope he doesn't expect me to keep.'

'What are you doing down here?'

'Thirty-seventh wedding anniversary. My wife wanted to browse at the consignment stores, so I dropped her off and went to the beach. She loves those stores. Lots of filthy-rich old people die down here and that's where their stuff ends up, dirt cheap. Nobody at home knows Myrtle is wearing a dead lady's clothes. They think we're loaded.'

'I meant, why were you parasailing in front of my house?'

'I slipped Pedro an extra twenty to take me for a spin over the big haciendas. I wanted to get some pictures from a bird's-eye view. We don't see homes much larger than a double-wide where we're from.'

One of the operatives stepped forward and handed Jake's disposable camera to Carter.

'I got a great deal on that,' Jake said, tipping his head toward the camera. 'Two for ten dollars at Walmart.'

Carter dropped the camera on the ground and crushed it under his foot.

'What the hell did you do that for?' Jake said.

'Consider it the price of trespassing.'

'It was an accident. You ought to be thankful that I didn't have a heart attack and die on your roof. My ticker isn't what it once was, and this has been a big shock to my system. You really don't want to give me any more stress. I could drop dead right here.'

'Then we'd better get you off my property before that happens.' Carter gestured to one of his men. 'Give Mr Saltz a ride back to his hotel.'

Twelve

Kate O'Hare had been trained by the military to be patient, and to endure many forms of torture, but nothing had prepared her for sitting through the next three hours of filming. It wasn't Carter reveling in his outrageous excesses, or Boyd's overacting, or Nick's comfort with his crime that was eating at her. What she couldn't stand was remaining at the scene of the crime after the heist was done. She desperately wanted to grab the rooster and run. The hardest part came near the end, when Carter showed off the home theater. It felt to her like the case with the rooster was glowing and radiating heat.

Carter and Boyd came out of the auditorium and were trailed into the lobby by the two cameramen. Boyd stopped and shook his head in wonder.

'You've got a small-town movie theater, an authentic English pub, a re-creation of the Sands casino with vintage slot machines, and the Grand Salon of Vaux-le-Vicomte. Who else has all of that in their house? It's incredible. Thank you for showing us all what it's like to live in one of *the most spectacular homes on Earth*!'

Boyd gave Carter a big smile, then they shook hands and remained in that stilted pose for a long moment.

'Cut!' Nick said.

The cameramen lowered their cameras and relaxed. Kate turned to the crew, who'd been waiting in the hall, and announced, 'That's a wrap. Let's break down the lights and clean this place up.'

Nick hurried over to Boyd and Carter. 'Outstanding,' Nick said.

'Thank you so much.' Boyd bowed theatrically.

Crew members swarmed in and began unplugging cables and taking down the lights, and Kate went into the auditorium with them.

Nick left the theater with Carter and went into the hall to get out of the crew's way. 'I think you'll be pleased with this,' Nick said. 'I think it went really well.'

Kate hauled the equipment case out of the theater and edged past them on her way out of the house.

'When do I get to see the first cut of the episode?' Carter asked Nick.

'Probably next week. I'll give you a call when it's ready.' Nick shook Carter's hand. 'Thank you again for letting us inside your home, Mr Grove. It's truly amazing what you have behind these walls.'

* * *

Joe drove his van to Carter Grove's house, picked up Boyd, and they drove straight to the airport, where they caught separate flights back to Los Angeles.

Neither Nick nor Kate could risk taking a commercial airline to Washington, DC, with a twenty-million-dollar Qing Dynasty bronze rooster in their luggage. So they went instead to the general aviation terminal, where a chartered business jet was fueled and waiting for them on the tarmac.

Once they reached cruising altitude, Nick went to the plane's refreshment center and brought Kate a tray with a glass of champagne and an assortment of appetizers.

'You plan for everything,' she said. 'Even the after-heist refreshments.'

'No detail is too small. Actually, they came with the price of the plane.'

She sipped the champagne and studied him. 'You seem very low-key when you should be reveling in your success right now.'

'Success would have been emptying that secret room,' Nick said. 'Leaving with just the bronze rooster is like breaking into Fort Knox and only stealing the paperclips.'

'Not if the paperclips are what you broke into Fort Knox for.'

'Who would break into Fort Knox for paperclips?'

'You know what I mean. We had a mission and we

accomplished it. We should celebrate. We can figure out how to get Carter Grove later.'

'We've missed our best shot. Once Carter discovers that the rooster is gone, he'll know his secret is out and he'll take extra security measures. He might even move the stash to another location. If I'd known ahead of time what else he had in that room, I would have taken an entirely different approach.'

'What would you have done?'

'I would have swapped a fake rooster for Carter's real one.'

'What would we have gained from that?'

'Time. We could have stolen the rooster from Carter without him knowing it was gone or that his dark secret had been discovered. That way, after we'd swapped his real rooster for the fake one in the Smithsonian, we could have come back and made a play for everything else he has in that room without him being prepared for it.'

Kate shook her head. 'You're a thief. What do you care if Carter Grove has a stash of legendary stolen art? In fact, I bet you have a secret room of your own somewhere. That's it, isn't it? You're jealous. His secret room has better stuff in it than yours does.'

'That's not it.'

'Okay, so it's ego. You're embarrassed that Carter wasn't on your radar before.' Kate lowered her voice, in case the pilots could hear them. 'And you're angry that he never bankrolled one of your heists or bought any of the stuff you stole.'

'Carter has a one-of-a-kind collection of stolen art treasures. It's got to be worth well over a hundred million dollars. It's a huge score and he's the perfect target, exactly the kind of guy I used to look for to swindle. Emptying his collection in a con like the one we staged today would have been one of my greatest heists ever.'

'You mean, if this was the good old days, before you got arrested and started working for the FBI,' she said. 'This is about you missing your previous life.'

'It's about doing what I do best,' he said. 'The old Nick Fox wouldn't have let an opportunity like the one we had today slip away.'

'The old Nick Fox got caught.'

'What about you? The Kate O'Hare who chased me all over the world wouldn't have let Carter get away with this.'

'True. And when we're done with this assignment, I'll make the case to Jessup that taking down Carter Grove should be our top priority.'

'And if Jessup says no?'

Kate went bottoms up with the champagne. 'That would be a challenge.'

Thirteen

They landed two hours later at the small regional airport in Manassas, Virginia, about thirty miles southwest of Washington, DC. Nick chose not to land at Dulles since it was, perhaps, the most security-conscious airport in the nation, crawling with cops, FBI agents, US marshals, military police, and all sorts of other law enforcement officers. Nick rented a car under one of his false identities, and he and Kate got separate rooms at the Manassas Holiday Inn.

Kate checked in to her room and contacted FBI Deputy Director Fletcher Bolton to let him know that the first stage of the mission was complete.

'That's great,' Bolton said, 'but we have a slight change of plan. Meet me at the Manassas Mall food court in one hour. Come alone, without the package.'

Bolton disconnected, and Kate stared at the phone. 'What the heck?' she muttered under her breath.

Nick was on the same floor as Kate, at the other end of the hall. Kate knocked on his door and sucked in some air when he opened the door fresh from a shower. His hair was wet and he had a towel wrapped low on his hips.

'Jeez,' Kate said, staring at the towel, her mind running amuck over what the towel was hiding, unable to drag her eyes to Nick's face.

'Is that a good jeez or a bad jeez?'

'It's just jeez. Don't you have a robe?'

'The room didn't come with a robe.'

'Okay, so that's why you're wearing the towel. I can see that. Makes perfect sense.'

A smile twitched at the corners of Nick's mouth. 'Is there something I can do for you?'

'No! Gosh. Absolutely not.' Kate stared at the towel. She was pretty sure she saw it move.

Nick tightened his grip on the towel. 'Kate?'

'Yep?'

'You're staring.'

'I know. I can't help myself.'

'Cute,' Nick said.

Kate squinched her eyes shut and wrinkled her nose. 'Ugh! I hate being cute.'

'Cute is good.'

'It's not. I'm an FBI agent. There's no cute in the FBI. Cute is goofy.'

'I'd grab you and kiss you, but I'd lose my towel, and I'm afraid you'd faint at the sight of me naked.'

'I think I could handle it.'

Nick dropped his towel, and Kate yelped and clapped her hands over her eyes.

'You're peeking,' Nick said. 'You're sneaking a peek between your fingers.'

He was right. She was peeking. 'This is embarrassing.'

'Maybe you'd feel better if you were naked too. Then we could stare at each other.'

'I don't think so. And why aren't *you* embarrassed? You're naked.'

Nick shrugged. 'Doesn't bother me.'

'Unh!' Kate said with another eye squinch. 'Men!'

'Yeah, we're pretty cool, right?'

Truth is, Kate was sort of jealous.

'I don't mean to throw a damper on this social interaction,' Nick said, 'but was there a reason for this visit?'

Kate thunked her forehead with the heel of her hand. 'Keys! I almost forgot. I came for the car keys. Bolton wants to meet with me. Alone.'

The Manassas Mall was a single-level enclosed shopping center built in the 1970s. There was a Walmart on one end and a Sears on the other. Coin-operated kiddie rides and vending machines were scattered along a turquoise-tiled promenade of vacant storefronts and bottom-feeding retailers like As Seen on TV and Dollar Plus.

Kate, the only customer in the food court, prepared a sampling menu of two pretzels from Auntie Anne's, two orders of fries from McDonald's, and two slices of pepperoni pizza from Sbarro.

Fletcher Bolton showed up at 8 PM sharp carrying a Walmart bag. He wore a starched blue shirt and crisply pressed brown slacks that were so stiff and wrinkle-free, they looked almost metallic. He was in his late fifties and very slim, with gray hair meticulously parted on the right.

He sat down across from Kate, set his Walmart bag on the floor beside the table, and regarded the food on the table as if it were a dismembered corpse. 'I hope you ordered all of that so we'd look like two shoppers meeting for a bite.'

'I thought we'd eat it, too.'

'Let's not go overboard,' he said, looking around. 'Nobody is paying any attention to us.'

'I'm a stickler for maintaining my cover,' Kate said, picking out French fries and laying them out in rows across a slice of pizza.

'How did it go in Florida?' Bolton asked.

'Without a hitch. There's a reason Nick is on our Ten Most Wanted list. We also made a big discovery. The rooster wasn't the only stolen art treasure in Carter Grove's collection. He's got a secret room filled with them.'

'Forget about the other stuff.'

'You don't understand, sir. These aren't little knick-knacks. We're talking Rembrandts, Picassos, you name it. If we arrest Carter and get him to talk, we could close the files on dozens of the world's most famous unsolved thefts.'

'Are you familiar with the concept of fruit of the poisonous tree?'

'It's a metaphor used for evidence that's thrown out of court because it was obtained illegally.'

'Then you know that we can't prove Carter Grove has stolen art without revealing how we obtained that knowledge. Therefore, we have no grounds for a search warrant or for an arrest.'

'So we'll find another way, a con of some kind. He's exactly the kind of crook you teamed me up with Nick to catch.' She broke off pieces of the pretzel and placed them between the rows of fries on her pizza.

'Carter is a former White House chief of staff and runs a security company that is a military contractor. If we arrest him and expose his crimes, it will create a massive scandal with serious geopolitical ramifications. That is exactly what we are trying to avoid here.'

'Is that our new job description, saving the government from embarrassment? Because if it is, sir, I'm out. You can find someone else to babysit Nick Fox. I'm in this strictly to nail bad guys.'

Bolton looked around the empty food court and then set his eyes on her. 'So am I. But Carter is not a typical crook. If we move against him, it will generate a lot of scrutiny. We have to carefully consider all of the possible ramifications of our actions before we do anything, or we could all go down with him. I will think about it. Right now, though, we have far more pressing matters with the Chinese to deal with.'

'That's as good as done,' Kate said. 'If you leave a door unlocked for us at the Smithsonian, turn off the alarm, and ask the guards to look the other way, we'll swap the real rooster for the fake one and then we can start thinking about going after Carter.'

'Making the switch is not going to be that easy.'

'I know that, but surely you can smooth the way for us a bit. We're doing the Smithsonian a favor here.' She folded the slice of pizza down the middle, trapping her new toppings inside, and took a bite.

'That's disturbing,' Bolton said, watching her eat.

'I call it the Fast Food Combo.'

'It's even more disturbing that you've given it a name.'

'About the change in plans . . .'

'Stanley Fu arrived two days early from Shanghai, and some overly helpful functionary at the Smithsonian already gave him the rooster.'

A piece of pretzel spilled out of the folded pizza onto Kate's shirt. 'You just found this out?'

'Obviously not, but Jessup and I felt that attempting to contact you in Palm Beach would have jeopardized your operation down there. Fu is one of China's *bao fa hu,* "the explosive rich." He's only thirty-five, and he's already made a ten-billion-dollar fortune in real estate. He treats the United States as one big shopping center. Fu comes here to buy hotels, restaurants, speedboats, racehorses, and American muscle cars. Apparently, there was a rare car that suddenly came up for auction yesterday, and he had to have it.'

'How much longer is Fu staying in DC?'

'He's leaving tomorrow morning, as soon as his car is delivered.'

'Where is the rooster now?' Kate asked.

'In a safe in the cargo hold of Fu's private five-hundred-million-dollar Airbus A380, which is parked on the tarmac at Dulles. It's imperative that you make the switch before he leaves for Shanghai.'

Kate looked incredulously at Bolton. 'How are we supposed to do that?'

'I've compiled detailed dossiers for you on Fu, his plane, his activities since he arrived in DC, and the security measures at Dulles.' Bolton slid the Walmart bag over to Kate's side of the table with his foot. 'At this point, I think it would be prudent to remind you that if you are caught, you are entirely on your own. This meeting never took place, and I will denounce you as a rogue agent.'

Kate wiped her hands with her napkin. 'What happens when Nick looks at this and says there's no way we can pull it off?'

Bolton stood up. 'That won't happen.'

'The rooster is in a safe in the cargo hold of an airplane that's behind the fence of the most heavily guarded airport in the United States. It's eight thirty-five PM and Fu is leaving tomorrow morning. It can't be done.'

'That's why Nick Fox won't be able to resist it,' Bolton said, and walked away.

She knew he was right.

Carter Grove sat on a stool in his casino, patiently feeding nickels into a vintage slot machine and pulling the lever. The mindless repetitive action was relaxing and helped him think through thorny problems, like plotting the military overthrow of a government or the kidnapping of a suspected terrorist from an enemy country. Tonight he was just enjoying the routine after the hectic day of filming in his house.

Rocco Randisi, an ex–army commando who was now a BlackRhino operative, joined Carter. Randisi had spent the previous day keeping an eye on the television producers and was now beginning his normal night shift heading household security.

'I hear you had some excitement today,' Rocco said.

'You'll be able to watch most of it on TV soon. But

if you want to see the outtakes, like the idiot who landed on the roof, you're welcome to scan through the security camera footage.'

'I'd like to do that, sir, but it's not there. That's why I came to see you. I thought maybe you'd offloaded the video for some reason.'

'Why would I do that? It's got to be on the hard drive somewhere.'

'I looked. The whole day has been wiped from the archive.'

Carter stopped feeding nickels into the machine and stared at Rocco. 'Why wasn't I told of this sooner?'

'It wasn't noticed. There was no reason for it to be reviewed.'

'Are there any other anomalies?'

'No. We're just missing a chunk of time systemwide.'

'I want you to comb the house for bugs and explosives.'

Rocco left, and Carter calmly and deliberately walked to the theater. He twisted the sconce that opened the hidden door to his secret collection, stepped into the room, and took inventory. All the major pieces were still there. It took him a few moments to realize the bronze rooster was missing.

The choice bewildered him. Although the rooster was worth twenty million dollars, it was hardly among the most valuable, beloved, or legendary pieces in the room.

In fact, there were very few people who knew the real rooster wasn't still on display in the Smithsonian. So why take the rooster and nothing else? Why take it at all?

Carter left the gallery, closed the secret door, and returned to the casino, settling in front of a slot machine.

Deposit the coin. Pull the arm. Let the wheels spin. Deposit the coin. Pull the arm. Let the wheels spin.

Carter repeated those actions robotically, establishing a mechanical rhythm that controlled his anger and allowed him to think clearly about the theft. Why the rooster? Why now? He could think of only one party that would want the rooster that badly. China. They'd recently found the missing bronze rabbit, and he was guessing they were determined to complete the collection.

First order of business would be to verify that his guess was correct. Second would be to determine the present location of the rooster. Perhaps he could somehow steal it back. Third order of business would be to make everyone involved pay dearly for their transgression. The full worldwide resources of BlackRhino would be devoted to it, starting now, until he had heads he could put on spikes.

It didn't take long for Carter's assistant, Veronica Dell, to get him the answers to his questions. A simple Google search turned up the news that Stanley Fu was in DC taking possession of his latest automotive toy, and would also be returning the treasured bronze rooster to China.

Twenty minutes later, Carter had one of his best operatives in the air, on her way to DC. Alexis Poulet was perfect for the job. She was beautiful. She was smart. She was tough. She could kill without remorse. And she had the added advantage of being able to recognize the thieves, since she'd done surveillance on them when they were in Palm Beach. Carter would plant her on Fu's plane, and she would have to figure it out from there.

Fourteen

Nick and Kate sat in Nick's hotel room and studied Bolton's files. Nick went over the schematics of the safe that held the fake rooster, and moved on to the floor plan of Fu's A380 Superjumbo. It was a triple-decked wide-body aircraft with a wingspan so large, it exceeded that of a Boeing 747-8 by nearly forty feet.

Passengers entered the plane through a three-story lobby featuring a floating spiral staircase that led up to the second and third floors. It was just a taste of the opulence to come. Fu's suite was on the top floor, along with four mahogany-appointed staterooms with private baths, a gym with changing rooms, and a luxurious guest cabin with thirty first-class seats that fully reclined into flat beds. The second level had a conference room, a library for quiet relaxation, and a nightclub with a giant video screen in the dance floor that mimicked transparent Plexiglas by showing the ground passing thirty thousand feet below. The lower level had a chef's galley, a wine cellar, and a vast cargo hold that doubled as a flying garage for Fu's Rolls-Royce. The cargo hold was also where the safe was stowed.

It was 10 PM by the time Nick and Kate had gone through all the material in the Walmart bag. Kate was working her way through a Snickers bar she'd found in her suitcase, and Nick was casually flipping through the auction catalog for Fu's new car.

'I can see why Fu rushed over here for this,' Nick said. 'The '69 Dodge Charger Daytona was a beautiful beast, the original winged warrior.'

He held up a picture of the curvy two-door coupe, with its front end that tapered down into a shovel point and a trunk that was topped with an enormous, staple-shaped spoiler.

Kate finished off the Snickers. 'That may be the ugliest car I've ever seen.'

'But it was the first car in NASCAR history to break two hundred miles per hour at Talladega. Chrysler only made seventy of these monsters with 426 CID Hemi V-8 engines, and this is one of them. It was a steal at three hundred thousand dollars.'

'It's not stealing when you pay for it.'

'It is when you pay much less than an object is worth.'

'That's called a bargain.'

'Otherwise known as a successful swindle.' Nick tossed the catalog on the bed. 'There's no way we can swap the fake rooster with the real one before Stanley Fu leaves DC. But we can do it before he gets back to China.'

It was almost midnight when Kate parked in front of Gelman's Haberdashery. The shop occupied the first floor of a handsome brownstone near Dupont Circle. Drapes were drawn on the bay windows, and there was no sign that lights were on beyond the drapes.

Nick was riding shotgun next to Kate, ending a call with the concierge at the Park Hyatt Shanghai. '*Xièxiè nǐ wǒ de péngyǒu,*' Nick said, and pocketed his phone.

'Well?' Kate asked him.

'Great news. Not only did I get my favorite ninety-third-floor suite, but the concierge got me a table at Ultraviolet. A dinner reservation there is harder to get than a Qing Dynasty bronze animal head.'

'I'm afraid we'll be dining at Tilanqiao Prison if this all goes wrong. So tell me again why we're visiting a tailor shop that's closed for the night?'

'Washington, DC, is the capital of the Free World. It's also the city with the most spies on earth. So naturally there's a robust underground economy that caters to their unique needs, which aren't that different from mine. This is one of those black-market businesses.'

Kate followed Nick up the short walkway to the front stoop and waited while he rang the buzzer. Two short bursts, one long, and one more short. The door was opened by Zev Gelman, an old man shaped like a question mark, his spine curved forward by age, bad bones, and too many years spent hunched over a sewing machine. His big glasses made him look bug-eyed, he wore a misbuttoned cardigan sweater and corduroy pants with breadcrumbs in the grooves. He leaned on a gnarled walking stick that could have belonged to Yoda.

'Nick Fox, international fugitive,' Gelman said. 'You don't look like a man on the run.'

'Have I ever?'

'That's one of the things I like about you. You're always relaxed. The Bing Crosby of thieves.' He studied Kate. 'And who is this?'

'An associate.'

Gelman shuffled back a few steps and Nick and Kate came inside, closing the door behind them. The room they entered was richly paneled with wood and had a masculine old-world British feel. A wide assortment of men's shirts, trousers, ties, and socks were neatly folded and stacked on shelves behind a central counter with bolts of fabric laid on top. There was a display case full of hundreds of different kinds of buttons, as well as a large mirror and two red-curtained changing rooms. Another red curtain covered the entry to the sewing room and the stairs.

'Bing Crosby? Really?' Nick asked. 'That's who you see when you look at me?'

Gelman gestured at Nick's reflection in the full-length mirror. 'Who do you see? Pitbull? Jay Z, maybe?'

'Do you even know who they are?'

'Just because I've had a hip replacement doesn't mean I'm not hip. What can I get you?'

'I have to get into a safe. A Hemmler J507.'

'That's a real nutcracker. The lock's wheel pack is protected by a cobalt-vanadium hardplate embedded with tungsten carbide chips that'll grind down most drill bits. But you don't have to worry about that, because you'll never get to it. The plate is behind glass as thin as Saran Wrap that will jam the lock with spring-loaded bolts if it's broken. So you're going to have to drill from the back of the safe to get at the lock mechanism from within. You'd better hope there isn't a thermal sensor inside that'll jam the locks the instant the interior is breached. Or you could just blow the safe open and hope you don't destroy what's inside.'

'All of that is too complicated, messy, and noisy,' Nick said. 'I'm going to open it using the combination.'

'Then what do you need me for?'

'I don't have the numbers.'

'So you're shopping for an autodialer rig and the software algorithm to crack the combination. That's top-of-the-line. It's going to cost you a hundred and fifty thousand dollars.'

Nick took out his iPhone, went online, and with a few

taps of his finger wired $150,000 to Gelman's Antigua bank account. A moment later, there was an electronic chirp from the pocket of Gelman's cardigan sweater. Gelman fumbled around in his pocket and brought out his own iPhone, along with a half roll of Tums and some lint. He glanced at the screen. The transfer was confirmed.

'Always a pleasure doing business with you,' Gelman said.

Gelman dropped the phone back into his pocket, shuffled up to the mirror on the wall, and pressed something behind the frame. Instantly a thin green beam of light shone from the glass and scanned Gelman's right eye. A retina identification system was built into the mirror.

'I've got to get myself one of those,' Nick said.

'They can be a pain in the ass. I got cataracts last year, and this damn thing locked me out. I couldn't get in again until I had eye surgery.'

Nick heard a series of bolts retract behind the wall, which slid open to reveal a showroom clad in sheets of polished metal. An astonishing array of weapons, surveillance devices, explosives, locksmith tools, and many devices Nick had never seen before were displayed within staggered, individually illuminated cubbyholes of various sizes. There were four flat-screen monitors, with mice and keyboards, swivel-mounted on a glass-topped counter in the center of the room. Gelman, Nick, and Kate stepped inside.

Gelman pointed his walking stick at an aluminum briefcase in a high cubbyhole. 'The dialing rig is in there. You run it with your smartphone.'

Nick pulled down the case. It weighed about ten pounds. 'Convenient.'

'Give me your iPhone,' Gelman said. Nick handed it to him and the old man plugged the phone into the keyboard on the table and hit a few keys. When the safecracking app was downloaded onto the phone, a stream of code flashed up on one of the monitors.

'The Hemmler has a six-number combination,' Gelman said. 'Even with the machine doing the safecracking for you, it will still take hours to determine the combination and get it open.'

'I've got the time, but I may be able to shave off a few hours by guessing a couple of the numbers.'

'You'll be taking a big risk.' Gelman unplugged Nick's phone and handed it back to him.

'That's the best part,' Nick said.

Gelman looked at Kate. 'And what do you think, missy?'

'Next time I get locked out of my apartment I'll give you a call.'

Barer Classic Motorcars was on Arlington Road in Bethesda, Maryland, a block south of a Mercedes dealership, an Apple Store, and an Urban Outfitters. The dealership marked the spot where prosperity abruptly petered out. On the next block were a derelict gas station and a string of fast food joints.

Kate parked their rental car at the curb a few feet south of the Barer showroom. She and Nick wiped the car down for prints, left the keys in the ignition, and walked away, each carrying a silver case.

The Barer lot held about a dozen mint-condition Camaros, Mustangs, Firebirds, GTOs, and Cougars from the '60s and '70s, chrome and sheet metal lures for suburban husbands in the throes of midlife crisis. The showroom contained more of the same, but the really good stuff was locked away in the garage.

Kate followed Nick around the building to the garage's back door and watched him pick the lock. They stepped into the pitch-black interior, and Nick turned to the security keypad on the wall by the door. The keypad was pulsing with light, counting down thirty seconds until the alarm went off. Nick typed in a code, and the light stopped pulsing.

'Nice work,' Kate said. 'How did you know the code?'

'It's a VeriSec 9000, the bestselling alarm system in the country for the last decade,' Nick said, closing the door and switching on the lights. 'I worked as a certified VeriSec repairman just long enough to get the access codes that all the repairmen use to deactivate alarms for servicing.'

'What if it had been a different brand?'

'I've worked for a lot of alarm companies,' Nick said. 'Everyone needs a hobby.'

The garage was as clean as an operating room, not a speck of grease anywhere. The tools and machinery gleamed almost as brightly as the three cars parked in the repair bays. One of the cars was the red '69 Dodge Charger Daytona that was going to be delivered to Stanley Fu's A380 Superjumbo in the morning.

'I'm having serious second thoughts about your plan,' Kate said.

Nick walked up to the car and opened the trunk.

'They don't make trunks like this anymore,' he said. 'If you take the spare tire out, there should be room for us. Unfortunately I don't think there's enough room for the two cases.'

Kate cut her eyes to the cases. 'So?'

'So we're going to have to remove the stuffing from the backseat and create a hidden compartment. It's an old smuggler's trick.'

'So old that everyone knows it. It's the first place they'll look.'

'*Who* will? The car is being loaded on the private jet of a highly respected businessman, not onto a commercial flight. It's not going to be searched. And once we're in the air, we're golden. Nobody is going to bother us in the cargo hold. We'll have eighteen hours of quality time to leisurely crack the combination on the safe, open it up, and swap the roosters.'

'You also didn't think there would be security measures in Carter's secret room.'

'Because I was going in completely blind and relying on guesswork. This time I know exactly what we're dealing with. I have detailed schematics of the cargo hold and the safe, courtesy of the FBI. This is going to be easy.'

'We're robbing a plane while it's in flight to Shanghai. You call that easy? As far as I know, it's unprecedented.'

'That's the beauty of it. It's grandiose and simple at the same time. It's a shame that nobody will ever know we did it.'

'You realize there's a major flaw in the plan. If something goes wrong, we'll be trapped with no possibility of escape, arrested on arrival, and tried for our crimes in China, a country known for sentencing criminals to a lifetime of hard labor or execution by firing squad.'

'What could go wrong?'

'Everything.'

'Well, if you're going to think like that, you'll never leave the house.'

'There's a big difference between walking out your front door and breaking into a safe at thirty thousand feet.'

'The difference is that *this* is a bigger rush,' Nick

said. 'This morning we were in Florida stealing a twenty-million-dollar artifact right under the nose of an ex–White House chief of staff, and now we're in Washington, DC, about to sneak onto a plane to Shanghai to break into a safe. What could possibly be better than this? Nothing. And you know it, too, or you wouldn't have gone into the Navy or joined the FBI or agreed to partner up with me. You're a thrill junky.'

'Okay, so I'm a thrill junky. That doesn't mean I have a death wish.'

'We'll be fine. Help me out by erasing the security camera footage while I gut the backseat, install a trunk release, and drill some holes so we can breathe.'

He's right, Kate thought. As dangerous and insane as his plan was, it was also daring and incredibly exciting. Hot, even.

'Someone has to be the voice of reason,' she said, knowing even as she said it that it sounded lame.

Fifteen

Alexis Poulet arrived at Dulles Airport at two AM and was met on the tarmac by a young BlackRhino operative from the DC office. The man's name was Bernbaum. He was an ex–CIA analyst, a desk-riding data cruncher and not an experienced field operative. And he wore his Ivy League education like a spray tan.

He's soft, Poulet thought. *I could kill him with my bare hands with less effort than it would take to wash them.* This was an important assessment for Poulet, since she judged everyone by how easy or difficult it would be to kill them.

Bernbaum gave her a warm smile, mistaking her appraisal of his potentially fleeting mortality for a different kind of physical interest in him, and began briefing her as they walked to the terminal from the BlackRhino private jet. A cold breeze redolent of jet exhaust whipped through their hair.

'We've been able to verify the news,' Bernbaum said.

'The Smithsonian has given the Chinese their Qing Dynasty rooster back. A businessman named Stanley Fu is delivering it to Shanghai in the morning. That's his private A380 out there.'

He gestured to a massive airplane parked on an outlying area of the airport. The plane was painted to appear as if an enormous dragon was wrapped around the fuselage and about to devour it whole.

'Nice ride,' she said. 'Where is the rooster now?'

'On the plane, along with Fu and his entourage.'

'He's on the plane now? But you said that he's not leaving until morning.'

'He owns two five-star hotels in town, but he'd rather stay on his jet while he's here. That's how lavish it is. He's waiting on some toys he bought here to be delivered, and for the arrival of a dozen senior executives from around the country who manage his US real estate holdings. Fu is bringing the executives on board for a big business meeting he's holding during the flight. The executives will stay overnight in Shanghai and then fly back to the States on commercial flights. First class won't seem half as nice after riding on Fu's flying cruise ship.'

Bernbaum knew only that his boss was interested in the rooster. Alexis knew that the rooster had been stolen from her boss, possibly by the two television producers, and that he wanted it back. How Fu and the Chinese government fit into the picture wasn't of any importance to her. Nor was it important to her that there were possibly two roosters on the plane, one fake and one real. Her mission was clear. Find the real rooster and return it to Carter Grove.

'Mr Grove is deeply concerned about US–Chinese relations,' Alexis said to Bernbaum. 'He feels there should be extra security on the plane, and he would like me to provide that security. How good are you at establishing a solid, verifiable cover in a short period of time?'

'How short?'

'Four hours.'

He smiled. 'Next time, give me a challenge.'

At 8:30 AM, the Dodge Charger Daytona with its huge spoiler sped across the tarmac at Dulles and raced up the loading ramp into the rear cargo hold of Stanley Fu's A380 Superjumbo. A moment later, two black Suburbans pulled up to the front of the plane, parked beside the stairway to the cabin door, and disgorged Fu's guests.

Fu could have cared less about the guests. Fu was in the cargo hold, watching the removal of the car's battery and seeing that the car was properly strapped onto a metal pallet. He flew with his cars all the time, but this was different. This was a new toy.

Alexis made her way up the cargo ramp to where Fu was standing. She was wearing a crisp, businesslike pantsuit that fit her like neoprene. The Smithsonian's official PROTECTION SERVICES patch was on the left breast pocket of the jacket. Her hair was pulled back at the nape of her neck.

'I'm Alexis Poulet with the Smithsonian's Office of Protection Services,' she said to Fu. 'The Smithsonian would like to extend its good wishes to you, and offer whatever assistance you might need in providing safe passage for the rooster.'

'I appreciate the gesture,' Fu said in perfect English, 'but I can assure you it is unnecessary for you to accompany the rooster. The rooster is already secure in a safe in the cargo hold of my plane.'

'Yes, but it's not yet on Chinese soil. The Smithsonian wants to be absolutely certain that the rooster arrives in its rightful home safely after so many years on distant shores. I'd like to travel with you today and accompany the rooster to its final destination, wherever that might be in China. Before you decide, though, I strongly suggest you contact the Smithsonian on your own to confirm my identity.'

'Is there a credible threat to the rooster?'

'No, none at all, but we'd feel terrible if something happened and endangered the relations between our countries. Wouldn't you?'

'Very well, it's the Smithsonian's money to waste,' Fu said. 'Assuming your story checks out, you're welcome on board as my guest as long as you don't interfere with the business being conducted.'

'Thank you,' she said. 'I can assure you that I will be invisible.'

'My staff will see to your luggage and your seat.' He nodded curtly at her and continued on to the front of the plane.

She watched him go. He was in good shape and had martial arts training. It might take five minutes of vigorous exercise to kill him if she ever had to, but it would be fun.

Nick and Kate had climbed into the Charger's trunk at dawn. She'd gone in first, squeezing into the back where the trunk narrowed against the tops of the wheel wells. Then Nick got in and lay down on his side, facing the taillights. In order for them both to fit in the trunk, she had to put one arm under her head and press tightly against Nick's back, her other arm draped around his waist. He pulled the trunk lid closed and they were alone together in pitch-darkness.

They'd hidden the two cases containing the safe-cracking rig and the rooster in the compartment they'd created under the backseat. They'd discarded the stuffing and foam in a Dunkin' Donuts dumpster.

'I've slept in some uncomfortable places,' Kate said, 'but this is right up there for first place.'

'It's not so bad,' Nick said. 'It's not freezing cold, and it's not raining.'

And he fell asleep.

Kate dozed on and off, and awoke for good when the first mechanics arrived in the garage. She was braced for the moment when the trunk would be opened and they'd be revealed. She even had her story ready. They were innocent tourists who'd been kidnapped and forced into the trunk. Then, at the first opportunity, she'd run like hell for the door.

She heard muffled talking, then after a while the driver's side door opened and closed, the engine cranked over, and the car was rolling. The ride was relatively smooth until the car raced up the ramp to the cargo hold and Kate and Nick were tipped at an angle. More muffled talking. She heard the hood creak open, and after some time it was slammed shut. Obviously, the ground crew was securing the car for the flight.

Kate heard the men leaving and then the hum of the A380's ramp closing, sealing the cargo hold. Nick didn't stir.

'Are you awake?' Kate whispered.

'Hard to sleep with this thing rumbling up a ramp at a forty-five-degree angle.'

'These are the worst seats I've ever had on a flight. I'm making the airline reservations on our next trip.'

'That's a deal,' Nick said.

A few minutes later, the plane taxied down the runway and lifted off. When it reached altitude, Nick cautiously opened the trunk and peeked out, scanning the area with a small Maglite.

'Looks like we're alone,' he said, pushing the trunk the rest of the way open.

'Great. Now if you could just get me out of here. I'm not sure I can uncurl myself without help.'

'I know what you mean. I can't feel my legs from the knees down.' Nick raised a leg and stretched it straight. He maneuvered himself over the edge of the trunk and hung there for a couple beats. 'This seemed like a good idea yesterday. Right now I'm not so sure.' He rolled the rest of his body out of the trunk, went down to the metal pallet with a *thunk*, and lay there spreadeagle for a moment.

'Are you okay?' Kate asked.

'I'm old.' He stood and looked in at Kate. 'Wrap your arms around my neck, and I'll haul you out.'

'My arms don't work.'

'Okay, then swing your legs over the side and I'll pull you up.'

'My legs aren't working either.'

'Is anything working?'

'Yes. My bladder's working. I need a bathroom.'

'Honey, I don't know if there's a bathroom in the cargo hold.'

'Are you kidding me? This is a long trip.'

'I don't have a problem with these things. I just need a jelly jar.'

'I can't use a jelly jar!'

'Don't panic. We'll get you out of the trunk and we'll look around.'

Nick got Kate's legs over the edge of the trunk, grabbed her under the arms, and tugged. Kate came out with a grunt, her legs buckled under, and the two of them went down to the metal pallet with Kate sprawled on top of Nick.

'I always had you pegged for a woman who would want the top,' Nick said.

'This was a stupid idea.'

'I'm starting to like it . . . a lot.'

'I can tell.'

'It's not what you think,' Nick said. 'You're lying on my flashlight.'

'Sure,' Kate said. 'I knew that.' She rolled onto her back and moved her arms and legs around. 'Some feeling is returning.' She got to her hands and knees and stood. She took her own flashlight out of her pocket and flicked the beam around the windowless cargo hold. She checked out Fu's Rolls-Royce Phantom, a thirty-one-foot jetboat, and two rows of the aluminum containers known as unit load devices curved to fit snugly against the contours of either side of the large hold. Three of the

ULDs held luggage and whatever else Fu had picked up on his trip. The fourth ULD held the safe.

A narrow space between the two sets of ULDs was just wide enough for a person to squeeze through and get to the access door on the far wall. Kate knew from studying the A380 floor plan that the door led to the landing gear compartment and, beyond that, to the rest of the lower level of the plane.

'Sixteen hours and counting,' Nick said. 'This is practically a vacation.'

'Easy for you to say.'

Kate went off to find a restroom, and Nick went to the Charger. He opened the passenger door, tipped the front seat forward, and lifted the seat cushion on the rear bench seat, exposing the two silver cases hidden inside, plus a coiled power cord with jumper cables on one end.

When Kate returned, Nick had the door to one of the ULDs open, revealing a dark gray safe about the size of a small refrigerator. Kate shined her light on the safe, and the silver combination dial gleamed.

'Hello, gorgeous,' Nick said.

He opened the case he'd gotten from Gelman, and Kate thought the device inside looked like a dismantled robot arm. The pincer-fingered 'hand,' the cylindrical armature, the cables, the suction cups, and the servomotor were all neatly placed in formfitting foam cutouts.

Nick set his flashlight on top of the safe and began to carefully assemble the pieces of the rig, which snapped together and were tightened with bolts he could turn with his fingers. The robotlike arm of the rig was surrounded by a skeletal sleeve that supported it and protected the delicate pincers at the end. Nick screwed suction cups to the front of the sleeve that encircled the pincers.

'Fu trusts this safe to guard items that he holds dear. He and that box share a big secret, the combination, something he won't share with anybody else. We can use that knowledge to improve our odds of cracking the combination.'

'I thought the machine you're putting together is supposed to do that.'

'Oh, it definitely will.' Nick attached the robotic arm to a small tripod and extended the telescoping legs beneath it so the rig was level with the combination dial. 'The safecracking software will try every possible combination, using those pincers to spin the dial and sensors to detect the subtle click whenever a tumbler slips into position. It could take two minutes or two days. You never know.'

'You're telling me that you don't know how long it will take to crack the safe?'

'It's mathematics, the process of elimination, and chance. You can't accurately put a timer on that.'

'I wish you'd told me that before we started this caper.'

'You wouldn't have agreed to do it.'

'That's right,' she said. 'Because where I come from, "you never know" is not favorable odds.'

'We can significantly improve those odds if we know a couple of the numbers in the combination.'

Nick slid the armature against the safe so that the pincers clutched the dial and the suction cups were flat against the door.

'That's like trying to guess the numbers in the lottery,' Kate said. 'What happens if we guess wrong?'

'It could take even longer to open the safe than if we'd relied only on pure luck and the software's algorithm.'

There were little tabs on the suction cups. Nick pressed the tabs, and the arm stuck firmly against the safe. He plugged one end of the power cord into the machine and ran the rest of the cord, the one with the jumper cables on the end, out to the battery that had been removed from the Rolls-Royce.

'We know that Fu is a successful Chinese businessman with a dragon painted on his plane,' Nick said. 'Dragons have enormous symbolic power in Chinese culture. A dragon is also the logo of his company. That leads me to believe that Fu is superstitious, since dragons represent power and good luck in Chinese culture.'

Nick took out his iPhone, plugged it into a socket on

the safe-cracking device, and tapped a vault-shaped icon on his touch screen, activating an app. 'If I'm right, then his combination will be comprised of numbers ending in two, six, eight, and nine. Those are very lucky numbers to the Chinese. Even numbers are usually considered better than odd ones, so we can rule odd numbers out. Traditionally, two represents harmony, six equals success, and eight symbolizes prosperity and high social status, which is why the Beijing Olympics opened on August 8, 2008.'

'Nine isn't an even number.'

'It's an exception. Nine represents permanence and security. Four is also an exception, in a bad way. It means death.' He gestured to the keyboard on his iPhone screen. 'So should I tell the app to favor numbers that end in two, six, eight, and nine?'

Kate sighed. 'Go 'head.'

Nick tapped the numbers into the iPhone, and the robotic arm came to life. The pincers immediately began spinning the combination dial with remarkable speed and agility. The unit emitted a smooth electric whirring sound and a *clickety-clack* as its robotic joints moved.

'Now all we have to do is wait for the door to open,' Nick said.

Sixteen

Alexis remained in her seat for the first couple hours and casually watched the other passengers move about the plane. None of them had introduced themselves or tried to engage her in small talk. In fact, nobody seemed to notice her at all. That's because she didn't make eye contact with anyone, and her body language screamed *not interested in any human interaction*. She might as well have been wearing Harry Potter's Cloak of Invisibility.

The two fake producers didn't appear to be on board, but that didn't mean they didn't have an accomplice or two among the passengers or the crew. Nothing jumped out at her as suspicious or unusual about anyone's behavior, so she eventually decided to get up and explore the plane along with everybody else.

She peeked into the gym and changing rooms that were aft of the passenger cabin. There were five executives marveling over the showers and taking pictures of themselves standing in them. The airborne showers didn't interest her at all. Her attention was drawn to the emergency door to a stairwell that led down to the two lower levels. Someone could use the stairwell to sneak down to the cargo hold, though she suspected that opening the emergency door would set off a warning light on the instrument panel in the cockpit, alerting the pilots.

Alexis walked back through the cabin toward the front of the plane and along the wood-paneled hallway that separated the four staterooms. The hall curved past the closed double doors leading to Fu's private suite and ended at the grand, winding staircase that went down to the first-floor lobby.

She went down the stairs to the second level, encountering two of Fu's statuesque young Chinese flight attendants carrying trays of dim sum and tea. She made her way past the doors of the conference room and through the elegant library to the nightclub. Several passengers were gathered around the nightclub's dance floor and gaping at the windowlike video display under their feet. It was a cheap thrill for people who'd never experienced any real danger, she thought. Only a genuine hole in the floor might have interested her. Even then, she wouldn't gape.

A door opened at the far end of the room, and a flight attendant emerged carrying a tray of assorted dim sum, fresh from the galley. Alexis peeked into the galley at the white-coated chef. He bowed in greeting and smiled. The galley was small but looked efficient. Elevator doors opened next to a prep area, and a second white-coated chef stepped out carrying a plastic container of food. Perfect, Alexis thought. The pantry was in the cargo hold. This would be her access point to the lower level.

She backed out of the galley and returned to her seat. She hadn't seen anyone yet who'd set off any instinctive alarm bells, but a pro probably wouldn't, and there were still a lot of crew members she hadn't laid eyes on. That was okay. She had more than fourteen hours to see if there were any thieves on board. She'd wait until the big meeting began, and once most of the passengers were behind those closed doors, she'd see if anyone tried to pay a visit to the safe in the cargo hold. And if someone did, he would find her there waiting for him with the stiletto that she called her 'conversation starter.' She'd found that people were a lot more forthcoming with her when she was slowly peeling their skin off.

And when she was certain she had a little time to herself, she'd take a good look at the safe, although she suspected it would be easier for her to steal the rooster after it was offloaded from the plane.

Kate was asleep in the backseat of Fu's Rolls-Royce, her head on Nick's shoulder, when a bump of turbulence woke her up. She lifted her head in the darkness.

'Is the safe open yet?' she asked.

'Afraid not,' Nick said.

Kate stretched, running her fingers along the car's cashmere headliner and then over the creamy chestnut leather seat. 'Who knew that flying in the cargo hold could be as elegant as first class?'

'This is much better,' Nick said. 'We're sitting on Bavarian bullhide. Everyone else uses cowhide for upholstery. Rolls-Royce won't, because cows get stretch marks.'

'I can relate. That's the same reason I insist on vinyl seats in my cars. There's nothing worse than a car with stretch marks. How long was I asleep?'

'About four hours.'

'I'm hungry.'

'We didn't bring food, but the food storage area is on this level.'

'I'll make a supply run,' Kate said. 'I need to stretch my legs anyway.'

'The wine cellar is down here, too. I understand Fu has some excellent Bordeaux. A vintage Pétrus would be nice.'

'I wouldn't know a Bordeaux from Hawaiian Punch.'

'Just grab a bottle of anything red. Some cheese would go well with that. Crottin de Chavignol if they have it. Maybe some chocolate, too.'

Kate got out of the Rolls, turned her flashlight on,

and squeezed through the narrow space between the ULDs to the access door at the front of the cargo hold. She opened the door and walked down a long, dark hallway to another door at the far end. It was pitch-black. Without her flashlight, she wouldn't have been able to see a thing.

She stopped, pressed her ear to the door, and listened for any sounds of people or activity coming from the other side. She opened the door a crack and peered out.

The lights were on. There was an elevator to her left and a hallway that led to a housekeeping storage area. Judging by the size of the door, the elevator appeared to be just wide enough to hold a person and a refreshment cart. Directly across from her was the pantry. A porthole window in the pantry door allowed her to see the bread, candy, cookies, and cans of food secured in cupboards with thick wire mesh to keep items from flying out during turbulence. She didn't see or hear anyone, so she stepped out, crossed to the storeroom, and slipped inside.

The room was roughly ten feet by ten feet wide, with a gleaming vinyl tile floor. To her right was a utility closet, a Sub-Zero refrigerator, and a huge temperature-controlled wine cabinet with a glass door that showed the dozens of bottles inside. A row of six empty food and beverage carts were lined up underneath a counter.

On top of the counter was a stack of one-inch-deep plastic trays for stocking the carts. Kate took one of the trays and began to do a little grocery shopping. She helped herself to crackers, several bottles of Evian water, and a bunch of Godiva chocolates and Toblerone bars, and she was just about to see if she could find some cheese and cold cuts in the refrigerator when she heard the elevator doors open.

Kate gripped her tray and ducked down, catching a glimpse through the porthole window of the person outside. It was the stunning blond BlackRhino operative who'd been watching her in Palm Beach. This didn't come as a total shock. There had always been the chance that Carter would discover the theft and put enough pieces together in time to place someone on the plane. Unfortunately it made an already complicated situation even more unwieldy.

Kate's rule of thumb was *Always better to be the attacker than the attackee.* So she pushed the door open and whacked the surprised woman in the head with the tray. Alexis went down to one knee, shook her head to clear it, and whirled around, catching Kate with a perfectly placed kick to the rib cage. Kate crouched and blocked a second kick.

The two women were now fully engaged in hand-to-hand combat, executing their attacks and defenses in rapid, dizzying combinations, with a deadly, almost balletic grace. Neither was able to deliver a decisive blow, but Kate felt a satisfying snap when one of her sharp lightning jabs smashed the woman's nose. The operative stepped back, licked the blood from her lips, and smiled.

It was unnerving. Kate's father had warned her that BlackRhino operatives liked killing. Now Kate knew that Jake was right, and that only one of two women would be leaving the storage room alive.

Alexis pulled a switchblade from a sheath in her sleeve, flicked it open, and slashed at Kate. Kate leaned away from the blade and tried to kick her attacker's knee, but Alexis dodged her, swung the blade again, and sliced into Kate's leg.

With her right hand, Kate grabbed the assassin's arm as it passed and drove her left elbow into the woman's bloody nose. Alexis seemed oblivious to the pain and countered with a furious series of devastating jabs into Kate's side with her free hand, weakening Kate's hold.

Alexis yanked her arm free and lunged at Kate with the knife again. Kate sidestepped the blade, but not fast enough. She felt the deep sting as the blade sliced her left forearm, which she'd instinctively raised to protect herself.

The parry gave Kate an unexpected opening. The assassin's body was momentarily exposed and unprotected.

Kate punched Alexis in the throat and grabbed her knife arm, yanking it down.

Alexis lost her balance. Kate pinned Alexis's right arm behind her back, driving the assassin facedown toward the floor, knocking the knife out of her hand. Alexis grabbed Kate's ankle and yanked.

For an instant, they were both down on one knee, facing each other like two opposing football players along the line of scrimmage. But Alexis was quicker, charging forward and wrapping her right arm around Kate's neck in a chokehold.

To tighten the vise, Alexis grabbed her own right wrist with her left hand, locking Kate's neck under her armpit, and then stood up, using Kate's weight against her to crush her throat. It was a brutally efficient way to kill.

Kate felt herself losing consciousness as her windpipe was crimped like a hose. She knew that in an instant, Alexis would intentionally fall backward, using the momentum to bring Kate down and snap her neck. Kate had a second or two left to live. Her years of combat training kicked in, she stretched her legs out in front of her, and abruptly sat down. The move dramatically shifted the balance between them, hurling Alexis face forward and dropping Kate backward. Kate let the momentum carry her, falling flat onto her back and flipping Alexis over her and headfirst onto the floor.

Kate gasped for air and realized the pantry was deadly quiet. Alexis wasn't moving. Kate crawled on her hands and knees and looked at Alexis. The would-be assassin's eyes stared straight ahead, unblinking, and her head was twisted at an unnatural angle. She'd broken her neck when she got flipped over Kate and slammed into the steel door of the fridge. Kate felt for a pulse. None.

Seventeen

Terrific, Kate thought. She was bleeding all over the pantry, she had a dead woman lying on the floor in front of her, and she was a millimeter away from vomiting. Breathe deep and focus, she told herself. Get it together. She reached for a Godiva candy bar that had fallen to the floor, peeled the wrapper away, and ate it while she caught her breath and did a more thorough assessment of her dilemma.

The gash in her arm wasn't deep. The gash in her leg probably could use a stitch or two . . . or forty. She picked her shirt up and looked at her side. Already turning purple. She didn't think she had a broken rib. Been there, done that. Still, it was going to be a monster of a bruise. The good news was that she was in better shape than the blonde. The blonde was dead.

Kate pocketed the switchblade and dragged the blonde over to the far wall where she'd be out of the way. She scanned the shelves for a first aid kit. Found none. She went to the utility closet and hit the jackpot. First aid kit. Paper towels. Garbage bags.

In minutes Kate had her arm Band-Aided and the wound in her leg pulled together with makeshift stitches and bandaged with gauze and surgical tape. She cleaned the floor with a bottle of Evian and a roll of paper towels. She tossed the towels into a big black garbage bag and tied the bag to the blonde's wrist.

She looked around, thinking she'd done a pretty good job of cleaning up. No blood splatters. No sign of struggle. She gathered up some candy, crackers, and bottled water in another trash bag, looking around one more time to make sure there were no signs of a fight or that an intruder had rummaged through things. She added a couple bottles of wine and a corkscrew to the contents of the trash bag, and satisfied that she'd covered her tracks she headed back to the cargo hold, dragging the blonde and the garbage bags behind her.

Nick was crouched in front of the safe, illuminating it with his Maglite, watching the rig spin the dial. He heard Kate's footsteps and saw the glow from her light radiating from the narrow space between the four ULDs. He turned to greet her and was momentarily blinded by her light.

'There you are,' he said. 'I was beginning to worry about you.'

She shoved one of the garbage bags into the cargo hold. 'Tell me the safe is open.'

'Not yet,' he said. 'But we still have lots of time left.'

'I'm not so sure,' Kate said. 'I had an issue in the pantry.'

'An issue?'

Kate grabbed the blonde by her heels and dragged her through the door, past the ULDs.

Nick jumped to his feet. 'Holy crap, what happened?'

'She's BlackRhino. I don't know what she was doing on the plane, but we sort of had a tussle.'

'Tussle? She looks dead!'

'Yeah, she sort of killed herself when I flipped her into the refrigerator.'

Nick flashed the light over Kate. 'Are you okay?'

'I could use a glass of wine.'

'I don't think we have glasses.'

'Just open the bottle, and I'll take it from there.'

'Honey, you've got blood all over you. Are you sure you don't need something more than wine?'

'It's not as bad as it looks.'

'That's good, because I don't have a prayer book handy to perform last rites. Do you want me to take a look at your arm or your leg? It looks like you got slashed.'

'Thanks, but I'm okay.'

'Consider yourself lucky that you don't have a tension pneumothorax.'

'What's that?'

'I have no idea,' he said, 'but I watch a lot of doctor shows on TV, and you wouldn't believe the number of patients who come into the ER with it.'

She looked into his eyes. 'We're screwed, aren't we?'

'I don't see how.'

'I just dragged a dead BlackRhino operative down the hall.'

'I'll put her body in a storage compartment on the boat.'

'That won't make what happened go away.'

'It will as far as we're concerned.'

'It means something that she was here,' Kate said.

'I think Carter took a shot in the dark with her. Someone stole his rooster and he figured the place to start looking for answers was the Smithsonian. So he sent her to DC to snoop around. She heard that Fu was taking the Smithsonian's rooster back to China, so she hitched a ride to stay close to the fake on the off chance that we planned to swap it with the real one. Or maybe she thought the swap had already been made and just wanted to steal the real rooster back.'

'We don't know if there are more BlackRhino killers on board, or if Carter has people waiting for us at the airport in Shanghai.'

'It doesn't make any difference.'

'Of course it does.'

'Not for us, not now,' Nick said. 'All we can do is continue as we planned. Besides, we're really no worse off than we were before. In fact, we're *better* off. Because if that woman hadn't been kind enough to reveal herself—'

'Kind?'

'We wouldn't know that Carter has discovered the theft and has already mobilized his forces. So now, instead of being in the dark about what we're up against, we can anticipate what's waiting for us in Shanghai and prepare ourselves for it.'

'So this is a good thing,' she said.

'Exactly.'

'I'd hate to be around when your idea of a bad thing happens.'

It was late afternoon in North Hollywood and 87 degrees in the shade. The smog was so bad that it was probably healthier to smoke a pack of cigarettes than to stand outside, breathing the air on Lankershim Boulevard. But that's where Boyd Capwell was anyway, milling around with a dozen other men, all of them studying their scripts outside a storefront casting office in a corner strip mall. The other tenants in the mall were a donut shop, a payday loan business, and a photographer who specialized in taking headshots for aspiring actors who would never fulfill their aspirations.

Like the other men, Boyd was waiting to audition for a commercial. The role he was up for was a burly fishing boat captain plagued with bad breath who finally finds relief, and the love of a fine woman, thanks to a new brand of mouthwash. Boyd thought of the commercial as a rich sixty-second character study of a heroically tragic, psychologically complex man and a scathing indictment of our economy. The bad taste in the captain's mouth was clearly a metaphor for the mistreatment of blue-collar workers. To truly embody the role, Boyd had cleaned a salmon in his sink that morning, getting fish scales all over his shirt, and he hadn't brushed his teeth since he'd left Palm Beach.

A black Mercedes pulled into a parking spot in front of the casting office. The car's windows were so dark, they looked as if they'd been painted black. Two muscular, grim-faced men got out of the Mercedes. They were wearing Italian suits as black as the car and sunglasses tinted as dark as the windows. The similarity between the men and the machine they emerged from reminded Boyd of *The Terminator,* only these guys were better dressed.

But then Boyd thought of another reason *The Terminator* might have instinctively come to his mind: These guys *were* killers. At that instant, one of the men faced him and asked: 'Are you Boyd Capwell?'

'No,' Boyd said. 'I'm Stieg Welkerdorf.'

'Wrong answer,' the man said, and he punched Boyd in the gut.

Boyd curled over the man's fist, all the air went out of his body, and he got shoved into the backseat of the car. The other man got behind the wheel, started the car, and they drove off. The entire abduction took less than thirty seconds, and not one of the actors on the sidewalk did anything to stop it. If Boyd survived this, he intended to file a complaint with the Screen Actors Guild. It was how he dealt with most of the indignities and outrages in his life, though it rarely did any good.

After a few long, painful seconds, Boyd was finally able to draw a breath. 'Why did you hit me?' Boyd asked.

'Why did you lie about your name?' the man beside him responded.

'Because you look like bill collectors.'

'How many bill collectors have you seen dressed as nice as us?' asked the driver, smiling at Boyd in the rearview mirror.

'I try not to see bill collectors.'

'We're with BlackRhino security,' the man in the backseat said. 'I'm Mr Smith and that's Mr Brown.'

Boyd took it as a good sign that they were bothering to use fake names. It meant they intended for him to survive the conversation and didn't want him to know specifically who'd abducted him.

'Two days ago you hosted a TV show that was filmed in Carter Grove's home,' Mr Smith said. 'Afterward, Mr Grove discovered that something very valuable to him was missing.'

Boyd had been warned by Nick and Kate that BlackRhino operatives might come calling, so he had his lines ready and rehearsed. But he hadn't expected to have to perform his part so soon after the heist. Still, it was comforting to have a script to work from. It gave him confidence, though he was careful not to appear any less fearful to his abductors, who were driving him leisurely up Lankershim Boulevard toward the Ventura Freeway.

'Is this about my slot machine winnings?' Boyd said. 'Because if it is, I didn't take a nickel. Ask him.'

'It wasn't money that was taken,' Mr Smith said.

'You can't blame me if some crew member lifted a knickknack. Most of them are Teamsters, and you know about them.' Boyd bent the tip of his nose with his finger. 'They're all mobbed up. But I'm not the one who hired the crew. The producers did. *They're* the ones you need to punch and throw into the backseat of a car.'

'We'd love to,' Mr Smith said. 'But they're in the wind. They don't exist. Their production company is a phone in an empty office.'

'The TV show you hosted was a fake,' Mr Brown said,

stealing a glance at Boyd in the mirror to gauge his reaction to the news.

'No, no, no. You're making a big mistake.' Boyd sat up in his seat. 'I've seen the show on TV. It's real. You can watch it yourself. It's on every week.'

'The show exists, but this wasn't a real episode,' Mr Smith said. 'It was a trick to get into Mr Grove's house.'

'Wait a minute,' Boyd said. 'Are you saying I'm not the new host of *The Most Spectacular Homes on Earth*?'

Mr Smith grabbed Boyd's hand and bent it backward. Boyd curled up in pain. 'Pay attention, Mr Capwell. This isn't about you. The important thing here is that something was stolen from Mr Grove and he wants it back. Your only concern should be helping us locate the object and the people who took it.' Mr Smith released Boyd's hand.

'You think I had something to do with it?' Boyd asked.

'You were the host of the show,' Mr Smith said.

'But you're telling me it was a fraud. If I was in on it, why would I use my own name? How stupid do you think I am?'

'You're an actor,' Mr Brown said, as if that explained everything.

'I'm a victim here, too,' Boyd said. 'I thought this was my big break, and now you're telling me it's not. I don't even have the footage to use on my reel.' Boyd saw Mr

Smith glance at his hand again, and he held it up in surrender.

'What can you tell us about the producers?' Mr Smith asked.

'Lucy Carmichael came to the set of a commercial I was working on and offered me the job. It was the first time I'd met her. A couple days later I was on a plane to Palm Beach.'

Mr Brown glanced at Boyd in the mirror again. 'Didn't that strike you as unusual? Wouldn't you ordinarily have to audition for a job that big?'

'I've sent my résumé and tapes to hundreds of casting directors and production companies over the years,' Boyd said. 'She said the current host had quit unexpectedly, right in the middle of production, and they had to move fast. They had no time for a lengthy audition process, so they watched some of the tapes that had piled up. They liked mine and that was that. It was a huge break for me, and they paid me SAG scale, and my per diem, up front. Why would I question my good fortune?'

'Where did you meet after that?' Mr Smith asked.

'We didn't. The next time we talked was over the phone, and it was to arrange my travel.'

'Did they give you a script or any special instructions?'

'There was no script. They didn't even give me any background on the house. They wanted everything to be fresh, for me to experience the house for the first time with the audience. The only direction I got was to keep things moving, and to pretend like the camera was a friend on the tour with me.'

'Were you aware ahead of time that the old man was going to land on the roof?'

'He was a fake, too?' Boyd asked.

'Of course he was,' Mr Brown said. 'What are the odds of a guy losing control of his parasail and landing on the roof the same day that a fake TV show is in the house stealing stuff?'

'Whatever they stole must really be special for you to go to so much trouble and expense to retrieve it,' Boyd said. 'I wish I could be more help.'

'You haven't been *any* help,' Mr Smith said.

'That's not fair,' Boyd said. 'I know Carter lost something here, but so did I. This is a crushing blow to me. I thought I'd hit the big-time.'

'Really?' Mr Brown said. 'Then why were you auditioning for a mouthwash commercial two days after wrapping your first episode?'

'Maybe it was to get some of that mouthwash,' Mr Smith said, turning his head away from Boyd. 'It smells like an unflushed toilet back here.'

'The producers said they'd call me in a week or so about shooting the next episode. What was I supposed to do in the meantime? I'm an actor, and actors need to act. It's like breathing.'

'You won't be doing either if we find out you've been lying to us.'

'Why would I? I'm not in on it. Isn't it obvious why they hired me?'

'Because you're desperate and cheap?' Mr Smith said.

'Verisimilitude,' Boyd said.

Mr Smith gave him a blank look.

'Reality,' Boyd said. 'I gave their scam instant believability by virtue of being the only one involved who was genuine.'

It was a good argument and Mr Smith seemed convinced, or maybe he just couldn't handle Boyd's bad breath any longer. He glanced at Mr Brown, who nodded, pulled the car over to the curb, and unlocked the doors.

'You hear from them, you call us,' Mr Smith said, handing him a card. 'Or your next role will be a corpse on *CSI*.'

Boyd got out and watched the Mercedes drive off down Lankershim. He didn't dare try to call the number he had for Kate to warn her. They were undoubtedly watching him closely. If the number still worked, he'd be playing right into BlackRhino's hands, revealing himself as a player in the con and leading them directly to Kate. All he could do was hope that Nick and Kate knew that they were already being hunted.

Eighteen

Nick and Kate were once again sitting in the dark in the backseat of the Rolls-Royce. It was six hours before Fu's A380 was scheduled to land in Shanghai. The dead BlackRhino operative was stashed in the boat, along with the trash bags. The safe-cracking rig was still whirring along. It was a waiting game now.

They'd gone through the candy, the crackers, and a bottle of wine. They'd played 20 Questions, sung songs, and taken turns napping.

'This is boring,' Kate said. 'This flight is never going to end.'

'Yes, but listen,' Nick said.

'I don't hear anything.'

'Exactly.'

The *clickety-clack* sound of the safecracking rig had stopped.

'The combination has been cracked and the safe is unlocked,' Nick said.

'And you're still sitting here?'

'There's no hurry. We have hours until we land in Shanghai.'

'I don't care,' Kate said. 'This is exciting. I have to see.'

Kate got out of the car, flicked her flashlight on, and led the way to the ULD that contained the safe.

Nick followed close behind and gestured to the iPhone attached to the rig. There were six numbers glowing on the screen. 'That's the combination.'

Nick crouched in front of the safe, carefully removed the rig, set it aside, and turned the latch on the door. He opened the safe, and there was the rooster, staring out at them.

'He looks fierce,' Kate said, shining the flashlight into the safe.

Nick took the rooster out and placed it gently on the floor. He opened the case containing the real one and placed it alongside the fake one. He stepped back and examined them under his Maglite.

'Whoever made the phony did excellent work. The patina of the bronze is perfect. I can't see any difference.'

'Don't get confused and mix them up.'

'I'm not new at this, you know. I'm an experienced professional. Maybe one of the best in the world.'

'I'm just saying.'

Ten minutes later, the real rooster was locked in the safe, the fake rooster was snug in its carrying case, and Kate and Nick were back in the Rolls-Royce.

'While you were napping I made a quick trip to Fu's wine cellar,' Nick said. 'I thought we needed something appropriate for a celebration when the safe got opened.'

'Champagne?'

'Of course.'

'Shall we open it?'

He smiled at her. 'It would be criminal not to.'

'You're the expert.'

Duff MacTaggert slept in an apartment directly over his pub in a heavy, hand-carved four-poster bed that was among the few surviving pieces of furniture pillaged from Kilmarny Castle over a century ago. The bed was big, sturdy, and a survivor, just like Duff.

The mattress, however, was brand new, hand-crafted in Aberdeen by blind artisans using the same techniques, and highly developed sense of touch, as their sightless ancestors who began the company in the mid-1800s. The British Royal Family slept on mattresses just like it at Balmoral Castle. It was an expensive, sumptuous mattress meant for kings and for Duff MacTaggert, the King of Thieves. Duff loved his bed.

So it took a lot to get Duff out of bed in the middle of the night. But on this night there was a distant rumble, and as it grew closer and louder his bed began to shake, something it had never done before, not even in the fiercest winter storm. The noise grew deafening and the whole building rattled. The shaking loosened from the ceiling a fine mist of stone dust that powdered his whiskers, and then a harsh light filled his room. That got him up.

He grabbed a robe, crossed the room, and squinted into the light outside his window. A helicopter hovered over the loch, aiming a spotlight at his pub. It had to be the police. They'd finally figured out what he'd done and had come to get him.

Duff went downstairs, marching through his pub, out the front door, and across the gravel to the edge of the beach to face the bastards head-on. The big black chopper hovered in front of him like some huge angry insect. It was an Apache attack helicopter armed with Hellfire antitank missiles, Hydra 70 rockets, and a phallic 30mm machine gun between its landing gear. The Apache struck Duff as overkill, but part of him was flattered the cops thought he was so dangerous that they needed one.

He gave the chopper the finger and cursed at it in Gaelic. The Apache opened fire on his pub with a barrage of 30mm rounds, shattering the windows, obliterating the doors, and riddling the stone façade. After a solid minute, the gun stopped. Duff looked back at his pub.

It stood as defiantly as he did. Then two Hydra rockets streaked from the chopper. The building exploded like a sandcastle kicked by a petulant child.

The blast knocked Duff off his feet and facedown onto the ground.

Armed commandos dressed in black peeled out of the darkness. Two of them lifted Duff to his feet. When Duff saw their balaclava-hooded faces and the stony look in their eyes, he knew it wasn't the police who'd come for him and now he wished that it had been.

The police would only jail him. But these guys were from BlackRhino. They would torture him to the edge of sanity and death to get what they wanted. He'd hold out as long as he could against the agony. It was a matter of honor and pride. But he'd eventually tell them what they wanted to know. He'd give them Nicolas Fox.

Hours after the events in Kilmarny, the A380 Superjumbo made a smooth landing at Shanghai Hongqiao International Airport and taxied to a stop. The local time was two in the afternoon, and it was drizzling. Nick and Kate were unaware of the local weather from where they sat.

'I feel like we're living the ending of *Butch Cassidy and the Sundance Kid,*' Kate said.

She was crammed into the trunk of the Dodge Charger with the two metal cases and a trash bag containing their bottles, candy wrappers, and soiled paper towels. They had done their best to clean up the cargo hold so there were no signs that a ULD had been opened, or that the safe had been broken into, or that there had been any stowaways on board. But they'd been working in the dark, using only their flashlights, and Kate knew they could easily have missed something.

'You mean that scene when Redford and Newman are stuck in some adobe hut, surrounded by the Bolivian army, and they decide to run out the door shooting into a barrage of bullets?' Nick asked. He'd stuffed himself into the compartment they'd created under the backseat.

'Yes,' she said.

'That doesn't apply to our situation at all.'

'We're a couple of outlaws stuck in an airplane, and the Chinese police and a squad of BlackRhino killers could be surrounding us right now, waiting for us to come out of the cargo hold.'

'Or there could be nobody outside this plane besides Fu's ground crew. Don't be so pessimistic. I'm counting on making my dinner reservation at Ultraviolet.'

'That's your priority right now, not losing your table?'

'I haven't had a proper meal in over twenty-four hours. It's a matter of survival.'

'What do you think is going to happen when that cargo hatch opens?'

'The ground crew will unload the cargo hold, someone

will drive this car to the underground parking garage at Fu's high-rise in Pudong, and we'll slip away unnoticed.'

'And if we're surrounded by police and BlackRhino killers?'

'We go to Plan B,' Nick said. It was why, as a precaution, he was hiding under the backseat instead of with her in the trunk.

'Plan B sucks,' Kate said.

'It's better than Plan C.'

'We don't have a Plan C.'

'Now Plan B doesn't seem so bad, does it?'

She would have shaken her head had it been possible without banging herself on the wheel well. 'I think you're even better at fooling yourself than you are at conning other people.'

'If you can't fool yourself,' he said, 'how can you expect to fool anybody else?'

Nineteen

Fu's A380 Superjumbo was parked outside a private terminal at the south end of the airport. Surrounding the airport was a dense concentration of warehouses, restaurants, office buildings, tourist hotels, sprawling apartment complexes, and the convergence of four freeways in an enormous tangle of overpasses.

Fu sat in his office aboard the jet and peered out the window at the murky skyline. Scattered rain clouds mingled with the thick brown haze of smog that continually hung over the city. The drizzle rinsed the gunk from the skies and soaked the ground and water with toxic chemicals. But once the rain clouds passed, at least the skies would be clear for a change and Shanghai would sparkle in the sunlight. Fu always tried to look at the bright side of things.

He was about to turn away from the window when several white police vans swarmed around the plane, and a dozen officers in their pressed olive green uniforms scrambled out, carrying rifles. He'd expected to be greeted by some low-level dignitaries, but not the police. He'd been told before he left for DC that the government wanted to keep the arrival of the rooster quiet and save the hoopla for the official unveiling and repatriation at the National Museum of China in Beijing. But now, with the Smithsonian woman on board and the arrival of the police, something had obviously changed the government's thinking.

Fu answered his phone, expecting it was the customary call from the pilot informing him that they'd arrived and inquiring whether Fu wanted to leave the plane before, after, or along with his invited guests.

'My compliments on a smooth flight,' Fu said.

'Thank you, sir,' the pilot said. 'The Ministry of Public Security has contacted us. They've surrounded the plane and have ordered everyone to remain on board until instructed otherwise. They've sent an official to the main cabin door to meet with you.'

'I'll be right down,' Fu said.

By the time Fu reached the bottom of the spiral staircase, the lower-level door was already open and a bureaucrat from the Ministry of Public Security was waiting for him with one of the flight attendants. The man appeared to be in his forties, wore a cheap, wet overcoat, and reeked of cigarettes. He had nicotine-stained teeth, bloodshot eyes, and a pointed nose that gave him a birdlike appearance.

'I'm police inspector Zhaoji Li,' he said, and shook Fu's outstretched hand. 'I apologize for the inconvenience, Mr Fu, but we've received a tip that Nicolas Fox, an international thief pursued by law enforcement agencies worldwide, might try to steal the rooster.'

'Now? While we're sitting here on the runway? That's ridiculous.'

Zhaoji grimaced, as if it pained him to even be discussing the topic. 'I'm told he's quite resourceful. In fact, there's a chance he's already stolen it in flight.'

'How could he get on board, and how could he possibly hope to escape with the rooster?'

The inspector shrugged. 'If I was imaginative enough to figure out how to accomplish such an extraordinary crime, I'd be a world-class thief like Fox and not the simple police officer that I am.'

'You sound like you admire him, Inspector.'

'I envy people with imagination. People like you, sir. I'm someone who sees only what he already knows and what is right in front of him.'

Fu appreciated Zhaoji's honest self-appraisal and subtle suck-up. Perhaps there was more to this inspector than met the eye. 'I assume this rumor about Fox is why a Smithsonian security guard approached us in DC and insisted on coming along on the flight.'

The inspector shrugged again. Fu got the impression

that shrugging was Zhaoji's primary form of communication.

'We'd like to keep everyone but you on the plane until we can confirm that the rooster is on board and genuine,' Zhaoji said. 'We have an antiquities expert with us from the State Administration of Cultural Heritage to authenticate the rooster. If everything is in order, we'll allow everyone off the plane and provide security for the rooster on its journey to the Shanghai Museum.'

'Suit yourself, Inspector, but I assure you it's a waste of time.'

The lights came on in the cargo hold, and Kate heard the ramp drop open. There were footsteps on the ramp. Maybe a half dozen men. They were engaged in a serious conversation. They walked past the Charger toward the ULDs. Kate didn't speak or understand Chinese, but she heard two words that chilled her blood. *Nicolas Fox.*

Fu led the inspector, four armed officers, and the antiquities expert to the ULD that held his safe. The expert, Lui Wei, looked frail and ancient enough to have seen the rooster the last time it was in China, one hundred and fifty years ago at the Old Summer Palace in Beijing.

Fu opened the ULD, revealing the safe inside. He

looked over his shoulder at Zhaoji. 'It appears untouched to me.'

The inspector nodded. 'That's encouraging, sir. Please proceed.'

Fu used his body to shield the dial from view so nobody could see the combination as he unlocked the safe. He spun the dial, opened the safe, and stepped back, presenting the rooster with a sweep of his hand.

'Here it is,' Fu said. 'Emperor Qianlong's bronze rooster.'

The antiquities expert crouched in front of the rooster and slipped on a pair of wire-rimmed glasses that made his eyes appear so enormous, he looked like ET in a wrinkled suit.

Zhaoji stepped away to give Lui some light and more room to work. He scanned the cargo hold, glancing at the two cars and the boat. He looked up at the ceiling and down at the floor. Everything was immaculate. Except for one tiny dark spot on the floor. He knelt to examine it and found another drop a couple feet away. One drop led to another. And another. A trail. The inspector was so intent on following the drops that he missed an even more significant detail. The straps and chains that should have been securing the rare Dodge Charger Daytona to the floor of the cargo hold were unfastened, and the battery was back in place, under the hood.

* * *

'We're going with Plan B,' Nick whispered to Kate when he heard his name mentioned by the Chinese official.

'Oh crap,' Kate whispered back.

Nick slashed the backseat open and crept out of his hiding place and into the driver's seat of the Charger, while all eyes were on the rooster. The keys were in the ignition. Nick released the parking brake and pumped the gas pedal to prime the engine.

Kate thought Plan B should have been called Plan D, for Desperation. Or Plan S, for Suicide. She braced herself in the trunk as best she could. Her fate was in Nick's hands now. Fortunately, if there was one thing she knew about Nick Fox, it was that he was very, very good at avoiding capture.

Zhaoji climbed onto the jetboat, following the tiny drops of blood to an aft storage compartment that was topped with a cushion and doubled as a seating area. He bent down, removed the cushions, and lifted the lid. Several plastic trash bags were crammed inside. He pulled the bags out and discovered a woman's stiff, dead body. She was blond, and her neck was twisted at an unnatural angle. He could see the Smithsonian patch on her jacket breast pocket.

'The rooster is authentic,' Lui Wei declared, rising to his feet in front of the safe.

'That's a relief,' Zhaoji said, his back to the men below. 'Tell me, Mr Fu, was the Smithsonian guard a woman?'

Nick heard someone on the boat say *Smithsonian* and *nǚrén,* the Chinese word for 'woman,' and knew the assassin's body had been found. He sat up, turned the ignition key, depressed the clutch, jammed the car into reverse, and flattened the gas pedal.

The Charger's loud, guttural roar startled everyone in the cargo hold. They were even more surprised when they saw the car speed backward down the ramp and smack onto the wet tarmac, setting off sparks and scattering the ground crew.

Fu ran after the car, waving his hands, yelling for the driver to stop. Zhaoji scrambled off the boat, issuing orders to secure the hold. And Kate held her breath and braced herself.

Nick executed a perfect half-spin as he hit the tarmac, turning the car around so it faced away from the plane and directly toward the chain-link fence that separated the airfield from the road. The Charger shot forward, a blur of red streaking over the asphalt, its 426 Hemi engine powering it through the fence and onto a side street that led into a warren of warehouses. He sped south, straight into oncoming traffic, dodging head-on collisions with the taxis, trucks, and buses. All those hours playing Asteroids at the video arcade when he was a kid had definitely paid off. He wanted to throw as many obstacles into the path of his pursuers as he could.

He glanced into his rearview mirror and saw cars

swerving wildly in his wake, but didn't see any police on his tail. He had the element of surprise, a big head start, and a car capable of hitting two hundred miles per hour. Still, he knew eventually they'd spot him from the air. And to make matters worse, he had no idea where he was going. He'd flown into Hongqiao International Airport before. He'd seen the Hongqiao streets from the sky and from the backseat of a taxi, but that wasn't the same as knowing his way around. What he remembered most about the area from those trips were the wide elevated freeways and roads that all seemed to converge in one spot.

He made a sharp, tire-squealing left in front of the Air China Shanghai Hotel and zoomed east on Yingbin Road, a wide boulevard lined with stores on the south side and the Shanghai Xintianlu Conference Center park along the north.

Nick saw a police chopper closing in ahead of him. He was out in the open on a wide boulevard in a bright red car with a huge spoiler on the trunk. They wouldn't be able to miss him.

The car that Inspector Zhaoji Li was driving was the last in a line of four police vehicles, sirens wailing, that were speeding south on Konggang First Road after a man he presumed was Nicolas Fox. None of the officers could see the Charger anymore, but Zhaoji wasn't worried. There was no other car like it in Shanghai. It might as well be on fire. In the meantime, they were following the wake of cars Fox had scattered when he charged through oncoming traffic. Zhaoji was surprised that Fox hadn't caused a single wreck and wondered whether that was by luck or by design.

Zhaoji was turning left onto Yingbin Third Road when a report came in from one of the police helicopters converging on the area.

'The assailant is a mile ahead of you, traveling eastbound on Yingbin Third Road toward the Outer Ring Expressway.'

The inspector smiled to himself. Whether Fox got on the elevated freeway or continued on the road toward the Shanghai Zoo, he'd be easy to corner now. Zhaoji would soon have the glory of catching an international felon. A promotion was definitely in his future. Perhaps he could afford a new overcoat. Maybe move into a larger apartment, too. The chopper pilot's voice cut into his brief reverie.

'We've lost him,' the pilot said.

Zhaoji grabbed the mike with one hand while he steered with the other. 'What do you mean you've lost him? How is that possible?'

'The car went under the freeway on Yingbin and didn't come out the other side. Maybe he crashed underneath the overpass.'

No, he didn't crash. Zhaoji knew what Fox was doing. The cunning thief was using the elevated freeway to hide from the choppers. Fox was undoubtedly heading south underneath the Outer Ring Expressway, taking it to where it met the Yan'an Elevated Road, the Huyu Expressway, and the Hu Qing Ping Highway in a massive four-level knot of overpasses, interchanges, and sweeping on- and off-ramps above a wooded median. By hiding under all of that concrete and brush, Fox might escape detection from the air, but not the ground. All Fox had managed to do was box himself in.

'All ground units, the assailant is below the Hu Qing Ping Highway exchange,' Zhaoji said. 'Seal it off. Air units, maintain surveillance of the freeways and surrounding roads for the red car in case he makes a break for it.'

The Charger blazed through the weedy, trash-strewn no-man's-land beneath the Outer Ring Expressway. Nick tried to avoid hitting the pillars that supported the freeway while also trying to keep control of the car as it bounced over the uneven ground.

Nick made an abrupt left, flew over a small embankment, and landed hard in the thick brush of the median that was hidden in the shadows underneath three looping overpasses.

He got out of the car, ran to the back, and popped

the trunk. Kate was curled up inside around the two suitcases. She was dazed and bleeding from a fresh cut on her head.

'Are you all right?' Nick asked, holding his hand out to her.

'Peachy.' She swatted his hand away. 'How did you ever get a driver's license?'

'I never said that I did.' He offered her his hand again. 'Come on, we have to make a run for it on foot.'

'You are, I'm not.' She handed him her cell phone, fake ID, credit cards, and passport. 'Close the trunk and go.'

'I know you're tired and hurting, but it's too soon to give up. The game isn't nearly over, and I've got plenty of moves left. There are twenty-four million people in Shanghai. Getting lost among them is going to be easy.'

'For you it will be, but not for me. I'm bruised and bleeding.'

'We can work around that.'

'I'd rather use it to my advantage,' she said.

Nick cocked an eyebrow and regarded her in a new light. 'You have a scheme in mind?'

'Plan C.'

'We don't have a Plan C.'

'We do now. You said we should trust each other to do what each of us does best. Well, now it's time for you to be a fugitive and for me to be an FBI agent.'

Nick could hear sirens closing in and helicopters streaking overhead. They didn't have much time left.

'Have you got an explanation for the dead body in the cargo hold and how you ended up in China in the trunk of a stolen car driven by the fugitive you're supposed to be chasing?'

'I do,' she said.

'I'd love to hear it.'

'I'll share it with you over drinks in LA.'

Nick grabbed her, and kissed her, and closed the trunk on her.

Twenty

Nick walked up the embankment to Hu Qing Ping Gong Road, which ran along the west side of the freeway interchange. There were no rickshaws, no pagodas, nothing that screamed he was in Shanghai. The signs on the hotels, freight companies, and restaurants were in Chinese and English, but otherwise this could have passed for any airport neighborhood in any city in the United States.

On the other side of the street was a Motel 168, one of a large chain of Chinese budget accommodations. It was a drab five-story building with MOTEL168.COM spelled out on the roof in huge letters that could be seen by anyone on the freeway interchange, and certainly by the two police helicopters now circling above it.

As Nick crossed the busy street, drivers barely made an effort to avoid him. He walked calmly, pretending to check his phone for email, so that he'd look like a fearless expat who had done this a thousand times, not a man running from the police.

Once he reached the other side, he walked past the taxis parked in front of the Motel 168 and strolled into the lobby just as several police cars streaked by the building, sirens wailing. He went directly to the front desk, where he exchanged some US dollars for Chinese yuan, then went back outside and hailed a taxi that took him to the airport Metro station.

Six police officers, led by Inspector Zhaoji Li, crept up on the Charger, their guns drawn. They could hear pounding and a muffled voice coming from the trunk. As Zhaoji got closer, he could tell that it was a woman's voice, and that she was calling for help in English.

Zhaoji sent four officers into the brush to look for the driver. He holstered his gun and slapped the trunk with the palm of his hand to get the attention of whoever was inside.

'This is the police,' he said in English. 'Be still. We're going to open the trunk.'

'Make it fast,' she said.

Zhaoji noted that she didn't sound scared. She sounded angry.

He told the remaining officers to cover him. The officers drew their weapons and stood off to one side as Zhaoji opened the trunk.

Kate blinked at the sudden light and wiped blood from her lower lip with the back of her hand. She was wedged in beside the two metal cases. Clearly, she had recently been beaten and bandaged. There was blood in her hair, and her shirt and jeans were blood-caked.

In spite of her bloody appearance, Zhaoji thought she didn't look like a victim. She was focused and angry.

'I'm Special Agent Kate O'Hare with the Federal Bureau of Investigation,' she said. 'Tell me you've got him.'

'Who?'

'Nicolas Fox. Who else?'

She tried to get up, but Zhaoji held up his hand in a halting gesture.

'Stay where you are,' he said to her, and then in Chinese he ordered one of the officers to call an ambulance and to alert the other units that Fox might be on foot. That's when Zhaoji realized that none of his officers knew what Fox looked like beyond the fact that he was a white male in his early thirties. By the time central command sent photos of Fox to every officer in every patrol car, the thief would be long gone, if he wasn't already.

The inspector turned back to Kate, and he could see her reading the defeated expression on his face.

'Damn,' she said. 'You've lost him.'

He shrugged. 'But we have you.'

Kate sat on a gurney in a windowless exam room at Shanghai United Family Hospital in Hongqiao. She wore a hospital gown, and her right wrist was handcuffed to the bed rail. She'd been examined and X-rayed by a Chinese doctor with the bedside manner of a mortician. Her wounds had been cleaned and freshly bandaged. The whole time, she'd remained under the stony gaze of two expressionless uniformed police officers she'd christened Rigor and Mortis, who stood now on either side of the exam room door. She hadn't seen the inspector since the ambulance had taken her away from the freeway median almost two hours ago.

She looked over at Rigor and Mortis. 'Could one of you run out and get me a hamburger or something? I'm starving.' Neither officer said a word. 'I'll settle for anything. Fried rice. An eggroll. A bag of Doritos. Whatever you can get from the cafeteria.' The men remained expressionless. She lifted her right arm and rattled the handcuff chain. 'I'm locked to the bed, and my ass is hanging out of this gown. I'm not going to escape if one of you goes to get me some food.' Neither man budged or gave any indication he'd even heard her. Maybe they didn't speak English.

The door opened and Zhaoji came in. His hair was wet, and his overcoat was soaked. The drizzle had apparently turned into a downpour. There was some mud on his shoes and the cuffs of his pants.

'How are you feeling?' Zhaoji asked. His English was good, though his Chinese accent was heavy.

'Hungry. Tired. Pissed off.'

The inspector said something in Chinese to Rigor, who nodded and left the room. Zhaoji faced Kate. 'The doctor says you've been slashed with a knife and that you've suffered numerous blows to your torso, resulting in substantial bruising, and you possibly have a concussion.'

Kate jangled her handcuff against the rail again. 'Why am I being treated like a criminal?'

Zhaoji took his wet coat off and draped it over the back of a chair. He wore a white shirt, black tie, and an off-the-rack gray suit that was beginning to fray at the cuffs from years of use. 'A woman was killed on Stanley Fu's plane, and an international fugitive is loose in our city.'

'I had nothing to do with any of that.'

'You were on the same plane.'

'So were Fu, his crew, and his guests. Are they in handcuffs, too?'

'You have no passport or identification of any kind.'

'Because they were taken away from me. I told you who I am. I'm FBI Special Agent Kate O'Hare. Send my picture and my prints to the US consulate. They'll confirm it.'

He shrugged. 'You stowed away on a private jet and entered this country illegally.'

'I was beaten and abducted.'

'You fled from the plane in a car with Nicolas Fox.'

'Against my will. I was locked in the trunk.'

'You were found in the possession of suitcases containing a counterfeit bronze rooster and sophisticated safecracking equipment.'

'It all belongs to Fox, and if you're smart, you'll stop wasting valuable time and uncuff me so I can help you catch him before he disappears.'

Zhaoji didn't appear to be in a hurry. He took a leather notebook out of his back pocket, dragged a stool in front of the gurney, and sat down. The deeply creased notebook was curved from being constantly pressed against his butt. All the male cops that she knew had notebooks shaped like that. He pulled a pen from his breast pocket, held it poised over a page, and looked at her with his bloodshot eyes. 'Let's start from the beginning, shall we?'

'I chased Nicolas Fox for years. I finally caught him and put him behind bars, but he escaped from custody on his way to trial. I've been searching for him ever since. Three days ago I got a tip that he was going to steal the bronze rooster, so I went to DC to try to catch him in the act.'

'Without telling your superiors? Without any backup?'

She narrowed her eyes at him. 'You've obviously talked to the FBI and you know who I am. So why am I still handcuffed?'

'They say you are supposed to be in Los Angeles and that they don't know why you're here. They say you've gone rogue.'

It was no surprise to her that Bolton had thrown her under the bus, but at least now they knew that she and Nick had pulled off the switch. Nick's cover was safe. He was a fugitive before and still was. But their covert operation was still at risk. Bolton probably had his intestines tied in knots worrying about whether she'd be able to walk away from this without being exposed as Fox's accomplice. It all rode on how this interview with Zhaoji turned out.

'They're pencil-pushing bureaucrats,' Kate said. 'I'm sure it's the same here.'

He shrugged again.

She knew it was his way of being noncommittal and keeping her talking. She was glad to play along.

'I knew the tip wasn't strong enough to get them to approve a trip to DC,' Kate said, 'so I went on my own. My bosses call it going rogue, I call it showing some initiative. It's the only way you're going to catch a man like Nicolas Fox.'

Rigor came back with a bowl of white rice and a set of chopsticks, which he offered to Kate. She nodded her thanks and took it, though she would have preferred a cheeseburger.

'If you believed the rooster was at risk,' Zhaoji said,

'why didn't you alert anyone at the Smithsonian, or in Stanley Fu's company, or in the Chinese government?'

'Because if I did that,' Kate said, 'they would have reacted by increasing their security or changing their plans in some way, which would have scared Fox off and blown my opportunity to get him. By the time I got to DC, the rooster had already been delivered to the cargo hold of Fu's jet and nothing unusual happened during the trip. So I assumed that Fox hadn't stolen the rooster yet, which meant that he had to make his move while the plane was on the tarmac at Dulles, or while it was in midair, or once it landed in Shanghai. It was obviously going to be in the air.'

Zhaoji looked confused. 'Why?'

'Because airports are high-security locations these days. He'd need manpower and weapons to pull off the theft at one of the airports, and that just isn't his style. But midair he wouldn't have to worry about security, and he'd have hours alone with the safe to crack the combination. Plus it was a ballsy play, pure Nick Fox. All I had to figure out was how he was going to do it.'

'You make it sound easy. Seems to me it would be the hardest part.'

'Not if you've been chasing Fox as long as I have,' Kate said, finishing her rice. 'I looked into Fu's activities while he was in DC and discovered that he'd purchased the Charger and intended to take it on his plane. If I was a thief, I'd hide in the Charger and sneak onto the plane. So the night before Fu was supposed to leave DC, I went out to the car dealer in Bethesda, slipped inside the building, and caught Nick Fox turning the backseat of the Charger into a secret compartment.'

Zhaoji had been taking notes as she spoke, but now he stopped and met her eye. 'You're an FBI agent and an ex–Navy commando. You could probably kill all three of us right now with those chopsticks. Do you really expect me to believe that Fox disarmed you, beat you up, and locked you in the trunk of the car?'

Kate set her chopsticks down in the empty bowl, and Mortis quickly snatched the bowl from her. Okay, she thought, now I know two things. The inspector is a lot smarter and more informed than he lets on, and the stone-faced guards clearly understand English.

'I got the drop on Fox,' she said. 'But what I didn't know was that he had an accomplice, a highly trained BlackRhino operative with a switchblade. She came out of nowhere and took me by surprise. We had a fight. She won. Next thing I knew, I woke up in the trunk of the car in the cargo hold of Fu's airplane.'

'Why didn't she kill you?'

'Fox must have stopped her.'

'Why would he do that?'

'Because he isn't a killer.'

'But Alexis Poulet was,' Zhaoji said. 'Before she joined

BlackRhino, she was a spy and assassin for DCRI, the French intelligence service.'

'That's irrelevant. Fox doesn't kill people. His con, his rules, that's how he rolls.'

Zhaoji took his cell phone out of his inside jacket pocket, tapped a few keys, then turned the screen toward Kate so she could see the picture of the dead BlackRhino operative stuffed into the jet-boat storage compartment. 'Then who did this?'

'I don't know,' Kate said. 'I was locked in the trunk. I was given a couple bottles of water, but beyond that I have no idea what went down. I heard some arguing, raised voices, but I don't know what was said. I had no idea the woman was killed. Like I said, it's not Fox's style. Maybe someone else is involved.'

'Was Fox the one who dressed your wounds?'

'I assume so. When I woke up, I was already bandaged.'

'It's one thing not to kill you, it's another to treat your injuries while he's in the middle of a heist.'

She shrugged. Two could play that game.

He cocked his head and looked at her as if seeing her in a new light. 'He cares about you.'

'Fox only cares about himself and his image. He wanted me alive and well to do what I'm doing right now, telling his side of the story.'

'Perhaps.'

The inspector's face betrayed nothing. She couldn't tell if he believed her or not, if she'd be sent home or to prison. Zhaoji stood up, slipped the notebook back into his pocket, and walked out, leaving her handcuffed and alone with Rigor and Mortis once again.

Twenty-one

The rain had stopped. The wet streets of Shanghai had a glossy sheen that reflected the lavishly illuminated buildings on both sides of the Huangpu River, the dividing line between the city's past and future.

On the western side of the Huangpu was the Bund, which in the mid-nineteenth century had been the Wall Street of the Far East. The surviving buildings were a trapped-in-amber artifact of the city's rich colonial past as a trading post. This nineteenth-century city had been carved up by the British, French, and Americans into districts that looked like their faraway mother countries.

On the east bank was Pudong, a booming Tomorrowland of skyscrapers rising from the swamps. The most iconic high-rise was the Oriental Pearl Tower, perfectly symbolizing Shanghai's aggressive new attitude on the global economic stage. There were 90 billionaires and 140,000 multimillionaires in Shanghai, and the majority of them lived, worked, and partied in Pudong. This was where Nick Fox liked to ply his trade when he came to town.

He stayed at the Park Hyatt Shanghai. The luxury hotel occupied the seventy-ninth to ninety-third floors of the 101-story Shanghai World Financial Center. It was a landmark building with a massive, rectangular hole at the top that made the sleek, shimmering tower look like an enormous bottle opener. The similarity was so striking that bottle openers shaped like the SWFC were sold as souvenirs on the tower's hundredth-floor observation deck and at tourist shops throughout the city.

Nick showed up carrying an Hermès suitcase and wearing some of the clothes he'd bought at Shanghai Tang. He wore a perfectly tailored black blazer, a light blue-and-white-striped chambray shirt, stretch denim slacks, and a pair of casual Ecco leather boat shoes. He registered as Sonny Crockett and took the elevator to his ninety-third-floor suite.

The suite's dim lighting, muted colors, and minimalist décor made the breathtaking view of the Huangpu River and the Bund through the floor-to-ceiling windows appear even more dramatic. But what really heightened the drama for Nick was the reflection of the man standing behind him holding a gun.

* * *

Inspector Zhaoji Li entered Kate's room carrying a neatly folded set of blue surgical scrubs, which he placed beside her on the gurney.

'If you were chasing Nicolas Fox in Shanghai,' he asked, 'where would you start looking for him?'

Zhaoji asked this in his politely enigmatic way, but Kate knew there was nothing trivial about the conversation. Just as she instinctively knew he already had the answer.

'I'd go to the five top hotels in the city,' she replied.

'Why?'

'He believes in hiding in plain sight, and he likes his comfort.'

'Would the Park Hyatt Shanghai qualify?'

Her heart skipped a beat. She knew that was where Nick was staying, and apparently so did Zhaoji.

'Is it a five-star hotel?'

He nodded. 'It's also one of the tallest hotels on earth.'

'Then yes, definitely, it would be at the top of my list.'

Her answer seemed to satisfy him, which only deepened her concern. He sent Rigor and Mortis out of the room with a nod of his head and unlocked the handcuffs on her wrist.

'Your shoes are in the closet, but you might prefer this clean set of scrubs I brought for you to the clothes you were wearing when you were brought in.' He pocketed his handcuffs. 'I hope they are your size.'

'Thank you,' she said. 'Does this mean that I am free to go?'

'Yes, though you won't get far without identification or money and wearing only scrubs. We could drop you off at the US consulate if you like.'

'I'd rather stick around and help you catch Fox,' Kate said. 'How is the search going so far?'

'It's over,' he said. 'We've found him.'

She tried to look happy, though she was filled with dread. 'Do you have him in custody?'

He shrugged. 'I suppose you could say that.'

The plaza outside the Shanghai World Financial Center was cordoned off with crime scene tape, though none of the passersby seemed the least bit interested in the police activity or the corpse under the blue tarp.

Kate, in her surgical scrubs, stared up at the building. The shattered window was on the ninety-third floor, but she couldn't see it. The room was too high up. She knew that a body falling from that height would hit the ground like an exploding water balloon, so she'd declined Zhaoji's invitation to look under the tarp. There would be nothing left to identify. But was the dead man Nick? And if it wasn't him, who was it?

Zhaoji exchanged a few words with one of the forensic technicians scurrying around the scene in their hooded white coveralls and plastic gloves. The tech handed Zhaoji several evidence bags, which the inspector brought back with him to Kate.

'We recovered this.' The inspector held up a baggie containing the pieces of two broken keys and an intact leather-strapped keychain with the word DAYTONA stitched in yellow on it. 'They appear to be the keys to the Dodge Charger.'

'That doesn't mean the dead man is Fox.'

Zhaoji nodded. 'I showed the concierge and the people at the front desk a picture of Fox. They knew him well here – not as Nicolas Fox, of course, but as Sonny Crockett – and gave him his usual ninety-third-floor suite, the same one the body fell from.'

'Sonny Crockett? Really?'

'Is the name significant?'

'He was a cop on *Miami Vice,*' Kate said. The inspector stared at her blankly. 'You know, the TV show? With Don Johnson?'

'I don't watch TV,' Zhaoji said.

'Fox likes to pick his aliases from TV shows. Usually the aliases are a little more obscure than this one. What do you think happened here?'

'I think he was murdered. There are signs of a struggle in the room, a chair was thrown out the window, and we recovered a bullet from the wall.'

Kate knew the list of people who wanted Nick dead was long and colorful. Carter Grove was up there at the top.

'What does the security video on the ninety-third floor show?' Kate asked. 'Who went into Fox's room before the fall, and who left afterward?'

'There is no video,' he said. 'The footage for that floor, as well as for the elevators and stairwells leading to it, has been erased, either by the killer or by an accomplice.'

'Or by Nick Fox.' Kate pointed to the tarp. 'I won't believe that's him until you have the DNA results to prove it.' Even then, she'd have her doubts. Nick was very good at fooling people.

'That could take weeks.'

'And in the meantime, I will keep looking for him.'

The inspector reached into his pocket and produced a Park Hyatt room key. 'Tonight you'll be staying here, courtesy of Mr Stanley Fu, who is grateful for your extraordinary efforts to prevent the rooster from being stolen.'

'I was stuck in the trunk of his car. I didn't do anything, extraordinary or otherwise.'

'Nevertheless, he would like to express his gratitude. Someone from the US consulate will deliver a temporary passport and a plane ticket to your room in the morning. You are to leave China by the end of the day tomorrow.'

'What about Fox?'

'He's dead.'

'And if he's not?'

'You can keep looking for him,' he said. 'But not in China.'

She was being allowed to leave the country, and the Chinese authorities were dropping the hunt for Nick. That was a big relief, and it gave Nick a real chance to escape, assuming he wasn't the corpse under the tarp. She believed he was still alive, despite the compelling evidence to the contrary, because she couldn't accept the alternative.

But Kate still had a role to play – the FBI agent obsessed with Nick's capture – and if she slipped out of character now, she might raise the inspector's suspicions. So she tried to work up a little rage.

'That's it? You're done?'

'There's nothing for us to investigate. The rooster is safe.'

'Two people are dead.'

'The woman was a French citizen killed in international airspace. The man who killed her is now dead himself. It looks to me that everything worked out.'

'Let's suppose you're right. What about Fox's killer? You're just going to let him walk?'

'We have limited resources that are better served solving the murders of innocent people, not felons from other countries.' It sounded to Kate like he was repeating verbatim what somebody else had told him, rather than expressing his own opinion.

'I see,' she said.

'I hope your flight home is more pleasant than your journey here.' He offered her a polite smile and turned to go.

'May I ask you one question?'

He stopped and looked back at her. 'You may ask, but that doesn't mean I'll have an answer.'

'Where did you get the tip that Nick Fox was after the rooster?'

He hesitated a moment before answering. 'The tip was given to one of my superiors. It came from BlackRhino Security.'

Kate went to her room on the eightieth floor and undressed. The bruise on her side was dark purple and had spread across her stomach. She started the shower, setting the temperature to its hottest setting, and stood under the rainshower head for thirty minutes, washing away the smudges of blood. She dried off, being careful not to disturb her wounds, making a mental note to get some giant-size Band-Aids. She was slipping into a bathrobe when she heard the pop of a champagne cork in the bedroom, and a wave of relief rushed through her so strongly it almost buckled her knees.

She'd worked hard to believe Nick was okay. And she'd pretty much convinced herself. So why were these tears suddenly running down her cheeks? For cripes sake, she told herself, there's no crying in the FBI. Get a grip!

She took a moment to get herself under control. She cinched the robe. And she stepped out of the bathroom, smiling wide, feeling as if it were Christmas morning.

Nick was stretched out in his new clothes on top of her king-size bed, his back against the headboard, his legs casually crossed at the ankles. His hair was lightly tousled, and she saw a tiny cut on his chin amid the stubble. A champagne bottle chilled in a bucket beside the bed. He held a crystal flute of bubbly out to her and smiled.

'I'm afraid they don't stock these minibars with Toblerones,' he said.

'I'll live.' She slid onto the bed beside him and took the glass from him. 'I'm glad to see that you will, too.'

He poured himself a glass. 'I had my doubts earlier this evening.'

'I didn't.'

'Really?'

'I have faith in your resourcefulness,' she said. That much was true.

'Likewise,' he said.

They tapped their glasses, sipped their champagne,

and took in the spectacular view of Shanghai through the window in front of them. They were quiet for a while, enjoying the peace of each other's company.

'Tell me what happened in your room,' Kate said. 'Who got killed?'

He shook his head. 'First I want to hear how you conned the police.'

'I was brilliant,' Kate said. 'I played the victim card. I told their inspector I was tracking you. You had an accomplice. I was caught by surprise. Blah, blah, blah. Spent the whole time locked in the trunk. Didn't know anything.'

'And he bought it.'

'Yes!'

'I'm seeing you in a whole new way. You could have a bright future in my line of work.'

'I'd rather do the dinner theater circuit with Boyd.'

'Wow, that's harsh. I thought we were a team. Until death do us part.'

'That's a marriage vow. We aren't married.'

'We took a vow in a monastery.'

'We made an agreement in a cave!' Kate said. 'We committed to work together on covert missions for the FBI.'

Nick grinned and refilled her champagne glass. 'It's sort of like a marriage, but without the benefits. You watch my every move and nag me. Unfortunately that's where it ends.'

'Good grief.'

'I'm sure you'll come around eventually,' Nick said.

Kate secretly worried that this was true. 'In your dreams.'

'Frequently,' Nick said. 'How about you?'

'I want to know who's down there on the sidewalk.'

'He didn't formally introduce himself, but I'm assuming he's a BlackRhino guy. I walked into my room carrying my suitcase and was admiring the view when a guy holding a gun with a silencer came up behind me. He made a big mistake not shooting me the instant he came out of hiding.'

'Because you're such a dangerous, ruthless individual?'

'Because it revealed that he needed me alive, at least for a few minutes. He probably had a list of questions he was supposed to ask me before putting a bullet in my head.'

'And then?'

'And then I spun around and swung the suitcase at him. He shot the suitcase, and I kicked him in the nuts.'

'Classy.'

'Yeah, but obviously I didn't kick him hard enough, because he still thought it was a good idea to shoot me. We struggled over the gun, a few shots went into the window, and I got tossed across the room. I'm no Kate O'Hare when it comes to hand-to-hand combat, so I threw a desk chair at him.'

'I'll use whatever weapons are handy. A chair counts.'

'Thanks. The chair slammed him against the cracked window, and he went through it. I tossed the keys to the Dodge Charger out after him.'

'Where have you been since then?'

'Dinner. I had to sacrifice my reservation and eat at a small café on the next block, but the steak was still excellent.'

Kate was torn between wanting to lose her bathrobe and have her way with him and ordering room service. She was starving, and the mention of steak had her salivating.

'Aren't you taking a big risk being here?'

'This is the last place anybody would think to look for me now, if anybody is even looking.'

'The staff knows you.'

'I can slip in and out of here without being seen. I know where every camera is, and I'm a master of disguise.'

'You have a disguise?'

'I'll color my hair and wear a false mustache.'

'You have a false mustache?'

'I never leave home without one.'

She wasn't sure if he was being serious or not, but the conversation brought up another question that had been nagging at her since he'd told his story.

'How did Carter know you'd be here?'

'I'm sure he questioned Duff MacTaggert. Duff knows that I travel in China as Sonny Crockett. Wouldn't be hard for Carter to find out if I was registered here. The question is, did Duff give me up for a price or was he coerced?'

'Does it matter?'

'I need to know,' he said.

'So tomorrow you're going to Kilmarny.'

He nodded and freshened her champagne. 'But we still have tonight.'

'I need food,' Kate said. 'Something other than rice.'

Kate ate a monster-size double cheeseburger and had a manly wedge of New York-style cheesecake as a chaser. The food, combined with her long day and several glasses of champagne, practically put her in a coma. When she awoke at 6:30 AM, Nick was gone. He'd washed his champagne flute and put it back on top of the wet bar in the living room. There was no sign that he'd ever been there. It was as if she'd dreamed the whole thing, though her dreams about him tended to be X-rated and their evening had been a chaste PG.

Kate sat up slowly, her side aching, her knife wounds stinging. She ordered a room service breakfast of fried eggs, sausages, pan-fried pork dumplings, fresh berries, deep-fried crullers, spring onion pancakes, steamed buns, and jellied, salted tofu topped with ground pork, cilantro, and glassy tree ear, a type of mushroom found on fallen trees. She washed it all down with a pot of tea.

It was midmorning when Susan Chow knocked on Kate's door and introduced herself as a representative from the US consulate. She was in her early forties, wearing a crisp gray business suit. Her hair was pulled back in a tight bun. She handed Kate a passport, a plane ticket to Los Angeles, and a shopping bag containing underwear, socks, a long-sleeve burgundy jersey top with a scoop neck, and black denim jeans.

'A car is waiting for you downstairs,' Susan said. 'Your flight leaves in three hours.'

'I'm sorry if I caused you any trouble.'

'On the contrary, our diplomatic spin on this is that you foiled an attempt to steal the rooster and prevented an international incident that would have strained the relations between our two countries.'

'So if I'm such a hero, why am I being hustled out of town?'

'You defied authority. That's not a popular attitude here. If you would do that to your bosses at home, the Chinese government is concerned about how you might behave in Shanghai. And so are we.' She handed Kate a bottle opener shaped like the building. 'Good luck.'

Susan left. Kate changed her clothes and went down to the lobby, where Rigor and Mortis were waiting with a car to escort her to Shanghai Pudong International Airport.

Twenty-two

Nick and Kate left Shanghai within a few minutes of each other, and from the same terminal, but they made no contact.

Nick departed on the 10:50 AM British Airways flight to London, and had booked a connecting flight to Glasgow. He traveled as 'Jonathan Hart' and sat in first class in a seat that gave him a soothing shiatsu massage.

Kate took an 11:00 AM Shanghai Airlines flight to Seoul, Korea, where she caught an Asiana Airlines flight to Los Angeles. On both flights, she was stuck in a center economy-class seat next to the rest-rooms. Still, it was an improvement over riding in the trunk of a car.

Nick arrived in Glasgow at 7:25 PM, rented a Range Rover, and made the three-hour drive northwest to Mallaig, where he spent the night at the quaint West Highland Hotel so he could take the first ferry to Kilmarny the next morning.

Kate arrived at LAX at noon and was met outside the terminal by Carl Jessup, who was parked in the red zone. She got into the front seat of his Chevy Impala and he drove off, heading east out of the airport terminal loop.

'Welcome home,' Jessup said. 'How are you feeling?'

'Great,' she said.

'Officially, you're suspended without pay for thirty days and you will be getting a written reprimand from the disciplinary board,' Jessup said. 'You're lucky your hunch was right about Fox being on that plane or you'd have been dropkicked right out of the Bureau.' Jessup eased onto the ramp that curled onto Sepulveda Boulevard north. 'Unofficially, *holy crap*, Kate. I don't know which is more amazing, pulling a heist in midair or getting caught by Shanghai police and talking your way out of it. You're becoming as good as Nicolas Fox, and that's scary.'

'Thank you, sir.'

She was well aware that some of Nick's con artist skills were rubbing off on her. She wondered what, if anything, he was learning from her.

'We knew you two would make a great team,' Jessup said, 'but is it over? Is Nick really dead?'

She shook her head. 'The dead man was a BlackRhino operative sent by Carter to kill Nick. The Shanghai police will know Nick is alive once the DNA results come back on what's left of the body.'

'I guess we underestimated how quickly Carter would

discover the theft and make the connection to the Smithsonian handing over the rooster to the Chinese.'

'Carter didn't rise to White House chief of staff by being stupid,' Kate said.

'Well, it's over now, the trail has gone cold. Nick can add Carter Grove and BlackRhino to the long list of enemies, bounty hunters, insurance investigators, and law enforcement agencies who are searching the globe for him,' Jessup said. 'Speaking of which, where the hell is he?'

'I don't know.' It was a lie, of course, but she'd promised Nick she'd protect Duff MacTaggert's identity and his role in the original theft of the rooster.

'Will he come back?'

'If he doesn't, I'll hunt him down like a dog.'

'Enjoy your thirty-day suspension first,' he said. 'You've earned it.'

She gestured to the In-N-Out Burger that was coming up on Sepulveda. 'Have I also earned a three-by-three with fries and a chocolate shake?'

'Definitely,' Jessup said, steering the car into the parking lot.

It was late afternoon in Palm Beach, Florida, when BlackRhino operative Rocco Randisi walked into Carter Grove's office. Carter was at his desk, going through the covert agreement for BlackRhino to purchase an aerial drone armed with Hellfire missiles. Attack drones were the new status symbol. Pretty soon, Tom Cruise, David Beckham, and Honey Boo Boo would each have one.

'What have you heard from Shanghai?' Carter asked.

'Fu has the rooster. Alexis Poulet was found dead on the plane. And Nicolas Fox escaped from the cargo hold by driving off in a vintage Dodge Charger.'

Carter couldn't believe that Fox, a mere grifter and thief, had managed to kill Alexis. She was a professional assassin. This was the last time he'd hire a castoff from France's Direction Centrale du Renseignement Intérieur. There was a reason nobody had ever heard of the French intelligence agency. They sucked. Carter buzzed Veronica Dell on the intercom. 'Make me a list of everyone on our payroll who used to work for the DCRI.'

Her reply came over the speaker in her wonderful British accent. 'We have only one.'

'Good to know.' Carter tipped his head toward Randisi. 'Continue. What happened next? Fox couldn't have gone far in a car that flashy.'

'You're right. He abandoned the car and fled on foot. But here's where things get really strange. When the Shanghai cops recovered the car, they found a fake rooster and an FBI agent in the trunk.'

That was distressing news. The last thing Carter

wanted was the FBI investigating BlackRhino's interest in Nick Fox. 'Was the agent dead?'

'No such luck. She was beaten up pretty bad, though.'

'What was the agent doing on the plane?'

'Her name is Kate O'Hare, and she's the one who arrested Fox a few months back. He escaped from custody, and she's been chasing him ever since. She told the police she discovered Fox was after the rooster and tried to catch him stealing it in DC, but his accomplice got the jump on her, beat her up, and threw her in the trunk.'

'Who was his accomplice?'

'It's not clear, but Alexis is looking like a possible. She told Fu she worked for the Smithsonian, so maybe we're still okay as long as her cover holds.'

If her cover *didn't* hold, Carter knew that the Shanghai police would believe that BlackRhino tipped them off about Fox because BlackRhino was trying to retrieve a rogue agent. It would be enormously damaging to BlackRhino's reputation if word got out that one of its operatives had gone bad.

'I assume this information came from our man in Shanghai,' Carter said.

'No, we got it from other sources. Our Shanghai operative hasn't reported in yet. He was supposed to have a chat with Fox if Fox showed up at the Park Hyatt.'

'And?'

'It appears Fox checked in under an alias and that a short time later someone took a ninety-three-floor swan dive from Fox's hotel room. The police are running a DNA check to identify the corpse. I gotta say, I don't have a good feeling about it.'

So Fox might be on the loose, Carter thought, and this time they had no leads on where he might be. But Kate O'Hare might. She knew Fox well enough to anticipate that he'd be on that plane. She could be an asset.

'Where's O'Hare now?' Carter asked Randisi.

'The Chinese threw her out of the country. She's probably back in LA by now.'

Carter buzzed Veronica again. 'Get me whatever you can on an FBI agent named Kate O'Hare.'

Carter turned his attention back to Randisi. 'You need to intensify the search. Keep looking for anyone ever associated with Fox. Squeeze them for every detail they know about him. Nothing is too small or insignificant.'

'How hard do we squeeze?'

'As hard as it takes,' Carter said.

Veronica walked into the office holding her open MacBook against her chest. 'I used our digital backdoor into the FBI's personnel database and got a picture of Special Agent Kate O'Hare.' She turned her laptop around so both men could see the screen. 'Look familiar?'

It was a picture of Lucy Carmichael, the fake producer.

* * *

Duff MacTaggert missed his bed. The mattress at the Bedford Hospital in Fort William felt like a stone slab, his pillows like sandbags. Suffering the pain and indignity of two broken arms and two broken legs wouldn't be so bad if he just had his own bed to sleep in. But that glorious bed was ashes now, and his pub a pile of charred rubble.

The story he'd told the doctors when his lads brought him in was that there'd been a gas leak, and that he was getting up to pee when the pub exploded, blowing him out of his second-floor window. Nobody questioned his story or went out to Kilmarny to investigate. But if anybody had, they wouldn't have found any witnesses who'd contradict his account.

For now he was a prisoner of his broken limbs, unable to leave his hospital bed or even feed himself. All he could do was press the buttons on the remote control in his right hand to raise the back of the bed, turn on the TV, give himself an IV jolt of morphine, or call a nurse.

A doctor came into the room, his head down, intently reviewing a chart as he approached the bed on his morning rounds. There'd been so many doctors, nurses, and orderlies coming in and out of Duff's room at all hours over the past few days that he no longer paid much attention to them. When he finally looked up into the doctor's brown eyes he knew he was in serious trouble. It was Nicolas Fox in a white lab coat with a stethoscope draped around his neck. Before Duff could press the call button, Nick snatched the remote from his hand.

'You're not going to be needing any help,' Nick said.

'Not where I'm going, you mean. I'm sure the Devil has been expecting me for a while. You too, Nicky boy. So what's it going to be? A pillow over my face or an air bubble injected into my IV?'

'I'm not here to kill you. What kind of man do you think I am?'

'An angry one.'

Nick put the remote back in Duff's hand and sat down on a stool beside the bed. 'I saw what was left of your place in Kilmarny, and I see what Carter's thugs have done to you. I don't blame you for telling them what they wanted to know.'

Duff sighed and shook his head sadly. 'I held out as long as I could.'

'Why did you hold out at all? You should have told them everything the first time they asked. You don't like me, and it was my fault they came after you.'

'The hell it was. It was my decision to sell Carter out to you. I got what I had coming to me. But I shouldn't have given you up. I should have let the bastards break every bone in my body and taken your name to my grave.'

'What for?'

'Honor, Nicky boy. You don't rat on your crew.'

'I haven't been part of your crew for years.'

'It doesn't matter. It's the thief's code. You never betray your crew. I've shamed myself and dishonored our profession. Go ahead, smother me. You'd be doing me a favor.'

'I'm not going to hurt you, it's not my style. At worst, I'd take you for everything you've got. But I'm not going to do that, either.'

'Then why are you here?'

'I had to know if you sold me out to Carter or if he forced you to talk.'

'What difference does it make?'

'Because if you'd been paid,' Nick said, 'you wouldn't hold a grudge against him. I need your help to take him down. I was in his house, Duff. He's got pieces from some of the biggest art heists of the last thirty years. It's incredible. His collection has got to be worth hundreds of millions of dollars.'

'You're crazy. He knows you've seen it, and he'll be ready for you. You won't be able to get *near* his collection. I guarantee that he's moved it all somewhere else and gone way over the top on security, booby-trapping everything.'

'He could bring in a ninja army to protect his collection and booby-trap it with a nuclear bomb and it wouldn't save him,' Nick said. 'Because I have an inside man.'

'Who?'

'Carter Grove.'

Duff grinned. 'I'm beginning to remember why I used to like you.'

'I have the beginnings of a plan, but I need some information. Did you deal directly with Carter?'

'No. He operates in complete secrecy. Not even his brokers know his identity. I found out by pure accident. Two days after the transaction was completed I was at the Watergate, doing some preliminary investigation for a jewelry heist, and I saw the rooster's case walk past me. I knew it was the case because it had a dented corner and a scratch the length of one side. Carter Grove was carrying the case. I'd heard rumors that he was secretly collecting. I made the mistake of approaching him and offering my services.'

'Did he take you up on the offer?'

'No. He broke four fingers and told me he'd kill me if I didn't forget I ever saw him.'

'Suppose I want to sell him something. How do I get to him?'

'I'd go to Julian Starke. My deal was finalized by Nelson Rhumann, but Rhumann is dead. Had a heart attack and went facedown in his morning oatmeal.'

Twenty-three

Jessup pulled up to Kate's apartment building and parked at the curb, and they both gaped at the red-and-white tent that engulfed the place. The tent was inflated so that it looked like a giant bounce house from a kid's birthday party. There were barricades on the sidewalk and signs warning people to stay away.

'Looks like you have bugs,' Jessup said. 'That's the kind of tent they put up when they have to fumigate a building.'

Kate got out, read the sign, and returned to the car. 'It says no one is allowed into the building for five days.'

'Good thing you're on leave. You can take a vacation.'

'I don't want to take a vacation. Where am I supposed to live? All my clothes are in there.'

Jessup looked at his watch. 'I have to get back to the office. Where do you want me to drop you? Are you good here?'

'No, I'm not good here. How about you drive me to the nearest supermarket so I can get a big cardboard box and live on the street?'

'Where's your car?'

'It's in the garage. It's a company car. I don't have my own car.'

'Bummer.'

'Can I have my company car?'

'No. What about your sister?'

Kate closed her eyes and slid down in her seat. She loved her sister, but living with her would be hell. Megan would have her fixed up with a new man every night. Accountants and produce managers and dentists. Kate gave an involuntary shudder.

Two hours later Kate pulled into her sister's drive court in a rental car.

'They're fumigating my building,' Kate said to Megan. 'I was hoping I could stay with you for a couple days.'

'Of course,' Megan said. 'The girls will love it. You're their favorite aunt.'

'I'm their only aunt.'

'Just throw your stuff in the guest room. If you have any guns, you have to give them to Dad. We don't allow guns in the house.'

'How about rocket launchers?'

'Not them either.'

The guest room was pretty, with peach walls and white curtains and bed linens. Kate had stayed there before, and it always made her feel girly. Her own apartment had a brown leather couch and a punching bag.

The apartment's previous resident had been a boxer, and she'd taken over his furniture.

Kate had a couple hours before dinner, so she left the house and walked across the driveway to her father's *casita.*

'They ran a piece on the news about the rooster going back to China,' Jake said, opening the door to her. 'It sounded like everything went as planned.'

'More or less.'

'You're in time for dinner. I think Roger's making smoked buffalo burgers. Ever since Megan gave him that smoker for his birthday, we've had smoked everything. Last night he smoked broccoli.'

'Something to look forward to,' Kate said. 'I moved into Megan's guest room for a couple days. They're fumigating my apartment building.'

'Your nieces will love that. You're their favorite aunt.'

'So I've been told. And I can spend quality time with you, too. You can teach me how to make improvised explosives out of household cleaning supplies.'

'I'd love to,' Jake said. 'We can include the grandkids and make it a family affair. We'll just have to wait until Megan and Roger aren't around. They're very uptight about making explosives in the house.'

Three days later, Kate was lying on a chaise in the backyard in shorts and a bikini top, reading *Star* magazine, while Megan patrolled the lawn, looking for dog droppings to pick up with her poop bags.

'What's Roger got in the smoker today?' Kate asked.

'Nothing. He's off the smoker. His doctor said all that smoked meat was eating a hole in his intestines. He's on the white diet now. He can only eat things that are white. So we're having cream of wheat for dinner. And wear something nice. I invited this wonderful man I met over for dinner.'

'No!'

'He's perfect for you. Okay, maybe he's a little short, but you know what they say about short men.'

'What do they say about short men?'

'They try harder.'

'Criminy, Megan.'

Kate's cell phone rang, and she glanced at the caller ID: UNKNOWN CALLER.

'Kate O'Hare.'

'Hello, Agent O'Hare.' It was a woman with a British accent. Her voice sounded vaguely familiar. 'Mr Grove would like to speak with you.'

Now Kate knew the voice. It was Veronica Dell, Carter Grove's assistant.

'Mr Grove is in a limo in the parking lot at the Commons. He'll be expecting you in ten minutes. I urge you not to keep him waiting. He has a tight schedule.'

Veronica hung up, and Kate stared at her phone, stunned.

Megan looked over at her. 'Is everything all right?'

'Yes, fine, something came up at work.'

'But you've been suspended.'

'Another agent needs me to brief him on a case. I'm going to run out and meet him for coffee.' Kate went to the guest room, changed into a T-shirt and jeans, and called her father.

'It's Jake,' he answered.

'Where are you?'

'Eighth hole, Calabasas Country Club, and I'm two swings ahead of the proctologist I'm playing with. Why?'

'Carter Grove is waiting for me in a limo at the Commons,' she said. 'I could use some backup.'

'I'll be there in five minutes. I've got a gun, a garrote, and a hand grenade in the nightstand beside my bed. Take them.'

'I'm going unarmed.'

'Do you think that's wise?'

'If he wanted to kidnap me or kill me, he wouldn't announce himself ahead of time and meet me in a public place.'

'I hope you're right.'

'So do I,' she said. 'But in case I'm not, I've got you.'

'You certainly do,' he said.

* * *

The Commons was designed to resemble a quaint European village. The developers wanted to give the shopping center some class so that celebrity Calabasas residents like Justin Bieber and the Kardashians would have a pleasant experience buying groceries at Ralphs.

Carter Grove's limo was parked at the far end of the parking lot, away from the trophy wives loading groceries into their BMWs and Mercedes. Rocco Randisi leaned against the limo, eating a Menchie's frozen yogurt. Kate parked her rented Taurus in front of the limo, got out, and acknowledged Randisi with a glance. She remembered him from the pool in Palm Beach.

'You carrying?' he asked.

'Nope.'

'Wearing a wire?'

'Nope.'

'What if I insist on patting you down?'

She shrugged. 'I'm sure BlackRhino has a pretty good health plan.'

'I bet you're not half as tough as you think you are.'

'Some dumb blonde recently made the same bet. She lost.'

He regarded her for a long moment, then walked to the back of the car, opened the door, and beckoned her in with a nod.

She got in and took the seat across from Carter Grove, who was also eating a frozen yogurt.

'You want a yogurt? I can have Rocco run over and get you one.'

'No, thanks,' Kate said.

'Okay, then let's get right to it, shall we?' He nodded at Randisi, who closed the door, leaving Carter and Kate alone. 'I know that you and Nicolas Fox are working together. But I'm going to let you off the hook. You're just a loyal government employee recruited for a covert operation run out of the FBI, or the CIA, or maybe the NSA. I really don't care. God knows I ran plenty of off-the-books operations like that myself when I was in the White House.'

'So what am I doing here?'

He picked at his yogurt with his little spoon, digging out the cookie dough chunks and eating them. 'I want you to bring me Nicolas Fox.'

'Why?'

'He's probably the best con man and thief in the world. I want to know the secrets behind every crime he's ever committed. I want his complete list of contacts and all of his resources. And then I am going to kill him.'

'What if he won't talk?'

'He will. I've got the top interrogators in the business working for me. Every single one of them has been convicted in absentia in The Hague for crimes against humanity.'

'That's a real laurel for any résumé,' Kate said. 'Look, the rooster wasn't yours to begin with. Nobody profited from this. You're giving me a pass, why not let Fox walk?'

'Because he made a fool out of me and he's probably the one person capable of stealing everything else that I have.'

'He wasn't alone. I was there.'

'But you don't worry me,' Carter said. 'You can't do what he does. That's why you and your masters needed him to begin with.'

'Forget it. I'm not going to get Fox for you. You'll just have to man up and accept the loss. You can't win them all, Carter.'

Carter finished his yogurt, dropped the spoon into the empty cup, and set it on the seat beside him. 'BlackRhino is often hired to assassinate people and make it look like natural causes or an accident. We're very good at it. I could arrange for your father to get hit by a runaway UPS truck. It wouldn't be the first time someone's brakes have failed on that steep hill your sister and her children live on. It could happen to one of them too.'

Kate leaned forward and spoke softly. 'I could kill you with that little yogurt spoon and end this right now.'

'I'm sure you could,' Carter said. 'But you won't. You have a conscience, ethics, and morals. You'd be a total failure in politics. Me? I pulled the strings in the Oval Office for eight years. I won't hesitate to go after your family. You have two weeks to deliver Fox to me.'

Kate got out of the limo and immediately spotted her father sitting at a table in front of the Corner Bakery Cafe. He was hard to miss. He was facing her wearing sunglasses, a Calabasas Country Club cap, a bright blue Greg Norman polo shirt, blazing white slacks, and Callaway reptile golf shoes. His right hand was inside a Nike gym bag on his lap.

She walked over and sat down in a chair beside him. Randisi got into the limo and drove away, waving to them both as he passed.

'You can take your hand out of the bag now,' she said.

Jake slid his hand out and zipped up the bag. 'How'd it go?'

'He's on to us.'

'That much I figured out.'

She gestured to the bag. 'What have you got in there?'

'Nothing much. Some golfballs, a handful of tees, a Glock, extra ammo, two hand grenades, a tear gas canister, a knife, Tums, clean socks, flares, and some Ensure chocolate shakes.'

'You took all of that with you to play golf?'

'When I first moved here, I saw a report on the news

that urged everybody to keep an earthquake kit in each of their vehicles. This is my earthquake kit. You never know when the Big One might hit.'

'I didn't know hand grenades were recommended for earthquake kits.'

'Carter wants you to give him Nick, doesn't he?' Jake asked.

She nodded.

'Did Carter threaten our family?'

'Don't worry, it won't come to that.'

'I'm sure it won't,' Jake said. 'Because I'm going to solve this problem for you.'

She shook her head and spoke to him in a firm but low voice so no one could overhear them. 'Forget it. You're not killing Carter.'

'I don't mind. I only have a few years left anyway. There isn't much difference between prison and a retirement home. At least in prison I'd be around people with similar interests. I have very little in common with proctologists.'

'We'll find another way to deal with Carter.'

'The easy way would be to give him Nick Fox.'

Kate's phone vibrated. She took it out of her pocket and glanced at the screen. It was a text from Nick.

Meet me at 7 pm. Hampton Inn. Room 216. Camarillo.

Nick's timing, as usual, was uncanny. It was as if he knew they were talking about him. She glanced around, half expecting to see him watching them from another table.

Her gaze returned to Jake. 'Do you have any gizmos that we can use to scan my car for bugs and tracking devices?'

'Of course I do,' he said. 'I sweep my *casita* twice a day.'

'Who do you think might be listening to you?'

'Nobody in particular. Old habits are hard to break.'

'Is that why you have hand grenades and a garrote in your nightstand?'

'They're sleep aids.'

Twenty-four

Camarillo is a farming community northwest of Los Angeles with vast fields of artichokes, strawberries, and tract houses, but the town's most lucrative crop by far was the cut-rate clothing sold at the 650,000-square-foot outlet center alongside the freeway.

The Hampton Inn was one of half a dozen budget hotels located near the Camarillo Premium Outlets. The hotels served the busloads of tourists who couldn't possibly get all their shopping done in a single day.

Kate knocked on the door to room 216 and the door to room 215 opened behind her.

'Over here,' Nick said, beckoning her in.

Giving out the wrong room number to people was a simple, age-old security measure, but it still worked. She turned and went into his room. He closed the door behind her and bolted it.

Nick wore a new Ralph Lauren polo shirt, new Levi's jeans, and new Nike running shoes. He looked like every other outlet shopper staying in the hotel.

Bags of clothes from several of the outlet stores were spread out on top of one of the double beds. The bags were set dressing to impress the maids. There were maps, blueprints, and photos of moving-company trucks scattered on the table near the window, which offered a breathtaking view of a McDonald's and a Carl's Jr across the street.

Kate gestured to the papers on the table. 'You're on the run, and I'm suspended, and you're planning something even though we don't have an assignment. That can't be good. What are you up to?'

'I saw Duff MacTaggert in the hospital. Carter's thugs blew up Duff's pub and broke his arms and legs to get my name out of him. I'm going to make Carter pay for that.'

'You can't,' Kate said. 'Our covers are blown. Carter came to see me today in Calabasas. He knows who I really am and that we're secretly working together for the government.'

'Of course he does. One more reason why we have to take him down now.'

'We can't. Didn't you hear what I just said? He knows who we are. He'll see us coming.'

'We aren't going to be the ones who take him down. Carter is going to do it for us. But to make that happen, there is one little thing we have to do first.'

She sat down on the edge of one of the beds. 'I'm afraid to ask.'

'We have to pull off the most daring and lucrative museum heist in Canadian history. And it has to be done in Montreal on July first in broad daylight.'

'That's only a week away. Why does it have to be that specific day?'

'July first is the Fête du Déménagement, the day when people in Quebec move to new homes. It's a tradition that goes back to the eighteenth century. A quarter million people in Montreal move on that day every year, clogging the streets with boxes, furniture, appliances, and trucks. It's also Canada Day, so you can throw a few parades into the mix, too. Those are the perfect conditions for committing the perfect crime.'

'But a week leaves you no time for planning.'

'I don't need any. I've been thinking about this heist for years. I just needed an excuse to do it. Carter is it.'

'You have my attention,' she said.

'We're going to steal some Rembrandt masterpieces from the Musée de Florentiny in a robbery so audacious that it will capture the world's attention,' Nick said. 'And especially Carter Grove's. We'll offer to sell the paintings through Julian Starke, the dealer du jour for stolen art.'

'It's clever, I'll give you that,' Kate said. 'But Bolton will never authorize it.'

'Don't tell him. You've been suspended, remember? Think of this as a vacation abroad with some friends.'

'What friends did you have in mind?'

'We're going to need Joe, Boyd, and Willie.'

Kate shook her head. 'We got them to believe we're two unconventional PIs with big expense accounts who will go to extremes to nail bad guys and undo wrongs. But now we're asking them to help us steal Rembrandts from a museum in Montreal. I don't see a way to spin this that doesn't make us look like crooks.'

'We're only borrowing the paintings. The museum will eventually get them back.'

'What makes you think they'll believe that?'

'What makes you think they'll care? Willie *is* a crook. As long as we give her something to drive, fly, or pilot she'll be happy. Boyd is an actor, all that matters to him is the part that he's playing. And Joe hates Carter even more than we do and will appreciate the lengths we're willing to go to nail him.'

'Why can't we just throw a grenade into Carter's house, dress up like firefighters, and discover his stolen art when we rush in with the *real* firemen to put out the flames? That will expose his crimes, ruin him, and bring down BlackRhino.'

Nick smiled. 'I like the way you think, but I'm sure his collection isn't in Palm Beach anymore. He's too smart to leave it where it was after we broke in. He has to realize that not only do we know about the collection, but someone high up in the FBI has to know as well.

Leaving it in that house would be like sitting on a ticking timebomb.'

'So you're saying that robbing a museum in broad daylight a week from now is the only way we can deal with Carter.'

'The alternative is to give me to Carter.'

She stared at him. 'How did you know that's what he wants me to do?'

'It's politics. He wants someone's scalp for stealing his rooster. You're an FBI agent. Taking you out could bring the United States government down on him. I'm an international fugitive. Nobody will come after him if I disappear. I'm expendable.'

'Not to me,' Kate said. 'I'll never let that happen.'

'You won't have to. I'll make a deal with you. If this plan doesn't work, I'll walk into BlackRhino headquarters and give myself up.'

'Why would you do a stupid, suicidal thing like that?'

'I won't let your family get hurt for something I've done.'

'*We've* done. I was as much a part of it as you were. I've got the scars to prove it.'

'Yeah, but that's because I've been a terrible influence on you.'

Kate gave up a sigh. This was true.

* * *

When Joe Morey returned from Palm Beach, he immediately quit his job at Best Buy, bought a new Camaro, and moved into a condo complex in Marina del Rey.

The complex was packed with flight attendants, who liked it because they were close to the beach and LAX. It was also packed with divorced middle-aged men, who liked it because they were close to the flight attendants. On move-in day, Joe was horrified to find that the parking garage was filled with Camaros, and that there were more potbellied men around the pool than hot young women.

That horror evolved into depression on his second day there. He sat on a chaise beside the pool, in a T-shirt and board shorts, watching those newly single men, their guts hanging over their Speedos like muffin tops, ogle the women in bikinis. Did those guys really think they had a shot at the women? Joe knew his luck wouldn't be any better. Sure, he had youth on his side, all his hair, and a flat stomach, but most of those men probably had good jobs and things happening in their lives that might make them attractive enough for a woman to overlook their man boobs.

What did he have going for him? Zilch. Even his financial independence was an illusion. The money from the Carter Grove caper wouldn't last long, especially in Los Angeles, so he knew he'd have to do something to make more money and occupy his mind. But he was unemployable in corporate America after what had happened at Gant Security. So what kind of job was he going to get? Two years from today he could be back in a Geek Squad uniform, teaching some old lady how to tweet.

And that's when an angel in the form of Kate O'Hare appeared in front of him in sunglasses, a tank top, and jeans. He blinked hard to make sure he wasn't dreaming.

'Hello, Joe,' she said. 'Have you got something in your eye?'

'No, no, it's the glare. Please sit down.' He gestured to the chaise next to his and propped up the backrest for her so she could sit straight. 'I didn't expect to see you again. I mean, I don't mind, it's just that I thought it was only a one-time thing.'

Joe realized it sounded like he was talking about a one-night stand rather than the robbery they'd committed together. Then again, the two situations did have some things in common. They were both illicit, exciting, and maybe a little shameful.

'So did I,' she said. 'The thing is, it bothers us that we got the rooster back but Carter didn't really get punished for what he did.'

'Guys like him never do,' Joe said.

'We think there might be a way to get him after all.' Kate leaned toward him, close enough to whisper in his ear. 'But we'd have to rob a museum in Montreal to do it.'

Joe's heartbeat jacked up as if he'd been shocked with defibrillator paddles. His depression vanished too. The idea of nailing Carter, and experiencing the thrill of another caper, was the antidote to all of his worries, at least temporarily.

'I'm in,' he said.

She whispered in his ear again, and that was almost as exciting as the words she was speaking. 'You do realize we're talking about committing a major felony in a foreign country, right?'

Yes, he did, and it was great. Larger than life. Well, certainly larger than *his* life. Just being asked to participate meant that he wasn't pathetic Joe Morey, ex–Geek Squad guy and prematurely middle-aged man anymore. He was slick Joe Morey, an international man of action possessing special skills. All of a sudden he was certain that he could easily pick up any of the women by the pool and give them the best night of their lives.

'Whatever it takes,' he said. 'That bastard has to go down.'

'We'll pay you another hundred and fifty thousand dollars, but I want you to think about the risk involved. You could end up in a Canadian prison if this goes wrong.'

How bad could a Canadian prison be? It was in Canada. Canadians were civilized. It had to be better than going back to the Geek Squad. And if he pulled this heist off, he'd have twice as much money socked away, buying him another two years to figure out what to do with the rest of his life.

'I understand that,' Joe said. 'But there's nothing I want more than to see Carter Grove behind bars.'

That was at least partly true.

She looked at him for a long moment. 'You used to sell security systems, but you sacrificed your career to expose criminal wrongdoing at your company. Now you're cracking security systems and stealing stuff. You've done a complete about-face for us. Has it occurred to you that maybe we're just a couple thieves taking advantage of you?'

Actually it hadn't, but he didn't want her to think he was so blinded by his hatred of Carter, hobbled by insecurity, and desperate for money that he hadn't considered all of the angles.

'Of course it did,' he said. 'But a real thief wouldn't be so bothered by her conscience that she'd keep trying to talk me out of the job she wants me to do.'

'Maybe I'm using reverse psychology.'

'Fine,' Joe said. 'I'd better see Carter Grove doing a perp walk when this is over, or I'll go to the feds. Feel better?'

'Much,' she said.

Of course he was bluffing. If he turned her in, he'd be confessing to a crime himself, which would probably get him sent to an American prison, and he knew they were bad. He'd watched *Lockup* on MSNBC. So no, he wouldn't do anything if he found out he was being tricked.

But Kate probably knew that. She just needed to hear him say he'd turn her in, and that had a powerful impact on him. It convinced him that she was honest, even if she was doing something inherently dishonest, and that she genuinely cared about his safety.

The needle on the Corvette Stingray V-8's speedometer was passing 150 miles per hour, and the tachometer needle was shivering near the 6500 rpm redline, when the car salesman in the passenger seat let out a frightened squeal and gripped Wilma Owens's thigh in terror.

Willie was in her mid-fifties but looked twenty years younger, if you didn't look too close. Her hair had been bleached to the color and texture of straw. Her boobs had been surgically hoisted and stuffed with silicone. And her taste in clothes screamed redneck slut. She had the uncanny ability and insatiable desire to drive or pilot anything with a motor in it, from a bus to a blimp, whether she owned it or not. Her tendency to borrow vehicles for joy rides often got her into trouble, which is how she'd come to Nick's attention. Getting Willie out of one of those jams was how Nick had recruited her for the first swindle he and Kate had pulled off together.

The Corvette salesman's hand had been doing a slow creep up Willie's bare thigh since they'd left the Phoenix dealership, where she'd shown up all cowgirl in short denim cutoffs, her shirt tied under her breasts, her power nipples pointing at the Stingray and hypnotizing every man in the showroom. A square-chinned salesman named Buddy, with a mustache like Hitler's, gladly stepped up and offered her a test drive before she could ask. She'd learned that alert nipples could get her into more cars than a slim jim, which was why she'd augmented hers today with a pair of Bodyperk silicone stiffies.

Buddy broke out of his nipple trance the instant she shifted into seventh gear on the two-lane desert highway and the scenery became a blur outside the windows. It was like the *Millennium Falcon* going into hyperdrive.

'You can't go this fast,' Buddy said. 'It's a test drive.'

'When you buy a Corvette, honey, it's for the 460 horses under the hood, and you aren't going to feel 'em parallel parking.'

'This car isn't meant to be driven this hard.'

'They didn't put seven gears in this transmission for dropping the kids at school and going grocery shopping. It should be against the law to sell this car to anybody who isn't going to make the tachometer lick the redline at least once a week.'

Willie's cell phone buzzed in the hip pocket of her short shorts. She squirmed in her seat to pull out the phone and the car veered into the next lane. Buddy yelped and clutched her thigh again. She answered the phone, slowing to ninety-five while steering with one hand. 'Hello?'

'It's me,' Nick said. 'Did I catch you at a bad time?'

'I'm having a great time,' she said. 'I'm test-driving the new Corvette Stingray.'

'Does the owner know it's missing yet?'

'I've got the salesman right here.' She held the phone out to him. 'Say hello, Buddy.'

'It's against the law to talk on a cell phone while you're driving,' Buddy said. 'You'll get a ticket.'

'A cop would have to catch me first, and if he can then you've got some balls selling this car for seventy-five thousand dollars.' Willie put the phone back to her ear. 'What's up?'

'I need you for a job.'

'What will I be driving?'

'A moving truck,' he said. 'I know it's not as sexy as a Corvette, but it pays better.'

'How much?'

'More than enough to buy yourself that car.'

'That would take the fun out of it, sweetie. I like cars the way I like my men. I pick them up, grab the stick, and drive them hard down the straightaways and fast around the curves.'

'Is Buddy panting yet?' Nick asked.

'Are you?'

'I'm taking a cold shower as soon as we get off the phone,' Nick said. 'Are you in?'

'Wouldn't miss it.'

'Great. You've got a reservation at one-thirty this afternoon out of Sky Harbor on United Airlines flight 1607 to JFK, where Joe Morey will be waiting for you. I need you two to pick up a van for me in the Bronx and drive it up to Montreal. I'll text you the addresses and details. Can you make it?'

She made a sharp U-turn and floored it, throwing Buddy hard against the passenger side door.

'With time to spare,' she said.

'Cut,' the director said, tears streaming down her cheeks.

Now everybody in the film crew let go of the sobs they'd been holding back while the cameras were rolling. They were crowded into a diner on the San Pedro docks and had just shot a scene about a waitress turning down a date with a lonely fisherman played by Boyd Capwell and, because of his bad breath, leaving him heartbroken and confused.

Boyd had given a powerful performance, though it had lasted only a few seconds. Relying almost entirely on the subtleties of body language, tone of voice, and facial expression, he'd conveyed how the waitress's rejection was yet another indignity endured in a lifetime marked by bitter disappointment. It was a moment that deeply resonated with the crew in every one of the sixteen takes of the scene he'd done so far.

The director was a young woman best known for a tampon commercial about women who didn't let their periods stop them from climbing mountains, running into burning buildings, or walking on a tightrope over Niagara Falls. She wiped her tears away, went up to Boyd, and gave him a hug.

'That was the most dramatic performance I've ever seen in a mouthwash commercial,' she said.

'Thank you,' Boyd said. 'I wanted people to feel his deep sorrow, to wonder if the next thing he might do is throw himself off his boat into the cold embrace of the sea.'

'I asked you after your last take to dial it down.'

'I did. I lost the humiliation and downplayed the utter hopelessness, so all he's doing now is staring into the dark abyss of his unrelenting loneliness.'

'I need you to get rid of the dark abyss and all the drama.'

'But then he wouldn't have any textures. He'd just be a one-dimensional cardboard character.'

'Perfect. Let's try that.'

He couldn't believe she wanted him to give a lousy

performance. Not only did he think it was beneath him, he didn't think he was capable of delivering anything less than fully layered, richly textured greatness.

'But you just praised my powerful portrayal.'

'The problem is that people don't watch commercials for stirring performances. What they want is a vision of a better life. But the way you're playing the fisherman, nobody will believe that mouthwash can change his life or anybody else's.'

'Of course it can't,' Boyd said. 'It's mouthwash.'

'But that's what we're trying to sell.'

'I'm an actor. What I sell is emotional truth,' he said. 'I quit.'

And on that overly dramatic note, Boyd turned his back on her and stormed out of the diner. When he took on a role, he embodied it, and if she and every other commercial director in town couldn't appreciate that, then so be it. He had more than $100,000 in the bank. He didn't need mouthwash money. What he needed was to perform, to indulge his raw, natural talent, without compromise or apology. He couldn't deny that need, or who he was, any more than a vampire could stop himself from sucking blood.

He was on his way back to his trailer when Nick called him.

'What a relief it is to hear your voice,' Boyd said. 'Are you and Kate all right?'

'Yes, we're fine. Why do you ask?'

'I had a visit from two nasty BlackRhino agents. Carter Grove is out to get you both.'

'Not if we get him first. I have a scheme, and there are two parts for you to play in it. One is a minor role, hardly worthy of your immense talent, but the other might just be the best character you've ever attempted. It will certainly be the most fun. The downside is that if you blow it, you won't go to jail. You'll probably be killed.'

The risk only made the challenge more enticing, the role more real. 'What's the big part?'

'A master thief,' Nick said. 'Suave, mysterious, and deadly.'

'In other words,' Boyd said, 'you want me to play myself.'

'If you're up for it.'

'Hell yes,' Boyd said.

Twenty-five

In the early 1900s, seventy percent of Canada's wealth was in the hands of just fifty men in Montreal who lived in mansions made of carved limestone in a neighborhood known as the Golden Square Mile. Two of those men, Walter Clagmann and Mecham Florentiny, were bitter rivals who ran competing railroads. Florentiny ultimately prevailed, driving Clagmann into bankruptcy and taking not only his railroad but his home, which he dismantled, shipping the stones across the St Lawrence River to build a hospital for lepers.

Florentiny was not a well-liked man, except by the owners of the world's finest auction houses, who'd helped him amass the most impressive art collection in Canada. Upon his death in 1938, his will directed that his mansion on Rue Sherbrooke be turned into a museum and that the bulk of his fortune be used to protect and preserve his collection. This came as a huge shock to his adult children, who were still living in the mansion at the time and had no vocations of their own beyond enjoying their wealth. The disgruntled heirs challenged the will, embarking on a doomed lawsuit of Dickensian proportions that was finally resolved against them in the 1950s, leaving them destitute. The Musée de Florentiny opened shortly thereafter.

The pride of the Musée de Florentiny collection were three Rembrandt oil paintings from the late 1630s that were displayed in what once was the mansion's grand dining room. The paintings were *Old Man Eating Bread by Candlelight*, *Two Men Laughing in a Tavern*, and an untitled self-portrait.

Kate and Nick were currently standing in front of the self-portrait, and Kate thought the painting should be titled *Rembrandt Hungover* because Rembrandt was pale and grimacing, his brow furrowed, turning his head ever so slightly away from the morning light as if it were causing him pain. She thought he must have been partying way too hard the night before he posed for himself.

There were about twenty people in the long gallery that Friday afternoon, all under the watchful eyes of three security guards who wore navy business suits with photo IDs clipped to their handkerchief pockets. One guard stood at the entrance and another at the exit on the opposite end of the room. The third guard roamed the gallery.

'At one time, this room had windows that looked out

over Montreal clear down to the St Lawrence River,' Nick said. 'Between the Rembrandts and the spectacular view, one prominent guest visiting from London remarked in his journal that "the greatest feast served by Monsieur Florentiny in his dining room was for the eyes, and it was glorious."'

'You should be a tour guide here,' Kate said.

'I like to know everything about what I'm stealing and where it's kept. Besides the cameras, this room is protected by motion detectors, thermal sensors, and two hundred infrared beams that crisscross the room in random, constantly changing patterns. Anything larger, heavier, and warmer than a fly moving through here will set off the alarms.'

'Is that all? No hidden machine gun turrets? Jets of poison gas? I'm not impressed.'

'But the security measures work. This museum has never been robbed. The biggest art theft in Canadian history happened in 1972 just a couple of blocks down the street at the Montreal Museum of Fine Arts. Thirty-nine pieces of jewelry and eighteen paintings, including a Rembrandt, were taken and have never been recovered. I've seen the Rembrandt, though. It's part of Carter Grove's secret collection.'

'That's why you think he'll be hot for these when they turn up on the black market.'

'He'd be interested in *any* stolen Rembrandts, but

the provenance of these, stolen in yet another historic Canadian heist, will be too sweet for him to resist.'

Nick and Kate walked through several more galleries to a wide corridor that led to the exit, where another guard sat on a stool by the turnstile a few feet away from the entrance. They walked past the solid double doors onto Rue Sherbrooke, which was Montreal's equivalent of New York's Fifth Avenue or LA's Wilshire Boulevard.

Most of the mansions that once made the Golden Square Mile so golden were now long gone, demolished to make way for the apartment towers, office buildings, and elegant brownstones that lined the wide boulevard in each direction. Directly across the street from the Musée de Florentiny was the Collège de Montréal and, behind it, the wooded hills of Parc du Mont-Royal.

'How did the thieves break into the Montreal Museum of Fine Arts?' Kate asked.

'They climbed a tree beside the building and got in through a broken skylight that was being repaired. The alarm attached to the skylight was deactivated.'

Nick led Kate around the corner onto Rue Saint-Marc, a narrow street with apartments on one side.

'They dropped into the museum, overpowered the guards, and went shopping,' Nick said.

'I guess that's why there are no trees near the Florentiny museum.'

'And no skylights,' Nick said. He gestured to a side door. Two cameras mounted on the building were aimed at it. 'That's the employee entrance, operated with a card key that's swiped over a reader. That's the only way in and out for guards when the museum is closed. The guards don't patrol the galleries or they'd set off all the security measures. So for a number of years they just sat in a windowless control room, watching a bank of monitors.'

'Sounds tedious,' Kate said.

'So tedious that the guards would nod off after a couple hours. So to alleviate some of the boredom and keep the guards alert, the museum brought in cable TV. It sounds like a great idea, but it's actually a huge mistake. The cable is a backdoor into their entire video surveillance system.'

Nick tipped his head toward the Bell Canada panel van parked on the other side of Rue Saint-Marc. The van blocked any of the museum's security cameras from seeing the technician working on the cable junction box that served all the buildings on the block. The technician was Joe Morey, a cap slung low over his face.

'They got rid of the skylights and cut the trees down for nothing,' Kate said.

'Not necessarily,' Nick said. 'You'd be surprised how often old-school approaches can still work.'

The back of the museum, and a rear door, faced

Avenue Lincoln and the block of apartment buildings across the street. Nick gestured to the door. 'That's where we'll make our escape.'

'With three Rembrandts in our hands,' she said. 'In broad daylight.'

He grinned. 'Exciting, isn't it?'

Exciting wasn't the first word that came to Kate's mind. *Terrifying* was the first word. After *terrifying* were words like *risky, stupid, crazy,* and *WRONG.*

They crossed Avenue Lincoln to Château Florentiny, a ten-story apartment building. It was a concrete monolith that didn't fit in at all with the smaller, more charming brownstone townhouses that flanked it. A sign in the lobby window read: APPARTEMENTS À LOUER.

Nick stopped on the sidewalk, pulled a ring from his pocket, and handed it to Kate. 'Your wedding ring.'

It was a platinum band inlaid with diamonds. Simple but elegant.

Kate put the ring on her finger. 'That's got to be the least romantic proposal in history. Where did you steal this?'

'I bought it,' he said.

'That must have been a new experience for you.'

'It was. Cost me ten grand.' He slipped a matching platinum band onto his finger. 'I want that ring back when this marriage is over.'

'No way,' she said. 'You can keep the dishes.'

They stepped into the lobby alcove of the Château Florentiny and pressed the intercom button to summon the manager. The speaker crackled, and a woman's voice said, 'Oui?'

'It's Jonathan and Jennifer Hart,' Nick said, smiling into the security camera. 'We have an appointment with Lorie to see Apartment 1007.'

'C'est moi.' She switched to English. 'I'll meet you on the tenth floor.'

There was a buzz, the door unlocked, and Nick and Kate went inside. The lobby had all the charm of an airport boarding gate. They got into the elevator, and as soon as the door closed Nick slid his hand around Kate's waist and pulled her close.

'What are you doing?' she asked.

'Getting into the part.'

'It feels like you're trying to get into something else.'

'That's because we're a young, vivacious couple who are passionately in love,' he said. 'This is probably the first time we've ridden in an elevator together without having sex.'

Before Kate could reply, the elevator doors opened, revealing a young woman with a big sugary-sweet smile on her lollipop-round face. She had pixie-cut blond hair and ruby red lips and wore a red-and-white-striped sundress that made her look to Kate like a candy cane.

'Bonjour, I'm Lorie,' she said, jangling the large key

ring she wore like a charm bracelet around her thin wrist. 'Let me show you the apartment.'

'Thank you,' Nick said. 'We can't wait to see it. We need to find a place to live right away.'

'Where are you living now?' Lorie led them down the hallway to a door that was already unlocked and ajar.

'Out of a suitcase,' Kate said. 'We've been crewing on yachts for the last five years. We're just getting used to having our feet on solid ground.'

'Jennifer is very eager to settle down,' Nick said. 'We've only been ashore a few days and we're already trying to get pregnant.'

'I hear that trying is the best part,' Lorie said, pushing the door open for them and beckoning them inside.

Nick squeezed Kate's waist, and Kate gave Nick an elbow to the ribs.

The living room, large and unfurnished, had freshly painted walls, new carpet, and French doors opening onto a long, narrow balcony.

Lorie gave them a quick tour, starting in the small kitchen, which had linoleum floors, fake granite countertops, and aging appliances. She showed them the two bedrooms, gushed over the his-and-hers sinks in the bathroom, and then brought them back to the living room.

'What do you think?' Lorie asked.

'Very nice,' Kate said. 'I like it.'

'Living here will make life convenient for you,' Lorie said. 'The rent is reasonable for this part of town, and everything you need for a growing family is within walking distance. The Guy-Concordia Metro stop, the Atwater Market, two parks, the Alexis Nihon Plaza shopping mall, and the best museums in Montreal are close by. And you can't beat the view.'

She opened the French doors and stepped outside onto the balcony. Nick and Kate went out with her. The balcony overlooked Avenue Lincoln, giving them a clear view of the two-story Musée de Florentiny and the streets that bordered it. Rue Sherbrooke to the north, Rue du Fort to the west, and Rue Saint-Marc to the east.

From their high vantage point, Kate could see an IKEA truck parked on the corner of Rue du Fort and Avenue Lincoln with a banner across the cargo trailer that read FREE BOXES. A dozen people were lined up behind the truck and walking away with flattened cardboard boxes of various sizes emblazoned with IKEA's distinctive logo.

'It's perfect,' Nick said. 'We'll take it.'

'I'm so glad to hear it,' Lorie said. 'I can see already that you're going to be marvelous neighbors. We can go downstairs and start filling out the paperwork. When would you like to move in?'

'Tuesday,' Nick said.

'You can have the keys today, but if you have more than a suitcase, you might want to pick another day to move in.'

'Why?' Kate asked.

'See that?' Lorie gestured to the IKEA truck and the woman handing out boxes. The woman was Willie Owens in a yellow IKEA shirt that was one size too small for her and clung to her body like spandex. 'Stores give away moving boxes at this time every year as a marketing gimmick. That's because this Tuesday is the unofficial national moving day in Quebec. Trucks are reserved for six months in advance. It will be impossible to book a mover now.'

'Getting a truck won't be a problem for us,' Kate said. 'All our stuff has been in storage in the US. We're bringing it in from there.'

'Even so,' Lorie said, 'it's going to be chaos on the streets on Tuesday.'

'We'll just have to be crafty,' Nick said. 'And steal a spot.'

'He's good at that,' Kate said.

Harry and Dottie Prestin of Albany, New York, were in their sixties and had served their time as parents, raising two rosy-cheeked girls. For most of their adult lives, Harry had worked on an assembly line at an all-weather-floormat manufacturer, and Dottie had been a cashier at Kmart. Now they were ready to retire and experience true freedom, hitting the open road in a used RV to seek out the best all-you-can-eat buffets in America. They were calling it their 'No Boundaries Tour' because from now on there would be no limits to where they could go or how much they could eat. So they sold their house, and on that last Saturday in June they put everything they owned up for sale on their front lawn.

Their stuff included four folding chairs, three TVs, his-and-hers matching vinyl recliners, two sets of dishes, 370 Harlequin romances, a dog bed, two stepladders, two worn-out couches, assorted lamps, a Hoover vacuum, a VCR, a wicker rocking chair, a birdbath, a lawn mower, a toaster oven, two hundred prerecorded movies on VHS, and almost all their clothing, with the exception of the matching NO BOUNDARIES T-shirts Dottie had made and that she and Harry were wearing. Whatever they didn't sell over the weekend would go to Goodwill or the city dump.

Harry and Dottie were sitting in their recliners on the front lawn under the shade of their maple tree, sipping iced tea and bemoaning their lack of customers, when a Toyota Camry pulled up to the curb, followed by a large moving truck.

A man in a bright blue blazer got out of the car with a spring in his step, spoke briefly to the three men in the cab of the truck, then strode over to the Prestins with a toothy, overly friendly smile on his face. It made Harry brace himself for a sales pitch, but it got Dottie excited, thinking that maybe, just maybe, they'd finally won the Publishers Clearing House sweepstakes. Maybe the Prize Patrol had arrived, ready to give them their million-dollar check.

Boyd Capwell would have been flattered to know what Dottie was thinking, because he was intentionally approaching his part like a game show host. In his mind, he wasn't walking across a lawn cluttered with junk, he was striding into the studio audience to pick out a costumed contestant for *Let's Make a Deal.*

'Hello, folks, how are you both today?' Boyd asked.

'We're selling,' Harry said. 'Not buying.'

'Indeed you are,' Boyd said. 'You have an amazing assortment of Americana. How much do you want for it?'

Harry glanced at Dottie, and Dottie shrugged. She had no idea what Boyd was talking about either.

'You'll have to bring the Americana over and let me take a look at it so I can give you a price,' Harry said.

'I'm talking about everything that's out here, my friend. From your bowling ball to that delightful ironing board.' Boyd reached into his pocket, pulled out a thick wad of cash, and started peeling off hundred-dollar bills. 'Will four thousand dollars cash cover it?'

Harry stared dumbfounded at the money. He'd never

seen so much cash in someone's hand before, and he didn't know how to put a price on all the belongings he'd spent a lifetime accumulating.

'You drive a hard bargain,' Boyd said. 'Five thousand, but that's my final offer.'

Dottie jumped out of her seat. 'Sold!' It wasn't a million-dollar check, but it still felt like the Prize Patrol had shown up at their door.

'I'm delighted,' Boyd said, and began counting the money out into her open palm.

With each bill that Boyd laid in Dottie's hand, the more excited she got, bouncing on her feet and letting out little shrieks, just like a game show contestant should. Harry, though, wasn't sharing her excitement. It had cost a lot more than five grand to acquire all of that stuff over the last thirty years, and even figuring for depreciation, wear-and-tear, and obsolescence, he still wasn't sure they were getting a fair deal, not that it mattered now. Dottie had already taken the cash and stuffed it into her cleavage alongside her Kleenex. It might as well have been deposited in Fort Knox.

'If you don't mind,' Boyd said, 'we'd like to box this all up and take it away right now.'

'Help yourself,' Dottie said. 'Would you like some iced tea?'

'That would be marvelous.' Boyd smiled and waved to the three movers, who'd already opened the back of the truck and came over carrying IKEA boxes and packing tape. This was the third garage sale Boyd had bought out that morning, having arrived at each one with a different moving company and plenty of IKEA boxes. He patted one of the movers on the back. 'Pack it all up. No need to waste time wrapping anything. I'm not concerned about any damage.'

'Are you sure?' the mover asked.

'It adds character,' Boyd said, and headed back toward his car. 'See you in Montreal on Tuesday. Apartment 1007 in the Château Florentiny on Avenue Lincoln. You can't miss it.'

Twenty-six

The Montreal Metro trains, many of them dating back to the 1960s, were the oldest still operating in North America. They were painted blue with a white stripe running down their sides, just like the baggy tracksuit on the old man who was riding the Orange Line into the city that Monday morning. It was one of the ways the old man tried to blend into the background like a chameleon.

The old man had a scarred face covered with little scabs from shaving with a dull razor held in a shaky hand. His palsy wasn't so much a physical condition as it was a psychological one. That's because he was a war criminal. Every time he looked in the mirror, he saw all the women and children he'd massacred in Serbia staring back at him. At least that's what Ralph Dennis imagined as he studied the old man surreptitiously from amid the crush of people in the aisle. The real story was far less colorful. The old man was actually a retired accountant going into town to see his dermatologist to have some skin tags removed.

Ralph wasn't interested in the reality. Creating lives for subway riders was how he kept his imagination sharp on his way into work as a security guard at the Musée de Florentiny. He had to keep the creative juices flowing during his day job if he ever wanted to make any progress writing his novel at night. If he didn't, his day job, which he'd had for thirteen years, would become his life, which was too depressing for the thirty-eight-year-old to even contemplate. So he focused his thoughts instead on the beautiful blue-eyed woman who was standing right in front of him, her open newspaper brushing against his dark sportcoat.

She had a dancer's lithe body, slim and sexy in a sensible pantsuit, her white blouse open to show a hint of cleavage. She was reading an article about an American spy satellite that had fallen in Halifax. The article was of special interest to her because she was an American spy, sent to Canada to retrieve a microchip from the satellite. She was in a race against time because spies from all over the world were converging on the crash site to recover the chip. One of the spies would undoubtedly be Sergei Blok, her former lover, a man she now had orders to kill on sight. But could she do it? That was the question that tormented her.

Ralph would have been shocked to know how close his imaginary backstory was to Kate O'Hare's real background, and how the romantic dilemma he'd come up with oddly paralleled her unusual relationship with Nick Fox. Ralph would also have been shocked to know that Fox was standing close behind him, preparing to pick his pocket.

The train rocked around a turn. Ralph was jostled from behind and briefly pushed up against Kate, crumpling her newspaper between them. He pretended not to notice, and so did she, a common courtesy all subway riders routinely performed to get past the awkwardness of being pressed up against one another in cramped trains. That courtesy made it easy for even the clumsiest pickpocket to snatch wallets and cell phones from subway riders, much the same way that Nick had just stolen Ralph's encrypted electronic identification card from his front pants pocket.

Of course, Nick had some help. What Kate had done was known among pickpockets as 'fronting the mark' and 'shading the duke,' using her newspaper to block Ralph and everyone else from seeing what Nick was doing. Nick had hooked a finger into the lip of Ralph's pocket, snagged the pleat, and pulled on the lining, bunching it up under the card and lifting the lining out for easy plucking. It all happened in a few seconds.

Once the snatch was complete, Kate turned her back to Ralph, who shifted his creative attention to a black man with shoulder-length dreadlocks who was intensely texting someone. Before Ralph could begin crafting a compelling story, the train arrived at Atwater station, a big transfer point, and he had to make his way to the door.

Ralph was carried with the flow of commuters out of the train and to the escalator. He looked up to see a bleached blonde on the next step. She was in skinny jeans and a flimsy tank top that could barely contain her huge breasts.

It was as if the breasts were magnetized and Ralph's eyeballs were made of steel. He couldn't stop staring at the breasts, not that he was trying very hard. He was so entranced by Willie that he didn't feel his security card being placed back into his pocket, and didn't realize the escalator had crested at the upper floor until he stumbled over the metal plate.

He regained his balance, and when he looked up again the woman was already lost in the crowd. He continued on through the turnstiles and out onto Avenue Atwater, then went to his left toward Avenue Lincoln and the Musée de Florentiny. He was totally unaware that his security card had briefly left his possession. Behind him, Kate, Nick, and Willie regrouped outside the station and headed in the opposite direction, down Atwater to Boulevard de Maisonneuve, which ran parallel to Lincoln. They were on their way back to the Château Florentiny apartment, which they were using as base camp until the robbery.

'Did you get it?' Kate asked Nick as they walked away.

He reached into his hip pocket and pulled out his iPhone, which had what looked like a credit card reader attached to it. He examined the display screen. It was solid green. That meant the app had successfully captured the encryption code from Ralph's security card when Nick had swiped it through the reader. Now the device could embed the same code onto a blank card.

Nick smiled. 'We're in.'

At 8 AM on Tuesday, July 1, Willie Owens parked a stolen United Van Lines moving truck behind the Musée de Florentiny. Joe Morey sat beside her in the cab, a MacBook on his lap. They were wearing matching moving-company overalls. And like the rest of the team, they were wearing tiny, barely detectable communications devices in their ears.

They weren't the only ones in the neighborhood getting an early start. Another moving truck was parked right in front of them, and three more were across the street. People were already out loading and unloading furniture and boxes and piling them on the sidewalks while they worked. Willie was pleased to see lots of IKEA boxes in play. The chaos was slowly building, which could only help them if things went tits up, as her mother used to say.

There were also lots of families walking down the

cross streets on their way to get good seats for the Canada Day Parade. The parade was to begin at 11 AM and run along Rue Sainte-Catherine, parallel to Avenue Lincoln. The festivities would create a long wall of humanity, cars, and barricades that would slow any police cars attempting to respond to an alarm at the Musée de Florentiny.

At 8:30, Ralph Dennis walked past Willie and Joe's stolen moving truck on his way to the museum's employee entrance on Rue Saint-Marc to begin his shift.

'Go,' Joe said, feeding his voice into everyone's earpiece.

The rear door of the stolen truck slid open, and Nick and Kate emerged, also in matching mover's overalls. Kate carried several unassembled IKEA boxes under her arms and against her sides. Nick carried a gym bag. They walked down Avenue Lincoln a few steps behind Ralph.

Joe lifted the top of his MacBook, and his screen lit up with a dozen live video feeds from the museum's security cameras.

'I'm in,' he said to Nick and Kate.

Ralph turned the corner onto Rue Saint-Marc and walked up to the museum's side door, smiled at the cameras, and ran his security card over the reader on the wall. The door unlocked and he went inside. The instant the door closed, Joe tapped into the camera feed and replaced the live image with one he'd recorded moments before Ralph walked up. The replay showed nobody at the door.

'You're clear,' Joe said to Nick and Kate.

They went up to the door. Nick took a white plastic card out of his pocket, wiped it over the reader, and unlocked the door. Nick opened the door, and he and Kate stepped into a corridor. The alarms in that section of the building had been deactivated for Ralph and wouldn't be turned on again until the officer he was replacing on the shift walked out. They had maybe one minute to act.

Kate set the boxes down, and Nick opened the gym bag. They took ski masks out of the bag, pulled them over their faces, and each picked up a Glock. The guns weren't loaded, but Kate's stomach still rolled. She'd sworn to uphold the law, and here she was all dressed up like a criminal, getting ready to rob a museum. It would be satisfying to take down Carter Grove, but truth is, she probably wouldn't be doing this if her family's safety wasn't at stake.

Nick grabbed the gym bag and Kate led the way down the corridor to the security station, stepping into the windowless room in a firing stance. There were six flat-screen surveillance monitors on the far wall, mounted over a broad alarm console, an array of switches, dials, and keyboards. Two guards, about the same age as Ralph, sat at the console, facing the screens. Ralph stood beside the men, talking about a soccer game. None of them were aware of Kate and Nick until Kate spoke up.

'Good morning,' she said.

The startled men whirled around and went wide-eyed when they saw the two hooded figures standing in the doorway, holding guns.

'Please do as you're told because we really don't want to hurt you. We'd like this to be a relaxed, stress-free robbery for everyone. Sound good?' she asked.

The guards nodded.

'Great. What we'd like you to do is get up very slowly, face the wall, and assume the position of someone under arrest.'

The guards did as they were told, put their hands against the walls, and spread their legs.

'Perfect. Now we're going to search you for weapons and zip-tie your hands behind your backs,' she said. 'Nothing to worry about.'

Nick put his gun in his pocket, went up to the men, and patted them down, taking their wallets and cell phones, which he placed in his gym bag. He bound their hands behind their backs with zip ties, stepped back beside Kate, and drew his weapon again.

'Don't worry about your stuff,' Kate said. 'We'll leave your things at the door before we leave. Now turn around, put your backs against the wall, and slide down into a seated position on the floor with your ankles crossed. What's going to happen now is that we're going to bind your ankles with zip ties, cover your mouths with duct tape, and then steal some paintings.'

Once Nick was finished taping and tying the guards, he went to the console and switched off the alarm system throughout the museum.

Twenty-seven

The employee restrooms weren't protected by any alarm systems, and as all the guards were men, no one ever went into the women's bathroom when the museum was closed. That mundane fact, combined with an obscure bit of Montreal criminal history, was the key element of Huck Moseby's elaborately conceived plot to rob the Musée de Florentiny.

Twenty-two years ago, a team of thieves had plotted to break into the basement cash room of the Bank of Montreal by tunneling in from the city's sewer system. They'd spent months digging tunnels and were only seven centimeters away from breaking through the bank's floor when, the day before the heist was to go down, a huge tree fell onto the street. The tree collapsed the tunnel and exposed their work. The would-be thieves were never caught, and if not for the fallen tree they might have succeeded in pulling off the crime of the century.

Huck had thought often about that failed robbery

during his ten-year career as a Montreal sewer worker. His fascination with the crime eventually evolved into a plan of his own to steal the Rembrandt collection from the Musée de Florentiny. His plot was so ingenious that he considered himself a criminal mastermind in the same league as Professor Moriarty, Auric Goldfinger, or the Penguin. This secret knowledge of his own incredible brilliance gave forty-one-year-old Huck the strength to go to work and slog through the day.

He had assembled his crack team with the same careful consideration as George Clooney had in *Ocean's Eleven*, had Clooney's circle of contacts been only people he'd met in the sewers and subway tunnels under Montreal. Huck's first recruits were two unemployed construction workers experienced with digging and demolishing tunnels.

Since Huck knew nothing about properly handling paintings or fencing Rembrandts in the international black market, he needed to find a professional thief, and he wasn't going to find one in the sewers. So he browsed through back issues of Canadian newspapers for stories about thieves convicted of committing art robberies and found one who'd recently been released from prison.

Two months ago, the men began digging a tunnel from the sewer collector line to a spot directly below the museum's employee women's restroom. They were on a tight deadline because Huck's plan was to break into the restroom, overpower the guards, turn off the alarms, and leisurely pillage the museum on July 1, national moving day. That way they could simply walk out the back door carrying their Rembrandts in moving boxes to the truck they'd parked behind the museum. No one would notice. They would blend in with everybody else on the street loading and unloading trucks and then quietly drive off into infamy.

At 9 AM, Huck's team cut a hole through the floor of the women's bathroom with a thermal lance, and the four men, their faces hidden by ski masks, quietly climbed out of the tunnel. They brought with them guns, packing tape, and several flattened moving boxes that IKEA had given away in the neighborhood.

As the criminal mastermind of the group, Huck Moseby was the first one to step out of the women's bathroom into the corridor. He'd barely emerged from the doorway when he felt something cold and hard pressed against his left ear.

'I've got a Glock pointed at your head,' Kate said. 'If my finger twitches, your head will explode like a water balloon, so you don't want to startle me.'

He didn't know what surprised him more, that there was a gun pointed at his head or that somehow he'd missed that there was a female guard on the museum's payroll.

'Does she really have a gun?' Huck asked. The question was directed at the three men behind him in the restroom, because he was afraid to turn his head and see for himself. But none of the men answered. They were already scrambling back to their hole in the floor.

Kate took Huck's gun from him and, keeping her Glock against his ear, peered into the restroom just in time to see the last man jump into the hole. They left behind their guns, boxes, and packing tape. She was glad to see them go. It made things a lot easier.

It wasn't a coincidence that she'd been standing there when they arrived. She'd been expecting them ever since she and Nick had walked by the Hydro-Québec truck on the street yesterday. Nick got suspicious when he saw a worker sitting on the back of the truck texting on his smartphone. Guys who spend most of their time working underground don't have blisters on their hands unless they're new hires. That made Nick study the man more closely, and when he did he recognized him as Michel Montoute, a mediocre thief who'd recently been released from prison. Montoute might have recognized Nick too, if he'd just once looked up from his tweeting.

Kate turned back to Huck and put his gun in her pocket. 'This is your lucky day.'

'It is?' He risked a look at her and was stunned to see that she wasn't a guard and that she was wearing a ski mask just like his own.

'Yes, because you were caught by another thief and not the law. You get to go free. But we're taking the Rembrandts.'

'Couldn't I have just one?'

'No, you can't.'

'That doesn't seem very fair. I put a lot of work into this.'

'You certainly did,' she said, glancing back at the hole. 'Way more than was necessary.'

'How did you get in?'

'Trade secret,' she said, and whistled for Nick. He came over a few moments later.

'Where are the others?' Nick asked.

She took a step back from Huck and handed Nick two zip ties. 'They scurried away like rats into their hole.'

'That was considerate of them.'

'Not as far as I'm concerned,' Huck said.

'They thought you'd been captured by a museum guard,' Nick said. 'They knew the heist was blown. You can't blame them for taking advantage of their one opportunity for escape. I have to congratulate you on your plan, though. Very clever.'

'Thanks,' Huck said. 'Since you clearly respect my skills, what do you say we band together on this?'

'The only thing we're going to band together are your wrists,' Kate said, keeping her weapon trained on him. 'Hold your arms out.'

'That's cold,' Huck said, but he complied. 'C'mon, give a guy a break.'

'We will.' Nick pulled the zip tie tight around Huck's wrists. 'We'll cut you free before we go. The guards will never know you were here.'

'You sure I couldn't have a Matisse or a Renoir as a consolation prize?'

That question was actually the subject of an argument Nick and Kate had had the previous night. Nick was in favor of letting the thieves take whatever they wanted from the museum, but the FBI agent in Kate couldn't let that happen. The only way she felt comfortable stealing the Rembrandts was because she was fairly certain the museum would be getting them back.

'We'll make sure you leave with a souvenir,' Nick said.

They sat Huck down, zip-tied his ankles, and returned to the Rembrandt gallery.

'I can't believe another crew tried to rob this place on the same day as us,' Kate said.

'At least I spotted them ahead of time.'

Nick removed the three paintings from the wall and wrapped them in plastic. He continued his work while Kate assembled the boxes. They then put the paintings into the boxes and sealed them with packing tape. Nick stepped out of the gallery and returned a few minutes later, pushing two of the museum's handtrucks. They loaded the boxes onto the handtrucks, then each took one and wheeled it to the back door. On the way, Kate stopped beside Huck, bent down, and cut his ties.

'I want to see you go back into your hole before we leave,' Kate said.

Huck stood up and faced Nick. 'You told me I'd get to take something with me.'

Nick reached into the box on the top of his handtruck and pulled out a Musée de Florentiny T-shirt with Rembrandt's *Old Man Eating Bread by Candlelight* on the back. 'Wear it in good health.'

'I was expecting something more valuable.'

'What could be more valuable than your freedom?' Kate said. 'Go before we change our mind, tie you back up, and leave you here for the police.'

Huck stuffed the T-shirt into his jumpsuit so it wouldn't get dirty in the sewer and reluctantly returned to the women's room. The sad notion wasn't lost on him that his tunnel robbery was as big a failure, and as doomed by bad luck, as the one attempted at the Bank of Montreal twenty-two years ago. At least he was getting away free and clear, just like those other would-be thieves did. But unlike them, he had something to show for it, even if it was only a lousy T-shirt.

Kate and Nick waited until Huck disappeared into the hole. They removed their ski masks and went outside. The two trucks parked behind the museum, the one left by Huck's crew and the other driven by Willie, served as a barricade blocking the rear of the museum from view on the street.

Willie and Joe got out of the cab and opened the back of the truck for Kate and Nick. They were just four more movers on Avenue Lincoln, loading IKEA boxes into a truck. Nobody noticed them. If anything was attracting attention, it was all the trucks from New York and their crews unloading tons of stuff onto the sidewalk in front of the Château Florentiny, much to the dismay of the other people trying to move in and out of the building.

The four thieves got into their truck and drove away with three Rembrandts worth $375 million.

It was a twenty-minute drive out of the city, over the St Lawrence River, and south to the suburb of Brossard and one of the many body shops tucked away amid the clutter of car dealerships along Taschereau Boulevard. Willie stopped the truck in front of the wrought-iron fence that surrounded a run-down body shop, leaned out the window, and typed a code into a security keypad. The gate slid open and she drove up to a garage door, opened it with a remote, and eased the truck inside.

There were four bays in the garage. A two-year-old Camry was parked in one. A late model Chevy Malibu was parked in another. The new Ford E-150 panel van

Willie and Joe had driven up from New York a week ago was parked in the third. Willie parked the moving van next to the E-150, and Kate opened the van's back door and jumped out. She took the smallest Rembrandt from Nick and carried it to a worktable. Joe took the second, and Nick took the last and largest.

Large sheets of construction-grade Styrofoam leaned against the table, plus preassembled cardboard boxes. The boxes were the exact size needed for the three paintings. The Styrofoam was cut and securely taped around each painting, creating a snug container, which was then slipped into a cardboard box. The packing would protect the paintings from shaking and damage on their short journey. Once the packaging was completed for each Rembrandt, Willie climbed into the Ford E-150, started the ignition, put the car into neutral, moved the passenger side mirror forward while pressing the brake, and then lowered her window halfway. That combination of specific actions activated the hydraulics that simultaneously opened hidden compartments in the ceiling and side panels.

Nick had bought the van for cash from an underworld contact with a body shop on Jerome Avenue in the Bronx. The street was known among smugglers, porn stars, rappers, major league athletes, and the very rich as 'the Rodeo Drive of Trap Cars.' Trap cars were vehicles outfitted with the latest innovations in secret stash compartments for hiding drugs, weapons, cash, stolen objects, jewelry, and other valuable goods. And it was entirely legal. There were no federal laws against altering cars to create hidden compartments, only against some of the things that might be put into them.

'That is so cool,' Joe said. 'I've got to get a stash pot like that in my Camaro.'

'What for?' Kate asked. 'You don't have anything to stash.'

'I have my cell phone and sunglasses,' Joe said.

'You could put them in the glovebox.'

'But that won't get me laid,' Joe said, gesturing to the secret compartment in the ceiling. 'That will.'

'He's got a point,' Nick said.

'No, he doesn't,' Kate said. 'What kind of woman would be turned on by that?'

'I'm kind of turned on,' Willie said.

Kate didn't think that was much of an endorsement. Willie was turned on by grass growing.

They placed a Rembrandt in each of the side panels and in the roof compartment. From the driver's seat Willie closed up the hiding places with another, different combination of switches and actions.

Nick leaned on the driver's side door and looked at Willie.

'Take it slow and enjoy the drive.'

'I can't do both,' Willie said.

She opened the garage door with the remote and drove out.

'Do you think they'll have any problems at the border?' Kate asked.

'Their passports are good, and it's the same small crossing at Hemmingford they drove through a week ago in the same car. Besides, it's not as if Customs has a dog that can sniff out Rembrandts.'

Nick had chosen that particular border crossing because it was small and rarely had a long line of cars. The last thing they wanted was for the van to be mired in a holiday backup at the border when word trickled down to Customs about the museum theft. Unless the Musée de Florentiny guards managed to wriggle free, the theft wouldn't be discovered for at least an hour, and it might be another few hours on top of that before Customs heard anything about it. By then Willie and Joe would be in the clear.

'There's no reason to suspect Willie and Joe of anything,' Nick said. 'They don't resemble us physically and their passports are authentic and in perfect order. Even if the van is searched for some reason, it's nothing to worry about. The secret compartments are undetectable to the naked eye, and they can't be opened unless someone is sitting in the driver's seat and hits the right combination of buttons in perfect sequence.'

'It feels risky,' Kate said.

'I've done dozens of border crossings like this before,' Nick said. 'And I've never been caught at it.'

'That was you,' she said. 'This is them.'

Kate left a few moments later in the Malibu, and Nick left twenty minutes after that. They were both headed to the Montreal airport to take separate flights to different places.

Kate took the 1:45 Delta Air Lines flight to New York City, and Nick departed on the 2:10 Air Canada flight to Washington, DC.

Kate arrived in New York at 3:30 and took a taxi to an unoccupied loft in SoHo that Nick had found. It belonged to an investment broker who was serving a fifteen-year prison sentence for fraud and embezzlement. The loft was one of the broker's many properties that were in limbo while his bilked clients, the brokerage house he worked for, and the government fought for his assets.

Kate settled in and waited for Willie and Joe to arrive that night with the paintings.

Nick arrived in DC a little after four in the afternoon and took a taxi to Gelman's Haberdashery in Dupont Circle, getting there just as Gelman was closing up shop for the day.

Zev Gelman greeted him at the door and leaned on

his gnarled cane. 'How did it go with the autodialer on that Hemmler J507?'

'A sky-high success.'

'Glad to hear it. Be sure to give me a good review on Yelp.'

Gelman stepped aside to let Nick pass. He closed the door and secured it with a simple deadbolt and turned around to see Nick grinning at him. 'What's so funny?'

'You relying on that simple deadbolt when you've got cutting-edge security systems for sale in that hidden showroom of yours.'

'Shows how little you know about locks. That deadbolt is the best theft deterrent I've got. If I had anything fancier on the door, people would think I had something more valuable in here than handmade shirts. Who's going to steal a shirt?'

'I would,' Nick said. 'Those are nice shirts.'

'You didn't come here for clothes, though you ought to let me make you a suit sometime.'

'I will, but tonight I'm looking for a small tracking device.'

'How small is small?'

Gelman stepped up to the full-length mirror and pressed the hidden button on the frame. The green beam of the retina scanner behind the glass passed over his right eye. He stepped back as the wall slid open to reveal the showroom, the polished metal paneling gleaming under the bright lights.

'Virtually undetectable to the human eye,' Nick said as they walked inside and stood beside the tall glass-topped counter in the center of the showroom.

'The smallest GPS tracker I've got is about the size of a quarter.'

Nick shook his head. 'That's way too big.'

'I see.' Gelman put both hands on top of his gnarled cane and thought about that for a moment. 'How much do you have to spend?'

'You're asking me to negotiate with myself.'

'I'm asking what you can afford.'

'Assume that money is no object.'

'Funny you should say that. Because "money is no object" is how much the Pentagon told defense contractors they were willing to spend on tracking technology after 9/11. They invested tens of billions of dollars to develop smartdust that tiny drones the size of hummingbirds could spray on Osama bin Anybody without him noticing.'

'What is smartdust?'

'It's sticky electromagnetic taggant particles that allow satellites to track your movements, or a predator drone to lock a missile onto you. It's highly classified technology.' Gelman pointed his cane at a slim silver briefcase on a high shelf. 'Can you get that for me?'

Nick reached up and brought it down, setting it carefully on the glass-topped counter. Inside the case, resting in foam cutouts, were a jam-size jar filled with what looked like black pepper and a device similar to a highway patrolman's radar gun but with a much larger display screen above the grip.

'What is this?' Nick asked.

'A covert operative's tagging kit. There's enough powder in that jar to target an entire terrorist camp. A few particles are really all you need to tag someone or something.'

'What's the radar gun for?'

'It's much more than a radar gun. It's advanced technology that can home in on a dusted object the same way a missile homes in. The gun can also be used by someone on the ground to tag an object with an invisible beam that guides a missile right to it.'

'That's a nasty game of tag.'

'It certainly is,' Gelman said. 'I assume that's not what you want this for, not that I am making any judgments, mind you.'

'I don't have any missiles.'

'I could get you some. The instruction manual would probably be in Russian, though. Do you speak the language?'

'It doesn't matter. I'm not in the market.' Nick tapped the case. 'How did you get your hands on this stuff?'

'It's on consignment from a spy with a lot of gambling debts and several mistresses to support.'

'James Bond without the expense account.'

'Or the luck at cards,' Gelman said. 'My eight-year-old grandson could beat him at poker.'

'What's the range of these taggants?'

'Five miles,' Gelman said.

'How long does the dust stay active?'

'Indefinitely. It's inert until activated by a radar signal.'

Nick nodded, impressed. 'What is this going to cost me?'

'Half a million dollars,' Gelman said. 'I'm afraid the price is firm and nonnegotiable.'

'Will you throw in a custom-made suit?'

'And a tie.'

'Done,' Nick said, and closed the case.

Twenty-eight

Carter Grove watched the national evening news on the large flat-screen television in his office. It had been a good day. The armed convoy containing his art collection had arrived safely at his Kentucky ranch, he'd become the owner of a fully armed Aero-System predator drone, and a fifty-million-dollar payment had come in from African dictator Muktar Diriye Abdullahi to protect his embattled regime from rebels.

The day went from merely good to officially wonderful when the news anchor announced that three Rembrandts had been stolen from the Musée de Florentiny in a brazen robbery committed in broad daylight on Quebec's national moving day. The museum guards told police that they were overpowered by half a dozen heavily armed thieves who tunneled in from the sewers. Art experts estimated that the combined value of the stolen paintings exceeded $375 million, making it the biggest art theft in Canadian history and the second largest in

North America, topped only by the five-hundred-million-dollar Gardner Museum robbery in March 1990.

Carter had visited the Musée de Florentiny many times and stared for hours at those Rembrandts, longing to have the masterpieces hanging in his home. Now he could make that dream come true. Unless those paintings had been stolen on demand for a particular collector, which Carter doubted, they would soon be available on the blackest of the black markets, the one reserved for the world's richest men. Only a few dealers catered to that elite clientele, and they all knew Carter's tastes in art, though they didn't know him by his real name. They knew him only by the alias 'Mr Wayne,' by the number to call to reach him, by the generous commissions he was willing to pay, and by the fatal consequences involved if they breathed a word of his existence to anyone. He didn't need to alert them to make him their first call if any of the Rembrandts came into their hands or remind them of the dire penalties if they failed to do so.

He'd allowed Duff to live with his broken bones as an example to those who would dare to discover or divulge his identity. And when the example had served its purpose, Duff would die an even more painful death.

Carter reached for the phone and dialed Veronica Dell.

'Yes, sir?' she said.

'Tell Rocco to make room for three additional paintings beside the Rembrandt when he installs my collection.'

'Of course,' she said.

Bad boy celebrity chef Razzie Olden was known as much for his addictions – namely sex, heroin, and alcohol – as he was for his daring dishes and outrageous restaurants. The bad taste of his décor often clashed with the exquisite taste of his culinary creations. Olden's newest restaurant was La Guerre, in Midtown Manhattan. The walls were exposed concrete, the ceilings were draped in camouflage netting, and the sound of distant explosions played from hidden speakers. The waitresses wore helmets, camouflage tops and shorts, and combat boots. The food was served on china that had been pillaged from one of Saddam Hussein's palaces during the war in Iraq. And all of Olden's signature dishes were seasoned or garnished with ingredients that could, if not prepared correctly, result in sickness or death, like Jamaican ackee, South American yucca, and elderberry leaves.

La Guerre wasn't just one of New York's priciest and trendiest restaurants, it was also considered by the city's cognoscenti to be a work of bold, politically incorrect performance art. So naturally the wealthiest members of the arts community flocked to La Guerre to be part of the experience, which was why Julian Starke was there. He didn't like the food, and he thought the décor was insipid, but like a shark drawn to blood in the water he was attracted to fools with money.

Starke was a fifty-year-old art blogger and dealer who generated a dependable cash flow selling forged Jackson Pollocks and Willem de Koonings to actors, athletes, rap singers, and all the other idiots who patronized La Guerre. He'd even sold chef Olden a Robert Motherwell abstract masterpiece for seven million dollars that was actually painted for forty-five hundred dollars by a Korean forger living in Queens.

But where Starke really made his money was selling big-ticket stolen masterworks to the megarich for megabucks. He just never knew when those paydays were coming. So there he was, sitting at a power booth in the back, stroking his impeccable goatee, dressed in his trademark black Versace turtleneck, slim-fit Maison Martin Margiela black twill jeans, and Krisvanassche black pebbled sneakers. He was trolling for clients who wouldn't know a Klimt from a Warhol when a new face walked into the room.

The stranger was dressed to kill in a perfectly tailored Tom Ford tuxedo with silk-trimmed lapels and Italian-cut trousers, his bow tie unbowed at the open collar of his white Turnbull & Asser shirt. He was accompanied by two drop-dead gorgeous women in their early twenties who looked like porn stars filling time between sex scenes.

He walked directly to Starke's booth and dismissed the women. 'Go warm up our table, ladies. I'll be right there.'

'Shall we order champagne?' one of the women asked, with a vaguely Russian accent.

'Order whatever you like,' the stranger said. The women went off, and the man slid into the booth beside Starke and smiled at him. 'What do you think of this place, Julian?'

Starke did a quick appraisal of the man beside him. The tuxedo. The Rolex Oyster Perpetual Datejust timepiece. The S. T. Dupont palladium cufflinks. The white moiré silk Albert Thurston suspenders with gold fittings. This man had spent more on what he was wearing than most people earned in a year. He had money and he liked to display it. He was just the kind of guy who'd spend seven figures on an abstract expressionist forgery and never know the difference. So whatever this man's game was, Starke was willing to play along.

'The cuisine is inventive, the wine list is adequate, but he's trying way too hard to be provocative with the atmosphere,' Starke said. 'I'm betting there will be a California Pizza Kitchen here a year from now.'

'You're probably right. But I like it.' The stranger smiled, ran his finger around the edge of a plate, and let it rest on the Iraqi seal. 'Reminds me of how I made my first million. I was boots-on-the-ground for the invasion.

Everyone else was fighting for apple pie, cheap gasoline, and a future without tyranny. Me? I'd heard that Saddam had crates of US cash buried all over Baghdad. It was like an Easter egg hunt in a minefield. Those were good times.'

Kate groaned. 'My God, does he always have to improvise? Why doesn't he just stick with the script?'

She and Nick were sitting in a rented Escalade parked across Fifth Avenue from La Guerre. They were listening on their earbuds to the conversation between Boyd and Starke. Nick pressed a button on a tiny remote control he held in his hand. It muted their voices so Boyd couldn't hear them.

'He's incorporating the setting emotionally into his backstory,' Nick said. 'It grounds the character in Starke's world and creates a stronger visceral connection to him. It's brilliant and it comes instinctively to him. You should be taking notes.'

'I took plenty of them in my undercover training course at Quantico. We were taught that the more you talk, the greater the risk you'll say something that will get you burned. He's riffing, giving Starke way too much information. It's dangerous.'

'To play a role, and be convincing at it, you have to lose yourself in the character and get caught up in the flow of the action. You need to be relaxed for that to happen, so you make it a game. The moment you approach the performance as a job, it stops being fun. You get anxious and start second-guessing every word you say and every move you make. You start thinking of all the things that could go wrong. And then they do.'

Starke didn't understand the point of the stranger's long, colorful story about his glory days smuggling Saddam's cash out of Iraq. What did he want? Was he here to buy or to sell?

'That's a terrific story,' he said. 'What's it got to do with me?'

'Finding you here is a good omen. Iraq was my first big payday, and now you're going to help me score an even bigger one.'

So he was selling. But Starke was immediately wary. He didn't like getting into business with anyone who didn't come with a recommendation.

'Do you have a collection to sell?'

'I do.' Boyd reached into his pocket and tossed a paper onto the table. It was a ticket for the Musée de Florentiny. 'Interested?'

Starke knew about the theft, of course. The entire art world was buzzing about it. But the last thing he expected was to be contacted the day after the crime by someone claiming to be involved, or at least representing the thieves. If this man really had the three

Rembrandts, then Starke stood to make millions in commission.

'Maybe,' Starke said. 'Who are you?'

'Names are for tombstones. But you can call me Al Mundy, if that makes you feel better.' He took a disposable cell phone out of his pocket and set it in front of Starke. 'I'll be in touch tomorrow. Be prepared to buy.'

Boyd slid out of the booth and strolled over to the table where his two escorts were waiting, having already polished off a bottle of Cristal together.

Starke stuck around, working the room for the next hour or so, as Boyd and his women gorged themselves on food and drink, racking up a bill that Starke pegged conservatively at three thousand dollars. When they were done, Boyd put his arms around the girls, who were giggly drunk, and led them to the door, winking at Starke as he passed.

Starke went outside just as Boyd climbed into a chauffeur-driven Rolls-Royce and headed toward Fifth Avenue. The odds were, Starke thought, that this Mundy was a flashy con man, trying to swindle him or a rich client out of millions. But on the small chance that Mundy could actually deliver the Rembrandts, it was a once-in-a-lifetime deal and Starke would need instant access to an enormous amount of money to clinch it.

He put his phone to his ear and called Mr Wayne.

* * *

Willie drove Boyd and his two five-hundred-dollar-an-hour escorts to the Four Seasons Hotel on East Fifty-seventh Street. Boyd led the women through the marbled lobby and up to his forty-ninth-floor suite.

Kate and Nick were watching from the lobby lounge.

'I still don't see the point of hiring two high-priced hookers,' Kate said.

'They're escorts, and we needed them because beautiful women are naturally attracted to successful world-class thieves who know how to have fun and enjoy the very best of everything.'

'Is that what your life was like before I came along?'

'You were always there.'

'One step behind,' she said. 'Did you ever hire hookers?'

'Escorts,' he said. 'Sure, if I needed eye candy for a con and didn't have time to find the right woman. Escorts are expedient. They arrive on short notice and play their role.'

This wasn't sitting well with Kate. Prostitution was illegal. She didn't like Nick's cavalier attitude toward it. She didn't like that a woman would have to turn to prostitution. And bottom line was that her role in all this made her feel . . . icky.

'The con was at the restaurant,' Kate said. 'Not in his suite.'

'You never know who might be watching. There could

be members of the hotel staff on Starke's payroll. It would be odd if he didn't bring the women back to his place to continue the party.'

'There are *two* of them.'

'And?'

'For crying out loud, isn't one woman enough? What *is* it with you men and the threesome?'

'No need to get emotional,' Nick said. 'It's business.'

She checked her watch. 'Boyd had better send them back down in an hour or I'm going up there and kicking them out.'

'No, you're not,' Nick said.

'We're paying for them.'

'Technically, the Vibora cartel is paying for them thanks to the two million dollars in drug money they gave me for the Malibu house.'

Kate nibbled on the cookie that had come with her cappuccino. 'So I'm using Mexican drug money to hire hookers to entertain a con man selling stolen Rembrandts?'

'Brilliant, right?'

She didn't bother to squelch the grimace.

'Boyd has earned some fun tonight,' Nick said. 'He could be killed tomorrow.'

Kate didn't understand that kind of fun. And in her present mood she thought Boyd was more likely to be killed by her than by Carter Grove.

'You could be killed, too,' Nick said.

She studied him over the rim of her coffee cup. 'Running with that line of thought, do you think I should get myself a gigolo tonight?'

'I'm available,' he said.

'I can't afford you.'

'I'll give you the FBI discount.'

'You aren't my type,' she said.

'What is your type?'

'For starters, a man who isn't on the FBI's Ten Most Wanted list.'

Nick gave her the cookie that had come with his coffee. 'If you keep being so picky, you'll die an old maid.'

Twenty-nine

Julian Starke's gallery on the Upper East Side resembled the drawing room of Lord Grantham's house in *Downton Abbey*. It was full of antique furniture, Oriental rugs, paintings of the English countryside, and bookshelves lined with leather-bound first editions.

It was 10 AM and Starke was in the gallery, sitting at his Biedermeier desk, doing the Daily Jumble, when Boyd called on the disposable cell phone.

'Meet me in my suite at the Four Seasons in a half hour,' he said.

Starke got to the forty-ninth-floor suite at 10:30 sharp and rang the buzzer. He was dressed in elegant black, as usual.

Boyd opened the door in a bathrobe, his hair wet and smelling of Bulgari shower gel. He seemed happy, relaxed, and refreshed. 'Come on in and make yourself comfortable,' he said.

Starke stepped into the spacious, luxuriously furnished

living room, which had silk padded walls and a commanding view of the city. There were plates of scrambled eggs, toast, caviar, fresh fruit, and bacon on the dining room table. It all looked as if it had been attacked by a flock of birds.

The door to the bedroom opened and the two women Starke had seen the night before came out like models hitting the runway. Boyd kissed them and handed each a thick packet of crisp hundred-dollar bills from his bathrobe pocket.

'It was a pleasure,' he said, leading them to the front door.

'Be sure to call us next time you're in town,' one of them said. 'And we'll party again.'

'I'll start training in earnest today, Natasha.'

'I'm Natalia,' she said, putting her arm around the other girl. 'She's Natasha.'

'Of course,' Boyd said, ushering them out the door and closing it behind them, then turning back to Starke with a smile. 'Would you like some coffee? Some caviar and eggs?'

'What I'd like is to know why I'm here.'

'You already know.' Boyd narrowed his eyes at him. 'Sounds to me like you're trying to get me to incriminate myself.'

'I can assure you I am not working for the feds,' Starke said. 'Nobody's listening but me.'

'You'll have to do better than that,' Boyd said to Starke. 'Strip.'

'What?'

'You heard me. I need to be sure you aren't wearing a wire. Take off all your clothes or walk out that door right now. There are other dealers I can find to do business with.'

Starke's immediate reaction was to tell Mundy to screw himself. But if Mundy had really just pulled off the biggest theft in Canadian history, Starke couldn't blame him for wanting to take every precaution. He also wasn't ready to walk away from the millions he could potentially earn from Mr Wayne on this deal. It could be his biggest payday yet. So Starke stripped down to his Calvin Klein bikini briefs, which were black, of course.

'Satisfied?' Starke asked.

'Can't be too careful.' Boyd spread some caviar on a piece of toast and took a bite. 'I want you to sell the three Rembrandts I stole from the Musée de Florentiny. They're worth three hundred seventy-five million dollars, but I'll settle for three hundred million. That's a no-dicker sticker. The price is a reasonable compromise between the rarity of the paintings and the restricted market for them. Add whatever markup you think is fair for your commission. That's between you and your buyer, anyway.'

'All I've got from you so far is talk, humiliation, and

a lot of flash,' Starke said. 'When are you going to back it up?'

Nick, Kate, Joe, and Willie were listening through Boyd's earbuds to every word that was being said. Nick and Joe were in the suite next door, where Joe was recording Boyd and Starke's conversation on his laptop. Willie was in the Escalade, idling on Fifty-eighth Street along with a line of other limos at the back entrance to the Four Seasons. Kate was also on Fifty-eighth Street, ready to shadow Starke once the meeting was over. She stood in front of the Duane Reade and pretended to send a text. The streets were clogged with people. But Kate noticed that a young couple that had been walking behind Starke as he came down Fifth Avenue were now standing in front of a gallery, admiring the artwork in the window. The woman touched her ear. A rookie move, revealing that she was wearing an earbud and listening to a transmission.

'Crap,' Kate said.

'What is it?' Nick asked.

She glanced to her left. There was a café across the street, just east of the Four Seasons, and it had tables outside. A man in an off-the-rack suit sat at one of the tables facing the hotel and reading a newspaper. He had a buzzcut, and he was staring at the hotel. He also touched his ear.

'Crapity crap,' Kate said.

'That can't be good,' Nick said.

'Starke was tailed and is under surveillance by cops of some kind,' Kate said. 'This could be a setup.'

Kate walked to Madison Avenue and then around the corner down to Fifty-seventh, keeping her head low and staying in the middle of the crush of people on the sidewalk. On the way, she passed an old Crown Vic idling at the curb with two men in suits sitting in the front seat.

'Crapity crap *crap*,' she said.

'How much worse is a *crapity crap crap* than a *crapity crap*?' Joe asked. 'I need a scale.'

Nick turned to Joe, who was on the couch, his MacBook on his lap, his screen split into thumbnail images of the dozens of feeds from the hotel's security cameras.

'Relax, everyone,' Nick said. 'There's no reason to panic.'

'Yet,' Willie said.

Boyd took his piece of toast, went into the bedroom, and returned carrying a Louis Vuitton valise, which he handed to Starke. 'This should do.'

Starke sat down on the couch and unzipped the valise. Inside was the Rembrandt self-portrait, the smallest of the three stolen masterpieces. He knew in an instant that it was genuine and congratulated himself on having the good sense to strip when he'd been asked. Otherwise, he might have missed out on what was sure to be the biggest deal he'd ever make.

'This could be a fake,' Starke said.

'Nobody knows that better than you. I've seen the Bong Chan-Wooks you've been selling as Pollocks. Good stuff.' Boyd gathered up Starke's clothes. 'You can examine the painting while I get dressed.'

'Why are you taking my clothes?'

'You're less likely to run out of here with the Rembrandt if you're naked.'

Boyd went back to the bedroom and closed the door. He tossed Starke's clothes on the unmade bed and whispered to Nick, 'What do I do now? I need some direction here.'

Asking Starke to strip was pure improvisation on Boyd's part. He was reacting to Kate's suggestion that the meeting might be a setup. The original plan was for Boyd to let Starke take the Rembrandt with him and authenticate it as a token of Mundy's goodwill. Boyd would call him later that night on the throwaway cell to set up the meet at a warehouse in Astoria to complete the transaction. But now Boyd was onstage without a script and had no idea where the story was supposed to go.

'I'll let you know in a minute,' Nick said. 'In the meantime, get dressed. Wear something casual.'

* * *

Kate reached the corner of Fifty-seventh and Madison Avenue and saw a man admiring the shoes in the window of the Geox store on the opposite corner. She saw another man across the street, outside of Turnbull & Asser, pacing as he talked on his phone but keeping his eyes on the entrance of the Four Seasons. She recognized him. He was an FBI agent out of the Manhattan office.

'The FBI have surrounded the hotel,' Kate said. 'This is bad.'

'It's not so bad,' Nick said. 'I've been in worse situations than this.'

'It doesn't get worse than this.' Kate turned around, walked smack into a man in a sportcoat and jeans, and discovered that she was wrong. It *could* get worse. Much worse.

'Kate?' FBI Special Agent Andrew Tourneur stared at her in disbelief. 'What the hell are you doing here?'

Thirty

As much as Nick wanted to listen to what came next, he didn't want Boyd, Willie, and Joe to hear it.

'Cut off Kate's earbud *now,*' Nick told Joe.

'Okay, okay.' Joe tapped a few keys on his laptop, but he clearly wasn't happy about it. 'Done. What don't you want us to hear?'

'It's the other way around. I don't want her hearing what we're doing.'

'Why not?' Joe asked.

'What she doesn't know she can't reveal, intentionally or otherwise,' Nick said. 'And we certainly don't want the FBI listening in on us if they get hold of her earbud.'

It was a lie. He didn't want his crew discovering that Kate was an FBI agent and that he was a fugitive on their Ten Most Wanted list.

'So now what?' Willie said. 'Johnny Cash knows we have the Rembrandts. You can't let him walk out, and you can't let the feds come in looking for him.'

'Johnny Cash?' Nick asked.

'You know, the Man in Black,' Willie said. 'Starke. It was a joke. I'm trying to lighten the mood, considering you're all screwed.'

'And you're not?' Boyd said.

'You're inside, surrounded by feds,' she said. 'I'm outside. I can just drive away whenever I like.'

'You'd do that to us?' Joe asked.

'Hell yes,' Willie said. 'The instant I see them move in, I'm gone.'

'It won't come to that,' Nick said. 'The Man in Black is what's going to get us out of this.' He turned to Joe. 'Can you erase all of the hotel's surveillance footage for the last forty-eight hours?'

It occurred to Nick that if the FBI went back and looked at the hotel's surveillance footage, they'd see him and Kate together in the lobby bar.

'With a click,' Joe said.

'Perfect,' Nick said.

Kate hadn't seen Andy in two years. He was from Montana, the son of a rural county sheriff, and wasn't comfortable unless he was wearing Carhartts. She'd told him, back when they were dating, that he'd made a mistake joining the FBI. He should have joined the US Marshals Service instead. They'd have let him wear jeans and cowboy boots to work. But Andy told her he wanted to hunt big game, not chase fugitives, escort prisoners, and protect witnesses, so it had to be the FBI.

'I'm on vacation,' Kate said. 'Experiencing the Big Apple.'

Andy took her by the arm and pulled her into the doorway alcove of the Coach store at the corner of Madison and Fifty-seventh. He yanked his earbud out and jammed it into the pocket of his jeans. He didn't want his team hearing this. 'I'm offline. I want to know what you're really doing here.'

'Seeing the sights,' Kate said.

'This New York trip is about Fox, isn't it? It's always about Fox with you.'

'Don't start in with me about that. I had enough of it while we were together.'

It was one of the things that had ruined the relationship. Andy had complained that Nick was all she thought about, and that it was like she was seeing another man. And it was true. Kate found Nick to be more interesting at a distance than Andy was up close and personal.

'I heard about you going rogue in China and getting suspended,' Andy said. 'I also heard you got hurt. Are you okay?'

'Yep, I'm fine. Good as new.'

'That's a relief. Now answer my question. Why are you here?'

* * *

Boyd came out of the bedroom dressed in a white silk shirt and khaki slacks and carrying some brightly colored folded clothes. 'Okay, Julian,' he said. 'You know the Rembrandt is genuine, and if you don't, you shouldn't be in this business. So do we have a deal, or do I find some other dealer to make outrageously wealthy today?'

'I'm in. I have a client who'll gladly take all three and at the price you proposed.'

'Do you have the money?'

Starke nodded. 'Once I've seen the rest of the paintings, I can access the money online and send it wherever you want it to go.' He knew that within an instant of his transferring the money to whatever account Mundy gave him, the cash would be broken up into smaller amounts and bounced all over the globe, from account to account, making the trail impossible to follow. 'But don't think about double-crossing me after the transfer. My client has a very, very bad temper and a long reach.'

'I'm sure he does, or he wouldn't be able to afford what I have to sell. Besides, what's the upside in burning him? I've got no intention of retiring. I may want to do business with you both again.'

'That's good news. If this works out, my client has a shopping list.' Most of the paintings on it were impossible to get. The Mona Lisa was item number one.

'I've never done work for hire before, but I could be

open to considering it.' Boyd set the clothes down on the couch beside Starke. 'Put these on.'

'What's wrong with my clothes?'

'Black is all you ever wear, so that's what people expect when they see you. If we put you in something colorful, and get rid of that goatee, nobody will recognize you when you walk out of this hotel.'

'Why do I want to be unrecognized?'

'Because I just pulled off the biggest heist in Canadian history and I'm taking you to see what I stole. I don't know if you were followed, and neither do you. If you have a tail, we're going to shake it.'

Starke thought Mundy was being paranoid, but he didn't argue. His clothes and goatee weren't worth the millions he'd be squandering now, and perhaps in the future, by making a stand over this. He stood up.

'Let's do this,' Starke said. 'I hope you have a proper straight razor and a black badger brush and not one of those obscene disposables.'

Kate sighed with resignation. Andy knew her well enough to see through a lie, so she decided her best shot was to stick as close to the truth as she possibly could.

'I saw the news about the museum robbery in Montreal, and it felt like Fox to me. So I took the red-eye here to shadow Starke on the chance that Fox might contact him to move the Rembrandts.'

She hoped her story sounded just crazy enough, and in line with what he knew about her, to ring true. And, she thought, he had a big psychological incentive to believe her. It would give him another chance to rag on her about chasing Nick and stick her with another implied *I told you so.*

'My God, Kate. It's only been a week or two since that mess in China. What's wrong with you?'

It worked. She was getting way too good at conning people. 'It's not me, it's Fox. He's the one who hit the museum. What was I supposed to do, just sit back and let him get away with it?'

'You aren't the only agent in the FBI.'

'I am the only one who can catch Fox.'

'You don't even know if he did it. Even if he did, there are a thousand art dealers in this world that Fox could use to broker the paintings. Why did you pick Starke?'

'Why did *you*?'

'I'm not chasing Fox,' Andy said. 'I'm building a case against Starke for selling tens of millions of dollars' worth of forged paintings to collectors around the world. We're sticking to him, hoping he'll lead us to his forger. So what put you on to him?'

'Starke's name came up once in the course of investigating another robbery that Fox pulled off,' Kate said.

'It's a long shot, but I figured given the proximity of New York to Montreal, it was worth spending some of my vacation watching Starke.'

'It's not a vacation, Kate. You were suspended for going rogue while pursuing Nicolas Fox. And now you're doing it again, crashing right into the middle of a two-year investigation. If the brass finds out about this, your career in the FBI is over.'

Starke came out of the elevator wearing a yellow T-shirt, white slacks, and flip-flops. He carried the Vuitton valise in one hand. Boyd carried a suitcase. He took Starke's free other hand.

'What are you doing?' Starke said, reflexively trying to pull his hand away. But Boyd held tight as they headed for the Fifty-eighth Street exit.

'You came in here a black-clad goateed heterosexual. You're walking out of here a clean-shaven brightly dressed gay man with his wickedly handsome boyfriend. You might as well be invisible.'

'So why does it feel like everyone is staring at me?'

'Maybe they are,' Boyd said. 'But they aren't seeing Julian Starke.'

As soon as they stepped outside, Willie pulled up to the curb in the Escalade. Boyd opened the door for Starke, patted him on the butt as he got inside, then climbed into the car after him and closed the door. Willie headed for Park Avenue and turned right at the corner.

'You're right, Andy,' Kate said. 'I don't know what I was thinking. But here I am.'

And there were Nick and Joe. She could see them over Andy's shoulder, walking out of the Four Seasons. Nick was wearing sunglasses and a baseball cap, the standard-issue disguise for celebrities everywhere. But while that might be good enough to keep a sitcom star or big screen superhero from being recognized, it was pitiful cover for a fugitive. He also carried the silver case that she knew contained the covert operative's tagging kit.

Andy was hands on hips, looking at something in the distance. This was just one of his many behavior tics. Kate called it his *thinking spot.* He was deciding what he should do about her.

'Well?' Kate asked. 'What's it going to be?'

He looked at her and shrugged. 'This isn't my problem. You're on vacation, seeing the sights of New York. You were strolling down Madison Avenue, back from a walk through Central Park, when you just happened to run into an old friend. We spent a few minutes catching up and you went on your way. How does that sound?'

'Really? You'd do that for me?'

'As long as you don't mess up my op,' Andy said, 'and promise me you'll keep on walking and not show up anywhere near Julian Starke again.'

This was an easy promise to keep. They were done with Julian Starke. Kate saw Nick and Joe get into the backseat of a taxi. The taxi merged into traffic, headed east on Fifty-seventh, and sailed past them.

'I'll give your regards to Lady Liberty,' she said, and walked away.

Andy was a nice guy, Kate thought. He was cute, and he could be funny, and he was a great kisser. He was so right and at the same time so wrong. Just like Nick Fox.

Thirty-one

The building in SoHo looked familiar to Starke as soon as they pulled up to the curb. Once he got inside the loft, and saw the Willem de Kooning painting on the wall, he immediately knew why. The big-busted, bug-eyed woman lost in a swirl of smeared colors was a fake.

'This is Hugh Sinclair's place,' Starke said.

'Indeed it is,' Boyd said. 'Since he's out of town for the next fifteen years, I didn't think he'd mind if I borrowed it for a showing.'

'Were you a friend of his?'

'If I was, I certainly wouldn't have let him buy so many fakes from you,' Boyd said, gesturing to the numerous pieces of abstract art in the loft. 'I read about his misfortune and the properties that had been left orphaned. Homes like this come in handy when you're looking for safe places to stay or to stash stolen artwork.'

Boyd led Starke into Sinclair's study, where the

remaining two Rembrandts were propped up on easels. The sight of all those masterpieces, and the fortune they represented, almost gave Starke an attack of irritable bowel syndrome.

Nick and Joe had the taxi drop them off at a Starbucks on West Broadway, a couple blocks away from the loft. They could hear the exchange between Boyd and Starke perfectly. Nick got them coffee while Joe got a seat and connected his MacBook to the free wifi so they'd be ready to move the money.

Kate didn't know if Nick had cooked up a scheme on the fly, or if he'd aborted everything and chosen a clean escape instead, but she knew where the Rembrandts were and that he wouldn't go anywhere without them. So she flagged a taxi and took it down to SoHo.

Starke took his time examining the paintings. There was no doubt they were real, but he wanted to appreciate them while he had the chance. He got up close to them and sniffed. Old paintings had a scent. He liked to think it was the smell of history, of the centuries that had unfolded around the paintings. These paintings had that unique scent. That is the sexiest fragrance on earth, he thought.

Boyd tapped his foot impatiently on the floor. 'Are

you authenticating the paintings or making love to them? You lick it, you own it.'

Starke turned around slowly. 'I am staking my life on the fact that these paintings are real and that my client is getting what he's paying for. Forgive me if I don't want to rush it.'

'Really? You think that I happened to have copies of the three Rembrandts lying around and was just waiting for the day when the real ones got stolen so I could swindle a collector? Stop stalling. You have thirty seconds and then I take my business elsewhere.'

Starke took out his cell phone. 'Give me a bank and an account number.'

'I'm in the bank and waiting for the funds,' Joe said, staring intently at his screen.

Nick sat beside him, his feet on the silver case, sipping a latte and picking at a slice of cinnamon coffee cake. It was all coming together now. He hoped Kate would make contact before they had to run.

The Escalade was parked in front of Sinclair's loft. Kate got out of the cab, walked over to the Escalade, and knocked on the passenger window. Willie unlocked the doors and let her in.

'I was wondering if you'd make it,' Willie said.

'You were afraid I got caught?'

'Last I heard through the earbud you met some guy. I thought you might have gotten a room.'

'Old boyfriend,' Kate said. 'Nothing more.'

'You can activate Kate's earbud again,' Nick said to Joe. 'She's with Willie.'

Joe nodded, absorbed in what he was doing. 'We've got the money. I'm moving it now.'

Nick punched a number into his cell phone.

Boyd's cell phone rang, though he didn't need the call from Nick to know the money had been transferred. He'd heard Joe on his earbud. This call was strictly for show. He took the phone out of his pocket, listened for a moment, then put it away again and smiled at Starke.

'Congratulations, Julian. You're a rich man.'

'Let's do this again sometime,' Starke said.

They shook hands and Boyd walked out. As soon as he was gone, Starke called Mr Wayne.

'The deal is done,' Starke said. 'You are now the owner of three new Rembrandts.'

Carter Grove was playing one of his vintage slot machines when Starke called with the good news and the address where the paintings were located.

'I trust you are absolutely satisfied that the paintings are authentic,' Carter said.

'I am,' Starke said, nervous despite his certainty. It was his life on the line. That was never explicitly stated, but he knew it.

'Stay where you are. I have people coming to secure the paintings.' Carter had kept an armed BlackRhino extraction team on call in Manhattan since last night to recover and transport the paintings. He had both air and ground assets in play. He was treating this as a military operation, no different than if he was kidnapping a terrorism suspect from Pakistan for the US government. There was too much at stake if things went wrong. 'Do not move until they get there, and do exactly as they say when they arrive.'

'Of course,' Starke said.

Boyd got into the backseat of the Escalade, and Willie drove off to pick up Nick and Joe at the Starbucks on West Broadway at Houston Street.

'That was the best part I've ever played,' Boyd said. 'I'm sorry it's over.'

'That's because you got screwed all night by two five-hundred-dollar-an-hour hookers,' Willie said. 'That doesn't happen when you're a talking pancake.'

'Of course not. Because it wouldn't be in character for Percy Pancake.'

'Because you couldn't afford those women and they wouldn't do a guy in a pancake suit,' Willie said. 'Then again, maybe they would if you paid them the fetish fee on top of their regular rate.'

'I didn't have sex with those women. Al Mundy did. I was simply playing my part. I'm really going to miss him. I believe there are a lot more facets of that character I could explore.'

'Un-huh,' Willie said.

'You have no understanding of what it means to be an artist,' Boyd said.

They pulled up in front of the Starbucks, and Nick and Joe got in beside Boyd in the backseat.

Willie pulled away from the curb and glanced at Nick in the rearview mirror. 'Where to, boss?'

'Four miles away in any direction,' Nick said. 'You pick it.'

Nick had carefully sprinkled taggant on all three Rembrandts, allowing the paintings to be safely tracked from five miles away with the special gun. It wasn't hard for Willie to follow them without being seen.

The paintings headed north on the Henry Hudson Parkway with a chopper following them. When the BlackRhino vehicles got onto the Sawmill River Parkway, Nick suspected they were going to Westchester County Airport to be loaded onto Carter's jet. Willie followed them all the way, parking on the airport access road until Carter's plane was in the air.

Next stop was LaGuardia to drop off Boyd and Joe. Their roles in the scheme were over. Joe took a flight from LaGuardia back to Los Angeles, where he was confident now that he could get lucky with one of the women around the pool. Boyd took a taxi from LaGuardia to JFK, where he caught a flight to London. He was planning to spend a couple weeks seeing plays in the West End.

Willie drove Nick and Kate to the private terminal at LaGuardia. They left the Escalade behind for the rental company and boarded a 'borrowed' Hawker Beechcraft King Air for the flight to Owensboro, Kentucky.

Kate hesitated at the steps leading up to the plane. 'Can Willie fly this?' she asked Nick.

'I hope so,' Nick said. 'She's the only one in the cockpit.'

'That's not making me feel good.'

'I sent her to flight school,' Nick said.

'So she has a license for this plane?'

'Maybe not a license, but I'm pretty sure she's got the instructional manual.'

'That's it. I'm not going.'

'Hey, Willie,' Nick yelled into the plane. 'Do you have a license?'

Willie stuck her head out the cockpit door. 'A what?'

'License.'

'Sure.'

'She's lying,' Kate said.

'It's a short flight,' Nick said. 'What can go wrong?'

Twenty minutes later they were in the air and Kate was able to unclench her teeth and loosen her grip on her seatbelt.

'See,' Nick said. 'We didn't even crash.'

'Yes, and since we didn't die, we need to talk,' she said. 'There's one part of this plan that really worries me.'

'I know,' Nick said. 'It's letting the paintings go and gambling that we'll be able to find them with the radar gun at one of Carter's properties. Of all the places he owns, I'm convinced his ranch in Kentucky makes the most sense. If we're wrong, we'll go to each one of his other places until we find the right one.'

Kate shook her head. 'That's not my fear. There's three hundred million dollars in one of your bank accounts. That's got to be your biggest score yet and an enormous temptation. Tell me you haven't thought about taking off.'

Nick smiled and did the twinkle thing with his eyes that he knew all women found irresistible. 'I know a beautiful island in Indonesia we could buy. We could live a carefree life of unrivaled luxury and total decadence in a tropical paradise on Carter's money, and my substantial savings, in a country without an extradition treaty.'

'You know I could never do it, but it worries me that you easily could.'

'No, I couldn't. I wouldn't be able to live with myself.'

'Don't tell me you've developed a conscience. You're a career criminal and this is the score of a lifetime. I know you don't feel any guilt about stealing the paintings or taking Carter Grove's money.'

'You're right, I could live with that,' Nick said. 'But not with what might happen to you, or your family, if you don't deliver me to Carter. I know you'd try to take him out. And you'd have Jake working with you, but even if you succeeded, neither one of you would come out of the experience unscathed. You'd both pay a price and that would be my fault. I won't do that to you.'

She knew Nick was a con man, that he was a master at manipulating people's emotions and telling them what they wanted to hear, but against her better judgment, she chose to believe him.

'Okey-dokey then,' she said. 'Does this plane have any Pringles?'

Thirty-two

Carter Grove flew on a BlackRhino corporate jet into Ron Lewis Field, a tiny municipal landing strip in Lewisport, Kentucky, landing a few hours behind the arrival of the three Rembrandts on the same airfield. He was met by Rocco Randisi, who picked him up in a black Cadillac DTS and drove him the ten miles south to Carter's ranch in Hawesville.

The ranch was Carter's getaway. A hundred and twenty acres set amid rolling hills, green pastures, rocky ravines, streams, and thick forests of oak, poplar, and hickory, it comprised a unique variety of habitats that sustained exceptional populations of deer and waterfowl for him to kill.

A narrow country road spilled down a wooded hillside and into the plain where Carter Grove's rustic eight-bedroom, seven-bath hunting lodge with a wraparound porch stood beside a picturesque five-acre fishing lake. The property also included a metal barn for storing vehicles, a six-stall horse barn and corral, a two-thousand-gallon gasoline tank and fueling station, a game-cleaning facility with meat processing room, and a secret art collection including some of the world's greatest lost masterpieces.

Randisi drove up the gravel driveway to the main house, which was patrolled by armed BlackRhino operatives dressed in jeans and scuffed boots so they'd look more like ranch hands and less like mercenaries, though nobody in Hancock County was fooled.

Carter got out of the car, bounded up the porch steps, and dashed into the house, heading straight for the great room and its massive stone fireplace. He pressed a particular stone, and a nearby built-in bookcase opened like an enormous door, revealing a staircase that led down to a storm cellar that had been converted into an art gallery.

The gallery was originally intended to showcase only a few select items, but now the whole collection was stuffed in there, including the three new Rembrandts, which were temporarily on easels in the center of the room. Even now, badly lit and haphazardly displayed amid what appeared to be the clutter of a billionaire hoarder, they were magnificent to behold. The sight actually brought tears to Carter's eyes.

He respectfully sat down on a step and admired the paintings. It was moments like this that made all the wheeling and dealing, bribery, kidnapping, and killing in his business worthwhile.

Willie buzzed Carter Grove's ranch before landing in Owensboro. Kate had satellite photos of the property, but she wanted to see it in real time. And Nick wanted to try out the taggant gun. Willie made a pass near the main house, and the gun picked up the taggant.

'Jackpot,' Nick said. 'We're in business.'

'Now comes the fun part,' Willie said. 'As soon as I can find the airport, I get to land this thing. Everybody hang on.'

Kate tightened her shoulder harness and bit into her lower lip. The plane swayed side to side on thermals at the low altitude for what seemed like forever to Kate. She squeezed her eyes closed and vowed to learn how to fly so she wouldn't have to rely on Willie ever again. The wheels touched down, the plane gave a bone-jarring bounce and smacked back down onto the runway, and Kate felt Willie put the brakes on.

'Next time I'm parachuting in,' Kate said.

They rented a Ford Explorer, and Kate had Willie drop her and Nick at the side of the road near Carter Grove's estate, in a wooded area. Kate had seen an elevated hunting blind from the air and thought it would be a good place to get the lay of the land. It was a half-hour trek to the blind, following a fire road. They reached the blind, climbed the rickety stairs, and looked out at the countryside.

'Carter picked a good spot for his hunting lodge and outbuildings,' Kate said. 'He's put a hundred yards of open field and a lake around them. You can't get near that house from the woods or the road without being out in the open.'

'True,' Nick said, 'but I have a plan.'

'You *always* have a plan. Where do all these plans come from?'

'This one came from you. When we were in Camarillo you wanted to toss a grenade into Carter's house and rush in disguised as firemen.'

It had been more of an offhand remark than a plan, but now that she heard it again, she saw the potential, as well as the considerable risk.

'Do you think it could work?' Kate asked.

'I think it's brilliant. Let's run with it. You're in charge now.'

'I've always been in charge.'

'Right,' he said. 'What I meant was that now you'll do the planning and organization, and I'll do the criticizing, worrying, and doomsaying.'

Kate surveyed the property again, as if something might have changed significantly about the topography and security measures in the two minutes since she'd last looked. No such luck.

'If the three of us try this alone, we'll be killed.'

'Whoa,' Nick said, holding his hand up. 'That's my line now.'

'We're going to need backup.'

'I'm afraid I don't have any mercenaries on my speed dial.'

'I do,' she said.

They left the blind and retraced their route to the road. Kate called Willie to pick them up, and minutes later they were in the Explorer. Their hotel was twenty miles away, conveniently located off the highway between a military surplus store and a strip club. As soon as Kate got into her room, she gave her father a call and briefed him on her plan.

'We can be boots-on-the-ground in Hawesville, fully equipped, in about twelve hours,' Jake said.

'We?' she said. 'Who is we?'

'There's me, of course, and Walter "Eagle Eye" Wurzel, the best sniper I've ever worked with. You remember him. He gave you some shooting lessons while we were stationed in Guam. You must have been eight or nine.'

'I remember Walter. I thought you told me he had cataracts.'

'That was ages ago. I'm sure he's had them removed

by now. But even with them, he could still shoot the whiskers off a kitten from two hundred yards away.'

'He shoots kittens?'

'It's an old expression. Very popular in Korea. Maybe it hasn't worked its way over here yet. The other guy is Clay Mandell.'

'You've never mentioned him before.'

'Because officially he doesn't exist and we never worked together. We did some black ops work in the Balkans in the nineties. He's become a survivalist out in Tennessee, preparing to survive the nuclear winter, the zombie apocalypse, or whatever else comes along. He's got all the weapons and tactical equipment we'll need.'

'Is he sane?'

'Reasonably,' Jake said.

'That's comforting. How much is all of this going to cost?'

'Nothing. They'll do it as a favor for me.'

'Are you sure? Assuming we get out of this, I don't want one of these guys calling in his marker and getting you to do something stupid and dangerous because of me.'

'Stupid and dangerous are my specialties.'

'I'm serious, Dad.'

'I've trusted these guys with my life many times. All they'd ever ask of me is the same thing I'm asking of them. To help me protect my family from harm. And that's something I'd gladly do in a heartbeat for any man I've ever served with, no questions asked.'

'They may have some, though. What are you going to tell them we're doing?'

'Nailing the bastard who threatened to kill me, my children, and my grandchildren. That will be all they need or care to know.'

Kate met Nick and Willie at the lobby bar, which didn't cater to hotel guests so much as to weary beaten-down locals. Nick and Willie were having hamburgers and beers.

'How'd it go?' Nick asked.

'He's in,' Kate said, helping herself to a bite of Nick's burger. 'And he's bringing a couple friends.'

Kate took a list of necessities out of her pocket and put it onto the table in front of Nick and Willie.

'This all looks reasonable to me,' Nick said.

Willie tapped an item on the list. 'How are we going to get two sets of official county firefighter's gear?'

'Arson,' Nick said. 'We'll set fire to a dumpster.'

Willie checked her watch: 9:30 PM. Nick and Kate had been gone for thirty minutes. Enough time for them to get into place. So she emptied a canister of gasoline into the dumpster behind the hotel, lit a newspaper on fire, and tossed it inside.

Then she went back to the bar and had another beer.

Nick and Kate were parked on Cedar Street, behind the fire station, when the trucks rolled out, sirens wailing, responding to the dumpster fire. Kate drove the Explorer into the parking lot and up to the back door, positioning the SUV at an angle so it blocked the security cameras' view.

Nick picked the lock on the door and they slipped inside, made their way to the equipment lockers, and helped themselves to a driptorch and two sets of firefighter gear, including masks, helmets, axes, and regulators. They were in and out of the fire station in less than five minutes.

'Stealing equipment from a small-town fire station is such an easy, petty crime,' Nick said. 'It feels anticlimactic after starting the day in New York selling three stolen Rembrandts and outwitting the FBI.'

'We could break into the International Bluegrass Music Museum,' she said. 'I hear that it's the Louvre of northwest Kentucky.'

That got Nick's attention. 'What have they got to see?'

'I was kidding! I was being sarcastic.'

'Sarcasm isn't one of your strengths,' he said.

Thirty-three

Kate woke up at 7 AM, showered, dressed, and made her way to the atrium, where free biscuits and gravy were being served poolside. Willie and Kate's father were already seated at a table. Jake was casually dressed in a bowling shirt, jeans, and Top-Siders and didn't look like a man who'd just traveled halfway across the country in twelve hours.

'You got here fast,' Kate said to her dad.

'I got a friend to fly Walter and me to Nashville last night. It's only about a four-hour flight. We met up with Clay and drove straight here. But if you'd told me that Willie Owens and a plate of hot buttermilk biscuits would be waiting for me, I'd have got here even faster.'

'I like that kind of talk,' Willie said.

Kate wanted to throw biscuits at both of them. She'd woken up feeling grumpy, and they were way too cheerful.

'Where are the guys?' Kate asked.

'Clay is in the pool,' Jake said.

Kate turned and saw a bearded old man who looked

like Santa Claus six months into a liquid diet. He was rail thin and swimming laps in his tighty-whities.

'He's swimming in his underwear,' Kate said.

'You're lucky I was able to talk him into swimming in anything at all,' Jake said. 'Walter is over at the buffet.'

Walter was in his late sixties and wore a pair of large-rimmed Buddy Holly glasses and a white patch over his left eye. He was dressed in cargo shorts, white tube socks, and leather sandals with Velcro straps. An untucked short-sleeve shirt did nothing to hide his big belly. He was busy collecting biscuits, stacking them onto his plate like poker chips.

'That's Eagle Eye the master sniper?' Kate asked. 'The guy with the thick glasses and an eyepatch?'

'He's having some thyroid problems that give him double vision, so he's got to wear the patch,' Jake said. 'But his good eye is fine.'

'How do you know which eye is his good one?'

'It's whichever one isn't patched,' Jake said.

'I can't believe this,' Kate said. 'Do you really think he's going to be able to watch our backs?'

'He wouldn't be here if I didn't,' Jake said. 'And he wouldn't have come if he didn't think he could do the job. He knows what's at stake.'

Walter came over to the table and sat down. He'd slathered his biscuits with gravy. 'This is my kind of grub. Just don't tell my cardiologist. He'd have a fit.'

'Do you remember Kate?' Jake said, tipping his head toward her.

'Of course I do.' Walter reached across the table to shake her hand. 'You grew up to be a knockout.'

'Thanks,' Kate said.

'You obviously got your looks from your mother,' Walter said, winking, though with one of his eyes patched, it was hard for Kate to tell for sure. It might just have been a twitch. 'You were the only kid I ever met who carried a Glock around like a teddy bear. I bet you're still a better shot than your father.'

'I'm a decent shot,' she said. 'How's your shooting these days, Walter?'

'I could shoot a grape off the head of a one-legged hooker from twice that distance.'

She didn't think that was an expression and was afraid to ask for more details, so she let it ride. 'Good to know. I appreciate you coming here and on such short notice.'

'Always glad to serve God and country.'

'This isn't for God and country,' Kate said.

'It is as far as I'm concerned,' he said.

Clay got out of the pool, wrapped a towel around his waist, and came over to the table, dripping water and leaving a trail of wet footprints in his wake.

'Does anyone remember if I locked the Humvee?' he asked.

Walter narrowed his good eye at him. 'You think you

might have left a vehicle unlocked that's loaded with assault weapons, explosives, hand grenades, and rocket launchers?'

'Actually, I was thinking about the iPhone I left on the seat,' Clay said. 'I'd hate to lose it.'

'I'll go check in a minute,' Jake said. 'This is my daughter Kate, by the way.'

Clay looked her over from head to toe. 'You're fit, fertile, and have fine birthing hips.'

'Birthing hips?' Kate asked.

'He's inviting you to ride out the apocalypse with him at his place,' Jake said. 'And then help repopulate the human race.'

'And you're okay with that?'

Jake shrugged. 'It's meant as a compliment.'

'Think on it,' Clay said. 'But don't take too long. The end of days could come at any time.'

Nick sauntered over with a rolled-up newspaper under his arm. 'I see the A-Team has arrived.'

'Good to see you, Nick.' Jake got up and shook his hand. 'This is a slick operation you've cooked up.'

'It wasn't me,' Nick said. 'This is all Kate.'

'Well done,' Jake said to his daughter. 'I could have used you in Costa Rica in '88.'

'What were you doing in Costa Rica?' Kate asked.

Clay wagged a finger at Jake. 'That's still classified.'

'Oops,' Jake said. 'Forget I mentioned it.'

Nick held out his hand to Walter. 'You must be Eagle Eye.'

'What gave me away?' Walter shook Nick's hand.

'Your steely gaze,' Nick said, then offered his hand to Clay. 'Thanks for coming down, Clay, and bringing the party favors.'

Clay grasped Nick's hand. 'It's a good opportunity to make sure everything is in working order for the day of reckoning.'

'You're not sure the ordnance works?' Kate asked.

'I've acquired a considerable stockpile but haven't had a chance to use most of it,' Clay said. 'Some of it dates back to Desert Storm.'

'I'm sure it's all fine,' Jake said, 'but I'll go see if it's still there.' And he headed out to the parking lot.

Nick turned to Willie. 'I need you to give me a ride.'

'Where are we going?' she asked.

Nick took the newspaper out from under his arm. 'To buy a pickup I found for sale in the classifieds and to case the Valor Oil refinery.' He turned back to Kate. 'What time do you want to do this?'

'Three o'clock,' Kate said. 'That way Carter's men will have the sun in their eyes if they look up toward the hunting blind where Dad, Clay, and Walter will be positioned.'

'We should swing by Kentucky Fried Chicken and grab a bucket on the way out there,' Walter said. 'I get dizzy on an empty stomach, and four o'clock is my dinnertime.'

Carter Grove sat on his porch in a rocking chair, enjoying a glass of iced tea as he gazed proudly at his property. In the mid-1800s it had belonged to Dr Hardin Davison, then one of the most powerful men in Hancock County. Able to act with absolute impunity, Davison was notorious for the day in 1859 when he walked into the Hawesville jail and emptied his gun into an injured unarmed sleeping man locked in a cell. No one dared raise a hand to prosecute Davison for the cold-blooded murder of a man who'd simply disagreed with him. And when a local lawyer criticized the town for letting the crime go unpunished, Davison slipped a bomb hidden in a basket of eggs into the man's office. The bomb didn't go off when it was supposed to, and Davison went back to check on it. And that's when it exploded.

Davison's four sons didn't fare much better in luck or intelligence. One accidentally shot himself while beating his dog with his musket. One fell off a boat while partying and drowned. One was shot while trying to blow up the Owensboro courthouse. Another was shot fighting for the Confederacy.

Carter Grove was a distant relative of Hardin Davison, and among his many reasons for buying the land was to bring it back into the family fold and to erase, by his own bold actions, the embarrassing legacy. There was no question that Carter was now one of the most powerful men in Hancock County, even as a largely absentee owner, so he felt he'd achieved his goal of erasing the stain left by Davison on his family line. He'd certainly proved to be smarter, and luckier, than his cursed ancestor and his sons.

At least he had until 2:55 that afternoon. That's when the squeal of rubber, shrieking like a woman in a horror movie, drew Carter's attention to the road. A Valor Oil gasoline tanker, the kind that regularly serviced all the properties in the area, was weaving wildly down the hill, the driver struggling to maintain control of the big rig.

Carter rose slowly from his rocking chair, his eyes on the road, as Randisi and the guards spilled out of the house onto the porch. The truck veered sharply across the roadway, crashed through Carter's picket fence, and barreled across the field like a runaway freight train. The driver's side cab door flew open and the driver jumped out, the only sensible thing to do since the truck was headed straight toward the gasoline tank and pumps thirty yards from the house.

Carter and his men hit the floor as the fuel truck smashed into the gasoline tank, setting off a tremendous explosion that rocked the ground like an earthquake, the concussive force of the blast shattering the windows of the house and lifting the big rig into the air atop a massive fireball.

* * *

At that same instant, from his perch beside Jake in the hunting blind, Walter 'Eagle Eye' Wurzel shot out the surveillance cameras on the west side of the house with his sniper rifle. The gunshots were completely muffled by the blast.

Walter lowered the rifle and reached for a chicken leg from the KFC bucket that was between them. 'Your daughter knows how to party.'

'She learned from the best,' Jake said, watching the scene through the scope of the rocket launcher he balanced on his shoulder.

The big rig plummeted to earth and broke apart, shaking the ground once again.

Carter Grove struggled to his feet and looked out at the raging fire that, for the moment, was isolated to the immediate area surrounding the gasoline pumps and wasn't yet threatening the house, the outbuildings, or the propane tank. The odds against a fuel tanker losing control and smashing into his gasoline tank, of all the structures on his property, were astronomical. That it occurred on one of the few days he happened to be there, with his entire collection of stolen art, seemed even more improbable.

Carter knew that the explosion was undoubtedly heard and felt all over the area and that the smoke from the fireball could be seen for miles. Soon volunteer firefighters from nearby ranches, and the fire truck from

Pellville, the nearest station, would begin converging on Carter's property, as well as the sheriff, his deputies, and curious neighbors. If something was going to happen, it would happen now.

'Secure the house and grab the driver,' Carter ordered Randisi. 'Find out what he knows. I'll be in the security center.'

'Yes, sir,' Randisi said, slipping a communicator into his ear and moving to gather his men.

Carter headed to the game-cleaning facility, where his security center doubled as a safe room. It was beneath the building and manned at all times by a BlackRhino operative. From there, Carter would be locked in a bunker beneath the floor, well-armed with guns and explosives, and able to monitor all the cameras on the property.

Randisi had three of the guards stay behind at the house while he took the other two men with him around the edge of the fire to apprehend the driver.

The three men surrounded the driver, who was lying facedown in the grass, and aimed their guns at him.

'Get up,' Randisi ordered. 'Very slowly.'

The driver rolled over, dazed, and Randisi was stunned to see that it was a woman, her big boobs just about bursting out of her Valor Oil shirt.

'Well, hot damn,' Willie said. 'I'm still alive.'

'For the moment,' Randisi said.

Thirty-four

Randisi trained his gun on Willie.

'Who are you working for?' Randisi demanded.

'Valor Oil,' she said, pointing to the logo on her chest. 'Isn't it obvious?'

'Why did you crash the truck?'

'It was an accident. My brakes failed. I lost control of the rig.'

'There are acres of wide open field, and yet you just happened to hit the one gasoline tank. You expect me to believe that?'

'Welcome to my life,' she said. 'I'm the unluckiest person on earth. They'll probably take my license and my double-wide for this. You think I did it on purpose? Why would anybody want to blow up your gasoline tank?'

'You tell me,' Randisi said.

'I have no idea.'

'Think of one.' He grabbed her by the arm, jerked

her to her feet, and pushed her toward the house. 'Or your luck might get a whole lot worse.'

Carter took a seat in the underground security center at the command console beside Vin Turbo, a bald, steroid-pumped BlackRhino operative whose real name was Irving Herkowitz and who'd got the inspiration for his name from actor Vin Diesel, whose real name was Mark Vincent.

'We've lost the cameras on the west side of the house,' Vin said, stating the obvious. Carter could see the dark screens among the two dozen monitors in front of them. 'The blast knocked them out.'

It made sense. That side of the house faced the gasoline tank. But it also faced the wooded hillside, which was the only place an attack force could approach the property without being seen, otherwise they'd have to come from the road or across an open field. It was another unsettling coincidence. There had been too many coincidences already.

'Pull up the feeds from all the working cameras around the house,' Carter said. 'And see if you can turn the cameras on the back of the barn toward the hillside so we aren't completely blind to the west.'

'Yes, sir,' Vin said.

Randisi radioed in. 'We've got the driver. It's a woman. She says her brakes went out.'

'Does she have ID?' Carter asked.

'It was in the truck.'

'Of course it was,' he said.

'We're taking her into the house for a forceful discussion.'

'Good. I think the explosion was a distraction. An attack could be imminent.'

'From whom?'

It could be anybody, Carter thought. Assassins from a banana republic he'd tried to topple. Terrorists seeking revenge for the extraordinary rendition of one of their leaders. Commandos sent by some dictator he'd helped depose. Crazed environmentalists he'd pissed off with oil drilling policies he'd championed as White House chief of staff. Carter had made a lot of enemies.

'I don't know,' Carter said. 'Just keep your eyes open and don't let anyone inside the house. If the deputies or firefighters ask what happened to the driver, tell them you don't know. When they're gone, bring her to the game-cleaning room.'

That was where Carter had held many forceful discussions with people who were reluctant to talk. He found that they became much chattier when they found out firsthand how game is cleaned and meat is processed.

The volunteers who comprised the Hawesville and Pellville fire departments were local farmers and merchants. They always carried their firefighting equipment in their cars so they could arrive prepared at a scene rather than waste valuable time rushing back to the station house to get suited up. In most cases, the firefighters would already be clearing structures of people, and fighting the blaze, when the fire trucks finally showed up.

Nick Fox was the first volunteer firefighter to arrive at Carter's ranch. He was driving a stolen rusted-out Ford pickup, and he was was wearing gear he'd stolen from the Owensboro fire station. He slipped a respirator over his face, put a helmet on his head, grabbed a fire extinguisher from the truckbed, and headed for the flames.

A moment later, Kate pulled up in the Ford Explorer they'd rented the day before at the Owensboro airport. She was also already in her protective gear. She added her respirator and helmet, grabbed a driptorch and a shovel from the backseat, and hurried after Nick, who'd started to spray the flames with his extinguisher.

More and more volunteer firefighters streamed to the ranch, rushing to battle the flames. They knew better than to try to fight a gasoline fire with water. They used fire extinguishers or shoveled dirt onto the blaze, but they weren't making much headway.

Nick and Kate split themselves off from the others and drifted toward the house. Nick went to the front porch, where Randisi stood. Kate headed to the west side of the house.

Randisi came down the steps to cut Nick off. 'Where do you think you're going?'

'My job is to clear all the buildings and get a head count of everybody who is here,' Nick said, salting his voice with a Kentucky twang and hoping Randisi wouldn't recognize him from his eyes. 'How many are inside and elsewhere on the property? We need to make sure everybody is safe and accounted for.'

'What you need to do is turn around and put out the fire.'

'The blast was pretty strong. There could be embers smoldering on the roof or under the porch. A fire could ignite at any moment. It's procedure to clear the buildings and check for smoke. So I'd appreciate it if you'd cooperate.'

'I won't tell you again.' Randisi opened his jacket, exposing the gun in his shoulder holster. 'Back off from the house.'

The gasoline tank wasn't the only flammable object on the west side of the property. There was also the white propane tank, which was positioned closer to the house, the barn, and the game-cleaning facility, since they used the gas for various purposes in each of the buildings.

Clay popped up in camouflage gear from his hiding place in the brush at the bottom of the hill, lobbed a grenade under the propane tank, and ducked down again.

Kate saw the grenade land and took cover behind the house, her back against the wall. Her sudden appearance startled the guard who was patrolling back there, but before he could ask her what she was doing, the propane tank exploded.

The blast rocked the property. It was a smaller explosion than the first, but it felt stronger, perhaps because of its proximity. All the firemen and guards, and even Willie and the two BlackRhino operatives in the house, instinctively ducked or dove to the ground to protect themselves.

Walter used the explosion to muffle his gunshots as he destroyed the security cameras on the barn.

The instant Randisi ducked, Nick swung his fire extinguisher into the operative's face, knocking him out and breaking his jaw.

The guard who'd been standing near Kate started to get up, and she took him out with a roundhouse kick to the head that flipped him over onto his back. She removed his gun, jammed it into her pocket, and ran to the front of the house.

A guard who'd been on the east side of the house ran around to the front and froze when he saw Randisi down and Nick standing over him. The guard whipped out his gun and aimed at Nick's head.

'Oh my God,' Nick said, staggering back from Randisi. 'Oh my God.'

'What happened?' the guard asked.

'He took a piece of shrapnel in the gut. There's so much blood. *Oh my God.*'

The guard came over to check, keeping his gun trained on Nick. The instant the guard stole a glance at Randisi, Nick slammed his extinguisher into the guard's stomach and whacked him across the head with it. The guard went down like a sandbag on top of Randisi.

When the propane blast hit, the feeds around the barn had abruptly blinked out. The camera behind the house was still working, so Carter saw the firefighter take cover just before the propane tank blew up. And then Carter saw the same firefighter kick a guard's ass. It was obvious now that the explosion was a trick to bring in commandos disguised as firefighters. He didn't know how many of the firefighters were real and how many weren't, but they all had to be considered enemy combatants. They all had to die.

Carter was just about to warn Randisi when he glanced at the feed from the camera in the front of the house and saw a firefighter take down the armed, stone cold BlackRhino killer with his fire extinguisher.

It was infuriating. His men were supposed to be the best of the best and they were being knocked down like bowling pins. There were only two BlackRhino operatives left standing, and they were both inside the house with the big rig driver, who was probably another commando.

'Call the house,' Carter told Vin. 'Hurry!'

Willie was sitting in a living room chair, two guards standing in front of her, when she shrieked and pointed at the French doors behind them. 'Fire!'

The guards turned and saw the rocking chair on the porch engulfed in flames, the fire licking at the window like an animal wanting to get inside.

The phone rang and someone began hammering on the front door.

'Fire department,' a voice called from outside. 'Open up or we'll break this door down with an ax! The house is burning!'

'Answer the phone!' Carter yelled, staring at the living room camera feed on the monitor, watching the guard ignore the phone and hurry to the front door.

'No!' Carter slammed his fist on the console. 'Fucking idiots.'

He saw the guard open the door, and saw two firefighters burst in.

One of the firefighters suckerpunched a guard in the throat, sending him choking to the floor.

The other guard reached for his gun and got sprayed in the face with foam from the extinguisher. Carter uttered an oath when the bimbo rig driver got up and hit the guard with a right hook so hard, it took him down and knocked the foam off his face.

'Nice,' Kate said.

'I'm not as sweet and innocent as I appear,' Willie said.

Nick handed Willie the extinguisher. 'Douse the fire on the porch with this and get out of here. Wait for me in the pickup.'

Carter watched it all go down in helpless fury. One of the firefighters took off his respirator mask, looked directly at the living room surveillance camera, and smiled.

It was Nicolas Fox.

The other firefighter removed his mask. It was Kate O'Hare.

Everything fell into place for Carter. They were here for his collection, which they'd use to send him to prison for the rest of his life, destroying him and BlackRhino all at once. But it wasn't over yet, not while he was still breathing and secure in his command bunker.

Nick removed the radar gun from inside his jacket, switched it on, and studied its screen.

'The paintings are under the chimney,' he said.

Kate took possession of the radar gun, and Nick

studied the fireplace stones. There was one that had a barely perceptible hairline gap around it instead of cement. He pushed and turned it. A bookcase swung open beside the fireplace.

'I'm beginning to feel like I'm the only person in America who doesn't have a secret door,' Kate said.

'That's because you don't have anything valuable enough to hide.'

'There's my Glock,' Kate said.

'You keep that under your pillow.'

'Maybe I'll get a secret compartment under my pillow.'

Kate stayed in the living room to watch Nick's back while he went down the stairs to confirm that the collection was there.

Carter stared at the screen, trying to conceive of an escape plan that would keep him out of jail, maintain his reputation, and destroy Nick Fox and Kate O'Hare.

'What do we do now, sir?' Vin asked, pointing at another screen. 'The sheriff just got here.'

Carter wasn't paying attention to Vin. Something had caught his eye. He leaned closer to the screen in front of him and studied the object in Kate's hand.

It looked like a radar-tracking, laser-targeting device, but he suspected it did much more. He suspected the Rembrandts were tagged. It gave him an idea, a way to save himself, but it would come at a staggering cost.

And yet it was a small price to pay for his freedom and his reputation.

Carter called Veronica Dell. 'Where's our predator drone right now?'

'On the AeroSystem airfield outside of Huntsville, Alabama, armed and ready for deployment.'

Huntsville was about 240 miles away. A drone armed with bunker-busting Hellfire missiles could cover that distance in less than two hours. Without the art collection, there would be no evidence to convict him of any crime.

'I have a target,' he said.

Thirty-five

When Sheriff Travis Villency, sitting at his desk in the Hancock County Administration Building in Hawesville, got the call about an explosion on a ranch, his first thought was that another meth lab had blown up.

There were over a thousand meth labs a year shut down in Kentucky, and rural Hancock County had more than its share. Villency estimated that 60 percent of the people in his county who bought pseudoephedrine at the drugstore were using it to cook meth, not relieve their colds. And meth heads weren't exactly cautious and meticulous people when it came to handling flammable chemicals, or anything else, so lab explosions were common.

When Villency realized that the address was Carter Grove's ranch, he tightened his suspenders and girded himself for trouble. He tried to have nothing to do with Carter and his BlackRhino bunch. Carter acted like he owned the county – though when it came down to it he essentially did, because he had the money and influence to sway every election toward the candidates of his choosing. Villency had been one of them, but he chafed at being treated like one of Carter's underlings.

Villency rounded up four of his deputies and they headed out to Carter Grove's place in three squad cars, sirens wailing. By the time they got there, two fire trucks had arrived from Hawesville and Pellville, paramedics were on the scene, and two dozen firefighters were at work trying to smother the flames around the twisted wreckage of a big rig. Twenty yards away was a blackened, smoking crater where a propane tank used to be.

Judging by the skid marks on the road, the flattened fence, and the wreckage, Villency assumed the big rig had lost control and smashed into the gasoline tank, setting off a blast that had also ignited the propane tank. What he couldn't figure out was why Carter hadn't called him directly, demanding action.

Villency parked on the roadway outside the estate. He pulled his considerable bulk out of the car, hiked up his pants even though they were already hiked up as far as they could possibly go, put on his stiff-brimmed hat, and ordered his deputies to control traffic and keep the looky-loos away.

Villency started down the driveway toward the house and was halfway there when he was intercepted by a firefighter.

'Hey, Sheriff, there's something in that house you've got to see,' the fireman said. 'We came across it when we were evacuating the house.'

'What's that, son?'

'There's a bunch of paintings in the basement. A couple look like the ones that were stolen in Canada.'

'Really?' Villency said, putting his hands on his hips. 'What are you, some kind of art expert?'

'I watch CNN. Go look for yourself.'

The last thing Villency wanted to do was start poking around in Carter's house. It was a good way to get himself thrown out of office in a Carter Grove-funded recall election.

'I didn't catch your name, son,' Villency said.

'Jethro Clampett.'

The name a rang a bell, but Villency couldn't place it. He was continuing on around the paramedic vehicle toward the house when it occurred to him that Jethro was wearing an Owensboro Fire Department suit. He glanced back over his shoulder, but the firefighter was gone. Villency turned his attention back to the house. Two paramedics were treating two BlackRhino guys who looked like they'd been hit in the face with bricks.

'What happened to these guys?' Villency asked the nearest paramedic.

'They've both sustained serious concussions and broken ribs. One of the men has a broken jaw. Neither one of them is in any condition to talk right now. But the two guys up on the porch say they were hit by part of the propane tank when it blew.'

Villency looked around. The nearest piece of the propane tank was twenty yards away. They'd been hit by something, but it wasn't the propane tank. What the hell had happened here? He went up to talk to the two other BlackRhino men, who were sitting on the porch, ice packs on their heads. One of the men was soaking wet.

'What happened to you two?' Villency asked.

'I got knocked down by the explosion,' the dry guy said.

Villency shifted his gaze to the wet guy. 'And you?'

'I fell in the lake,' he said.

'You both look like you've been in fights and lost.'

'It was the explosion,' the dry guy said.

Villency knew he wasn't getting the whole story, but he wasn't sure he really wanted to know the truth. 'Where is Mr Grove?' he asked.

'I don't know,' the wet guy said.

'Neither do I,' the dry guy said.

'Was he here when the accident happened?'

The two men looked at each other, trying to decide how to answer. They both looked back at Villency.

'Maybe,' the dry guy said.

'We aren't sure,' the wet guy said.

'We were elsewhere,' the dry guy said.

Villency glanced at the open front door and was trying to decide whether or not to go inside when his attention was caught by the sound of a car approaching. He turned and saw a Ford Explorer speed down the driveway and come to a stop behind the paramedic truck. A woman in a V-neck T-shirt and jeans stepped out, a holstered Glock clipped to her belt. She walked up and flashed an ID at him. It was federal tin.

'Sheriff,' she said, 'I'm FBI Special Agent Kate O'Hare.'

'What brings you all the way out here?'

'Three stolen Rembrandts,' she said. 'I've been chasing the guy who took them from a Montreal museum. The trail led here. I believe Carter Grove has them now.'

So Jethro was right after all. Villency noticed that the agent's comment seemed to stir an angry glare from the BlackRhino guy with the broken jaw. He thought on the situation for a moment. Stolen Rembrandts in Carter's house would be the biggest crime he'd ever uncovered. It would make his career, ensuring he'd keep his job as long as he wanted it, and he'd never have to answer to Carter Grove again. But if the paintings weren't stolen, Carter would ruin him. Or worse. He decided to go with his gut, which was the majority of his body.

'Funny you should say that,' Villency replied. 'One

of the firefighters saw some paintings he thought he recognized from a news report on CNN.'

Kate looked past him to the open front door. 'Let's go look.'

'We don't have a warrant.'

'Exigent circumstances,' Kate said. 'There's a raging fire, and if there are still people in that house, they could be in grave danger.'

The fire didn't seem to be raging anywhere near the house now, but Carter was missing and several people had already been injured in the blast. It would hold up in court, at least in Hancock County. Even so, he decided it would be best if he didn't take the lead.

'After you,' Villency said.

Kate marched past him into the house, and he followed. The first thing Villency noticed was the bookcase yawning open like a door. That was cool, like something out of a Batman movie. Kate took a small Maglite out of her pocket, drew her gun, and stepped into the opening. Villency drew his gun too, just to be sociable.

A staircase led down into a storm cellar. 'This is Kate O'Hare, FBI. Is anyone down here?'

No one answered. Kate found a light switch. The lights came on, revealing a room stuffed full of paintings, sculptures, pottery, and some jewelry in display cases.

Kate gestured with her gun to some paintings on

easels. 'Those are the Rembrandts. The rest of these are stolen, too. There's got to be hundreds of millions of dollars' worth of art in here.'

'Hot damn,' Villency said. This would put him on the national stage. He'd be the small-time sheriff who'd helped solve an international crime. His political future in Kentucky suddenly seemed very, very bright. 'You know, I always thought there was something fishy about Carter. I've been unofficially investigating him for months.'

'I'm not surprised,' Kate said, knowing things would go much smoother from here on out if Villency decided she was okay. 'Lawmen have a sixth sense about this kind of thing.'

'We certainly do.'

'This will be a joint effort now between your office and the FBI.'

Villency liked the sound of that. 'How do you want to play it from here?'

Kate holstered her gun. 'I suggest we restrict this entire property as a crime scene and clear those fire-fighters out of here as soon as the blaze is under control. Meanwhile, based on what we've learned, you obtain a search warrant from the friendliest judge you've got. I'll contact the US Marshals in Lexington and get them out here to guard the evidence until I can get a full FBI operations team and forensics unit here from Louisville.'

'Works for me,' Villency said. 'What do we do about Carter? Nobody knows where he is.'

'He's probably got a safe room somewhere on the property,' Kate said. 'If he's still here, he's not going anywhere. And if he's fled, we'll have to deal with it.'

'We've never had a catered field mission before,' Walter said.

He'd set down his sniper rifle when the sheriff arrived, and he was now eating the KFC biscuits. Somehow they tasted better in Kentucky than they did in LA, even though they were probably made from the same recipe and ingredients throughout the chain.

'This is the way to go,' he told Jake. 'Speaking of going, shouldn't we be getting out of here?'

Jake surveyed the scene with binoculars. The rocket launcher was propped up on the wall beside him. 'As long as Kate is still down there, and Carter is in his bunker, we stay.'

'Fine by me.' Walter dabbed his lips with a napkin. 'I've still got the Little Bucket Parfaits to eat.'

Carter watched Kate and the fat sheriff come out of the house. He knew they'd be securing the scene, filing for a warrant, and bringing in more federal agents.

'Shouldn't we get out of here?' Vin asked.

'Just sit still and shut up,' Carter said.

'What's the point of staying down here now?'

Carter held out his hand to Vin, palm up. 'Can I see your gun, please?'

Vin took the gun from his holster, handed it over, and Carter shot him in the head.

Carter set the gun on the console. He wasn't worried that anyone outside had heard the gunshot. The security center was underground and the walls were thick. And he wasn't concerned about being found with the body. Nobody would be coming down to the bunker. He was going to blow his house and all the evidence in it to kingdom come, then emerge after the smoke cleared. And he'd talk his way out of this mess, just as he'd done many times before. And then he'd seek revenge. The thought of that kept him happy and occupied as he waited for the drone to arrive. It wouldn't be long now.

Kate was feeling pretty pleased with herself. She sat in her car in front of Carter's house, watching the firefighters shovel dirt onto the smoking embers that remained in the wake of the blaze. She was waiting for the warrant and the marshals to show up. Once they got here, she'd roust Carter out of his bunker, arrest him, and oversee the cataloging and confiscation of the paintings. Any accusations he might make later about her and Nick working together for the FBI would be dismissed as utterly absurd. Nobody would take Carter seriously after what they were about to find in his basement.

The BlackRhino operatives had been taken away and were being held for questioning by deputies. By now, Nick and Willie were waiting at the hotel for word from her that it was all done, then they'd fly back to LA on the 'borrowed' King Air with Jake and Walter while she stayed in Owensboro until everything was wrapped up.

It had been about two hours since she'd introduced herself to Sheriff Villency, and an hour since she'd phoned Jessup to fill him in. She smiled to herself thinking about that call.

'I thought you'd like to know that I'm in your home state of Kentucky and about to arrest Carter Grove for possession of stolen goods,' Kate had said to Jessup. 'Most notably, the three Rembrandts stolen this week in Montreal.'

'Wait one damn minute,' Jessup had said. 'You've been suspended. You were supposed to be on vacation, recuperating from your injuries. You have no authority to conduct an investigation into Carter Grove or anybody else. In fact, you were explicitly told to stay the hell away from him.'

'I wouldn't mention that in the press conference.'

'What press conference?'

'The one Bolton will be having tomorrow to explain Carter's arrest and the recovery of the Rembrandts and dozens of other masterpieces stolen in some of the most notorious art thefts committed in the last thirty years.'

'How did you do that?'

'I'll give you the details when I see you.'

There was a beat of silence on Jessup's end. 'You're a credit to the department,' he finally said. 'Good thing your suspension was lifted yesterday.'

It had been a good conversation, but time was dragging now. Kate did some housekeeping, sorting through the junk she had in the car. A couple empty water bottles, some confiscated guns, her FBI windbreaker, the high-tech taggant gun she'd forgotten to give back to Nick. She was checking email on her smartphone when the taggant gun started beeping. The beeps started slow and then became more and more urgent. She was initially puzzled, and then a jolt of fear coursed through her body. She knew what the beeps meant from her years as a Navy commando. A Hellfire missile was coming.

Thirty-six

From the safety of the security center beneath the game-cleaning facility, Carter Grove watched the video feed from the camera mounted on the nose of the predator drone. He could see the Hellfire missile homing in on his house below. Retribution was coming from the skies. In a few seconds, Kate O'Hare and all the evidence against him would be obliterated and only a smoking crater would be left behind. *That* was how he rolled.

Kate grabbed the radar gun and jumped out of the car. In the distance, beyond the house in front of her, she could see an object streaking through the sky toward her like a fiery meteor. She checked the readout. Ten seconds until impact.

She aimed the taggant gun at the game-cleaning facility and squeezed the trigger, using the laser function to create a target on the wall, hoping it would attract the missile.

* * *

Carter watched the missile closing in on the house. An instant from impact, it abruptly acquired a new target and made a sharp turn.

Carter had only a split second to comprehend what had happened, but that was long enough for him to experience true, bone-chilling terror before the missile hit.

The bunker-busting missile was so close to the house when it turned, it sheared off the shingles on the roof before it slammed into the game-cleaning facility.

The building burst apart in an eruption of fire, chunks of concrete, and jagged sheets of metal that frisbee'd through the air like flying buzz saws. The metal sheets sliced into tree trunks, the barn, and the side of the house.

On the missile's impact Kate and the remaining firefighters had flattened themselves on the ground, and they were so busy kissing the dirt, they didn't see the predator drone as it streaked overhead, then banked to make another pass at the house.

Jake O'Hare saw the course change from his position in the hunting blind. He picked up the rocket launcher and aimed at the drone. He knew he had only one shot, a split second of opportunity, before the drone released another Hellfire missile on the house. This missile wouldn't miss.

Jake centered the target and squeezed the trigger. The rocket shot out, the backfire on the launcher punching a hole in the wall behind him.

The rocket slammed into the predator drone and it exploded in midair, the flaming debris spiraling through the air and splashing into the lake behind the house.

There was a long moment as the sound of the two explosions dissipated, the ground seemed to still, and all that was left was the ringing in Kate's ears and the smell of smoke.

She staggered to her feet and looked up at the wooded hillside. She couldn't see her father, but she knew he could see her in his sights. He'd saved her life. She smiled and gave him a thumbs-up.

Clay climbed up into the hunting blind where Jake and Walter were high-fiving each other.

'Just like old times,' Jake said.

'Even better,' Walter said. 'I thought I'd never get another chance to feel this way before I died.'

'Kate is one tough daughter-of-a-bastard,' Clay said. 'I think I'm in love.'

'You'll have to move to the back of the line, buddy,' Jake said. 'Somebody has already beaten you to her.'

After the weeks of international travel and dangerous heists, it was hard for Kate to go back to the procedural drudgery of routine FBI work, tying up the loose ends of the Carter Grove case and wading through a seemingly endless amount of paperwork.

She felt like a prisoner in her cubicle at the Wilshire Federal Building, but getting some of the credit for bringing down Carter, returning the Rembrandts to the Musée de Florentiny, and repatriating the scores of long-lost masterpieces to museums worldwide made it easier to take.

Director Bolton grabbed a big chunk of the credit for himself, claiming that the investigation into Carter Grove had been ongoing for some time but had gained momentum when it dovetailed with Kate's pursuit of Nicolas Fox. Even Kate's ex-boyfriend, FBI Special Agent Andrew Tourneur, got his share of the limelight for arresting Julian Starke as part of a wide-ranging conspiracy to sell forgeries to wealthy suckers and for dealing in stolen art.

The big rig accident that led to the exposure of Carter's cache was blamed on some unknown person, probably a kid, who'd stolen a gasoline tanker for a joyride, lost control of the large vehicle, and then fled the scene.

Two teeth and a Cartier belt buckle were found on the driveway a quarter mile from the game-cleaning facility and were identified as belonging to Carter Grove. No other remains were found.

* * *

Kate heard from Nick two weeks after the events in Hawesville. He invited her to a mansion on Broad Beach in Malibu. The place belonged to an actor who was shooting an eight-hour gothic miniseries in Bulgaria. Nick was an actor friend from England who was house-sitting. At least that's what he told the neighbors.

Kate wore her favorite date-night outfit of jeans, Glock, and navy FBI windbreaker. Nick had Toblerones and caviar set out.

'If I didn't know better I'd think you were trying to seduce me,' Kate said, eyeing the Toblerones.

'You could be right,' Nick said.

One

FBI Special Agent Kate O'Hare slouched back in her tan leather executive office chair, looked across her desk, and surveyed the lobby of the Tarzana branch of California Metro Bank. The desk actually belonged to the assistant manager. Kate was occupying it because she was waiting for the bank to get robbed. She'd been waiting for four days, and she was wishing it would happen soon, because she was going gonzo with boredom.

The boredom vanished and her posture improved when two businessmen wearing impeccably tailored suits walked through the bank's double glass doors. One of the men wore Ray-Bans and had a Louis Vuitton backpack slung over his shoulder. The other man was stylishly unshaven and had a raincoat draped casually over his right arm. It hadn't rained in LA in two months, and no rain was expected, so Kate figured these might be the guys she'd been waiting for, and that at least one of them wasn't all that good at hiding a weapon.

The man wearing the Ray-Bans went directly into the manager's glass-walled office, and the man with the raincoat approached Kate's desk and sat down across from her. His gaze immediately went to her chest, which was entirely understandable, as she was wearing a push-up bra under her Ann Taylor pantsuit that made her breasts burst out of her open blouse like Poppin' Fresh dough. This wasn't a favored look for Kate, but she was *the job*, and if it took cleavage to capture some slimeball, then she was all about it.

'May I help you, sir?' Kate asked.

'Call me Slick,' the man said.

'Slick?' she said. 'Really?'

He shrugged and adjusted the raincoat so that she could see the Sig Sauer 9mm semiautomatic underneath it. 'Keep smiling and relax. I'm simply a businessman talking to you about opening a new account.'

Kate glanced toward the office of the manager. FBI Special Agent Seth Ryerson was behind the manager's desk, and the real manager was working as one of the bank's four tellers. The Ray-Bans guy was giving Ryerson instructions. Ryerson turned to look at Kate, and she could see that sweat was already beading on his balding head. As soon as any action started, Ryerson always broke out in a sweat. In five minutes, he'd be soaked. It was never pretty.

Kate and Ryerson had been working undercover,

following a tip, hoping the men would show up. The bank fit the profile of the six other San Fernando Valley banks the Businessman Bandits had held up over the last two months. The Tarzana bank was a stand-alone building in a largely residential area and was within a block of a freeway on-ramp and a major interchange.

Kate knew there was a third 'businessman' in a car idling in the parking lot. She also knew that an FBI strike team was parked around the corner waiting to move in.

'What do you want me to do?' Kate asked Slick.

'Sit there and be pretty. Here's how it's going to work, sweetie. My associate is telling your manager to take the backpack to the vault and bring it back filled with cash or I will put a bullet in your chest. My associate will then leave the bank, but I will stick around for a minute flirting with you. If any dye packs explode, or any alarms go off, I will shoot you. If nothing goes wrong, I'll simply get up and walk out the door, no harm done. All you have to do is stay calm, and this will all be over soon.'

It was the same speech he'd given to the women at the six other banks the Businessman Bandits had held up. Slick always picked a young woman with cleavage to threaten with his gun, which was why Kate had worn the push-up bra. She'd wanted to be his target.

Kate looked past Slick to the lobby and the bank

tellers. There were seven customers in the bank, four at the counter and three in line. No one seemed to notice that anything unusual was happening. Ryerson left the Ray-Bans guy in his office and took the Vuitton backpack to the vault.

Kate's iPhone vibrated on her desk. JAMES BOND showed up on the caller ID.

'Ignore it,' Slick said. 'Look at me instead.'

Kate shifted her gaze back to Slick's carefully unshaven face, his stubble a shadow on his thin cheeks and sharp chin. The phone went still. After fifteen seconds it began to vibrate again. James Bond wasn't a man who gave up easily.

'That's annoying,' Slick said. 'Do you always take personal phone calls during work hours?'

'If they're important.'

The phone continued to vibrate.

'Shut it off,' Slick said. '*Now.*'

Kate shut the phone down. A moment later her desk phone rang.

'I don't like this,' Slick said. 'On your feet. We're walking out of here.'

'It's just a phone call,' Kate said. 'It's probably my mother.'

'Up!' he said. 'And start walking. If anyone approaches you, I'm shooting you first and then whoever else gets in my way. Clear?'

This isn't good, Kate thought. There were customers conducting business, coming and going, and there was a possibility that one of them would accidentally cross their path.

'Should I take my purse?'

'No.'

'Won't it look odd if I walk out of the bank without my purse?'

'Where is it?'

'The bottom drawer, to my right.'

'Stay where you are, and I'll open the drawer. Do *not* move.'

He stood and moved around the desk, all the while keeping his eyes on Kate. He held the Sig in his right hand and reached down to open the drawer with his left. The instant his attention shifted from Kate to the drawer, she smacked him hard in the face with her keyboard. His eyes went blank, the gun dropped from his hand, blood gushed out of his smashed nose, and he crashed to the floor, unconscious.

Kate picked the gun up and aimed it at his partner in the manager's office.

'FBI!' she yelled. 'Don't move. Put your hands on your head.'

Mr Ray-Bans did as he was told. Everyone in the bank froze, too, startled by her outburst and shocked by the sight of her holding the gun.

Ryerson rushed out of the vault, his gun drawn, big sweat stains under his armpits. He looked confused. 'What happened?'

'I had to go to Plan B,' Kate said. She turned to the customers in the bank. 'Relax, everyone. We have the situation entirely under control, and you aren't in any danger.'

Kate's desk phone wouldn't stop ringing. She kept her gun aimed at Mr Ray-Bans in the manager's office, and snatched at the phone with her other hand.

'What?' she said.

'Is that any way to talk to James Bond?'

'You're not James Bond.'

It was Nick Fox, and truth is, Kate thought Nick was pretty darn close to James Bond. A little younger and mostly on the other side of the law, but just as lethal and just as sexy.

Fox was a world-class con man and thief. Kate had tracked him for years and finally captured him, only to have her boss, Carl Jessup, and Fletcher Bolton, the deputy director of the FBI, arrange Nick's escape. In return for conditional freedom, Nick had agreed to use his unique skills to nail big-time criminals the Bureau couldn't catch using conventional means.

Kate had been given the unwanted responsibility of helping Nick neutralize the bad guys. She was also supposed to make sure Nick didn't go back to his life of crime. The Bureau didn't have Nick under constant surveillance or wearing a tracking device between assignments, so it was up to Kate to keep him on a loose leash. It had been a few days since she'd last spoken to him.

'Did I catch you at a bad time?' Nick asked.

'Yes. What do you want?'

'I didn't do it.'

Kate went silent for a beat. She had no clue what he was talking about, but whatever it was, at least he hadn't done it. That was good, right?

'I'm kind of busy right now,' she said.

'No problem. I just thought you'd want to know.'

Kate hung up, and the phone rang again. It was Carl Jessup.

'Your cellphone isn't working,' Jessup said.

'That's because I'm in the middle of a bank robbery thing.'

'We've got a big problem,' Jessup said in his distinctive Kentucky twang. 'Yesterday, Nicolas Fox stole a five-million-dollar Matisse from the Gleaberg Museum of Art in Nashville.'

'Are you sure it was Nick?' she asked, watching as Ryerson called in the troops and cuffed Mr Ray-Bans.

'I've just texted you a photo from one of the museum's security cameras.'

Kate turned her phone on and clicked on MESSAGES.

The photo showed a man in an oversize hoodie holding a painting under his arm. The man's face was partly obscured by the hood, but she could see enough to recognize that it was Nick.

'I've never seen Nick in a hoodie before,' Kate said.

'I'm not interested in his fashion choices,' Jessup said.

'You don't understand, sir,' Kate said. 'Nick shops on Savile Row, not at the outlet mall. He wouldn't wear a hoodie from Old Navy.'

'He was trying to blend in with the local yokels.'

'How did he steal the painting?'

'He walked into the museum in broad daylight and took it off the wall.'

'Where's the fun in that?'

'He got away with it, didn't he?'

'Yes, but that's not why he steals or swindles. It's all about the challenge of the crime or the person he's targeting. What's the point of just lifting a painting? Anybody could do that.'

'Maybe he lacks impulse control,' Jessup said. 'The reason doesn't matter. What matters is that he did it. He broke our deal.'

'It doesn't add up. If he wanted to break the deal, he'd pull off something really big, an ambitious hustle with a payoff in the tens of millions of dollars. This is small-time.'

'Five million dollars isn't small-time to me,' Jessup said. 'We've kept him too busy to pull off anything more elaborate. So he grabbed the low-hanging fruit.'

Kate thought about it as she looked through the bank's double glass doors. The strike team agents, guns drawn and wearing Kevlar vests, were converging on a BMW and pulling a man out of the driver's seat. Five million dollars would probably be a dream score for the three guys they were arresting today, but not to a master criminal like Nick Fox. He'd had the chance to run off with a half billion dollars during their first assignment together, and he'd resisted the temptation. This felt wrong. Not to mention he'd just called, and she assumed that this theft was the thing he hadn't done.

'Nick is smart and discreet,' she said. 'Why would he let himself be caught on camera?'

'To give us the finger. The Gleaberg is only a block from the Davidson County Sheriff's Office. He's really rubbing our nose in it.'

This was the first aspect of the crime that felt to Kate like a Nick Fox caper. It took chutzpah to take a painting from a museum so close to hundreds of cops. Even so, she wasn't sold.

'I want you to get on a plane to Nashville and take him down fast,' Jessup said, ending the call.

Kate blew out a sigh, hung up the desk phone, and

stuffed her iPhone into her pocket. She looked down at Slick, who was still on his back, bleeding from his nose. His eyes were open but unfocused.

'Hey,' she said to him. 'Are you okay?'

'I don't know. How do I look?'

'Like a train wreck.' She stuck his gun under her waistband and yanked him to his feet. 'Let's go.'

Kate turned Slick over to the strike team and joined Ryerson.

'So what's the big crisis?' Ryerson asked.

She pulled her phone out and showed Ryerson the photo. 'Fox has come out into the open again.'

'Lucky you.'

Kate walked to her car, a white Crown Vic police interceptor she'd bought at an LAPD auction. Like many FBI agents, she kept a go bag, a packed duffel bag of clothes and toiletries, in the trunk. The bag had been in there for three months and her clothes probably smelled like her spare tire, but she could head straight to LAX and catch the next flight to Nashville. Before that happened, she needed to talk to Nick.

He answered on the second ring. 'Remington Steele, at your service.'

'Remington Steele? You've got to be kidding.'

'Is it too on the nose?'

'I thought you were James Bond today.'

'I'm trying to keep things interesting.'

'My fear is that you're trying to keep things *too* interesting.'

'Everything I've done lately I've done with you,' Nick said.

'Not everything.'

'Not for lack of trying. But a man has his needs.'

There was a time not so long ago when Fox's sexual banter annoyed Kate. Now she was annoyed to find that she was enjoying it.

'Where are you?' she asked him.

'On my yacht.'

'You have a yacht?'

'I do this week,' he said.

'I suppose you're somewhere with clear, blue skies and no extradition treaty.'

'Marina del Rey.'

'Really?'

'Come see for yourself,' he said, and gave her the slip number. 'I'll open a bottle of Cristal.'